The author is a happily married man, aged 60 years, and is the proud father of five children, who are now all adults. He has four beautiful grandchildren. His main home is in Northern Ireland, and he has a flat in Spain. Hilton prefers Spain, it's warmer.

He was a serving police officer in Northern Ireland from 1983–2010. During his service, he performed both uniformed and plain-clothed roles in both; city and rural settings. Hilton experienced many of the province's atrocities first-hand, but also the marvellous spirit of its people.

He always wanted to write but never found the time until the Covid lockdown arrived. The author hopes you enjoy his humble creation. He can assure you that this fiction is closer to the truth than one might think. This is not a book about politics, it's about people.

Mountroyal is dedicated to all those police officers who got out of bed each day to walk towards the dangers in service of their people. Several close friends paid the ultimate price for the freedoms we enjoy today. This collection of words is dedicated to them and their families. I also wish to dedicate this book to the wonderful and courageous people of Northern Ireland, to their huge heartedness and their love of life and laughter.

Hilton McCabe

MOUNTROYAL

AUSTIN MACAULEY PUBLISHERS™

LONDON * CAMBRIDGE * NEW YORK * SHARJAH

A CIP catalogue record for this title is available from the British Library.

ISBN 9781398443471 (Paperback)
ISBN 9781398443488 (ePub e-book)

www.austinmacauley.com

First Published 2022
Austin Macauley Publishers Ltd®
1 Canada Square
Canary Wharf
London
E14 5AA

I wish to give heartfelt thanks to my wife and best friend Kim who has been the Ying to my Yang. She has been by my side for over 25 years and has been my North Star and my constant through many of life's storms. Mercifully, Kim is a keen reader and has proven herself to be a prodigious beta reader and critic. I throw the words at the pages and Kim makes them form an orderly queue. *Mountroyal*, like our lives together, has been a team effort. Love you lots x.

As rooftop views of Belfast City Centre went, this was hard to beat. For the month of May, the weather was glorious. The sun had his hat on as a soft breeze nursed the marshmallow clouds along their merry way. George had left his cluttered desk with all his problems for a few minutes to take in this vista. He was top of the house on the fourth floor, his nose pressed against a large three-inch-thick glass reinforced window. Below him, a huge metal gate was manually opened and closed clanging hard as vehicles and people came and went. If he craned his neck hard to the right, he could just about see Goliath, a giant yellow crane dominating the landscape of East Belfast. Goliath was located at the world-renowned Harland and Wolff Shipyard. Slowly scanning across to his left, the Albert Clock came next, then further left the aqua green domed roofs of the Belfast City Hall eased into view. Hiding just behind them and slightly to the left, he could also make out the Europa Hotel, the most bombed hotel in the world. George wasn't in his shoes; it was his wee treat to himself as he enjoyed the feel of the soft carpet under his feet. His high-end brogues were tucked neatly away under his desk. Wriggling his toes in excitement, he quickly checked his watch. A bit to go yet. George then hollered over his shoulder. "Debbie Dean, get your ass in here!" A vision of thirty something elegance entered. A blonde bobbed beauty.

"What is it, George? I'm up to my ears."

George smiled. "Sorry, Debbie. A wee game. Let's call it Plume of doom."

Debbie shook her head looking puzzled but then noted the exhaustion in his sixty something face. "Jesus George, there's wiser eating grass."

George laughed. "Right. You have to guess where the smokes going to appear from on the skyline. Loser makes the tea. Deal?"

Debbie shrugged. "I suppose!"

A white van packed with explosives had been abandoned in High Street. Downtown Radio Station had received a call from the IRA giving twenty minutes warning before it was due to go off. A recognised code word had been used. Police on the ground frantically cleared buildings and ushered the unwary to safety. The surrounding area had been cordoned off. It was like the scene of a Cecil B. DE Mille epic except this was for real. This was 1983 and this was what normal Belfast life looked like. George and Debbie marked their chosen spots by tiny smudges on their blast proof window. Then stood and waited. First came a plume of black acrid smoke then a deep BOOOOOOOOM! Their window rattled in protest. A thousand startled pigeons took flight from out of nowhere. George shrugged his slight shoulders in defeat then clicked the switch on the kettle. Debbie's face was still staring out of the window. She watched as the smoke increased and thickened before billowing heavenward across their skyscape. The sound of multiple sirens wailing could now be heard in the distance accompanied by a chorus of burglar alarms triggered by the blast. Dogs howling and the familiar sound of bin lids banging on the pavements arrived. The all too familiar Belfast Opera was in full swing, and the natives were happy.

George smiled at his secretary and good friend. She was always immaculate considering she worked in a shit hole like this. Strand RUC Station was no palace or place for a lady like her. "What's it to be big time winner?"

Debbie was still engrossed. "Coffee for me, George. You know how I take it. Oh, I hope everyone's all right, especially our boys. Some of them are so young."

George nodded, feeling his stomach tighten as he added half a sugar and stirred. Two chocolate digestives were sneaked onto her saucer.

Debbie turned and gave a slight hint of a victory in her smile. "Thank you, George. I love a man that settles his bets."

George paddled over to the corner of his office and dragged a large armchair through his thick pink shag pile. He plonked it beside his desk and sat down. Debbie slipped into his green leather recliner in Persian cat fashion and purred. They supped their tea and ate their digestives in the quiet of his office. Both wishing the wailing world outside would go away.

George was the boss. His official title was Superintendent George Sewell. He was the commander of strand subdivision. He was based at Strand RUC Station and was also in charge of Mountroyal RUC Station a quarter of a mile or so on up the road. Both stations were located in East Belfast.

With their party over, Debbie got up to leave and was gathering up the dishes. George spoke, "Would you get a communication out to all the Duty Inspectors in the Sub. I want them all here Monday night at 7.00pm. I've arranged for the

Collator to give a full briefing on these bloody attacks. I want CID here as well. No excuses. Make it read like a rocket, you're good at that."

Debbie laughed. "Your wish is my command oh mighty one." She left him alone, closing the door gently behind her. George slumped wearily onto his green recliner and stared at all his current worries. Spread across his desk were sensitive documents from a dossier. These documents contained explicit details of vicious sexual attacks on females in the Mountroyal area over the past couple of months. The local press and politicians were now onto it and all over him. Both were demanding answers and results. Up to now, he had nothing to give them.

It's 1983 and in Northern Ireland, the TROUBLES are raging. It's a powder keg of Sectarian hatred and mistrust. Emotions are fed and fuelled by the terrorist gangs of the time.

It's the day of the bomb and the bullet. Life is cheap and your religion could be the difference between life and death. Good people existed. They went to their work, churches, pubs and clubs. When darkness fell, most remained indoors. NO GO areas existed. These were based solely on your faith or political tribe. Death stalked the streets looking for easy prey. If you chose to go out, you were fair game. Death dined lavishly at the all you can kill buffet. No one could ever accuse it of being a picky eater.

The role of peacekeeper and upholder of the law fell to the RUC. The force was 12,000 strong made up of 8000 regulars and 4000 reserves. It comprised of both men and women. Their average age was under 30. Age wise, it was a very young force but well trained and highly professional. In those days, the average response time from when you called for police to a police officer standing at your front door was just three minutes.

Its stations were scattered throughout the province, some in busy towns, others in more rural settings.

The Force was broken into divisions which in themselves were further broken into subdivisions. Each subdivision consisted of two or three individual stations. Strand subdivision had Mountroyal RUC Station as its satellite station. Its patrol area was around four square miles and catered for the mainly working-class Protestant people. Strand RUC Station had an even smaller patrol area of no more than two square miles. Its people were also working class but mainly Roman Catholic, very republican and all things anti British and anti RUC. Strand RUC Station had the dubious record of being the most attacked police station in the world. If you were posted to Strand RUC Station, it was usually as a punishment. The chances of you being blown up or shot increased greatly with a move there. Both these stations were open 24 hours a day, 7 days a week, 365 days a year.

I think it best if we keep things simple and stay with one Section for the duration of this story or collection of stories. Call it as you see it. We will follow A. Section of Mountroyal RUC Station. They're quite an eclectic bunch. You'll catch my drift. Their Inspector is a great guy called Derek Grant. He's nearing retirement. His Sergeant is newly promoted Tony Speers. Tony arrived on promotion from Cookstown, County Tyrone. There he had 140 square miles to get lost in. Now he's only got four. He's got the stripes and is very wet behind the ears. The lone wolf is having to transform himself into a doting mother hen. Here is their story and the story of those lives they became involved with.

...Dot to Dot...
Saturday 14 May 1983...

Occurrence Am 3285/83

Dorothy Walker, known as Dot, stepped out of the Rosemount Bar shortly after 10.00pm. The gunky smell from the River Lagan had crawled up the Woodstock Road and was lingering with bad intentions. Dot breathed in. "Poo yuck, that's disgusting." Farting back in an act of defiance. She was a bit tipsy she thought, *Hic!* But she felt great. The night out with the girlies had done her the world of good. For the first time in her dull life, she had felt the rush of excitement at being ogled at by a bunch of hairy arsed men. Up until now, she had been invisible to them. Not tonight though, no siree, the male species had been full on gawping at her!

The money she had splashed out on her hair do had all been worth it. Why hadn't she done it sooner? Dot was dipping her porky toe into her early forties but claimed mid-thirties. A man on a galloping horse wouldn't have taken issue. She was a spinster by title and never had any serious relationships. Dot was just over 5' 2" in height and fluctuated between average to pleasantly plump. Comfort eating was her hobby of choice. Dot could best be described as drop dead slightly below average. She was a closet romantic, a Mills and Boon groupie if you like. Love would seek her out and find her. Her 'sheikh of the dessert' was just a sand dune away.

She was known and loved as Dot by all who knew her. There was really nothing more to say about Dot, full stop. Dot never knew her dad. He had done the great disappearing act when news of a baby surfaced. Her mum never mentioned him, and he was quietly swept under the carpet of God's forgetfulness. Her mum had died a few years back and Dot now lived alone at the family home. She lived at number 14 Frank Street, East Belfast. There were no cats or dogs, not even a goldfish for company. A radio and an old TV were her sole companions when she got behind closed doors.

Dot's mother had been a wonderful mum and a delightful human being. Her name was Tessie and Dot missed her very much. Tessie had been a larger-than-life character both in size and spirit. They said that you could hear her from a mile away either laughing or singing. Tessie had been employed as a school dinner lady at Mersey Street Primary School all her working life. She just loved the children especially during her later years. Serving dinners to the children of the children she once served. Tessie had been a stalwart at Mersey Street Baptist Church. Should any church functions require catering she would be found in the middle of it all, cooking, baking and tidying up. Tessie had nothing much of worldly value except for an ornate silver T shaped necklace, as in T for Tessie. This was presented to her by the school on her retirement. She adored this gift and never took it off.

One evening shortly after her 62nd birthday, Tessie and Dot were in the front living room watching as they always did their favourite programme Coronation Street. Len and Rita were splitting up again. However, in a final twist Len saved the day. He bought Rita a bunch of flowers and a Chinese take away, closing the show with a smooch and a cuddle. The famous cobbled street music began to play. Dot dabbing away at her tear-filled swollen eyes went 'Awwww' and turned to her mum who appeared to be peacefully sleeping on her favourite recliner with a chocolate éclair resting on her lap. But Tessie wasn't sleeping, she was gone, with no word of goodbye.

The doctors thought Tessie's death was caused by a clot to her brain and that her passing would have been quick and painless. Dot was heartbroken. Her mum had been her everything, her life, her protector and her guardian. Dot had hidden under the shadow of this wonderful larger than life woman, now suddenly she was gone. Dot cherished her mother's beautiful T for Tessie necklace, and just like her mother she never took it off. She would often touch it for comfort or when she was troubled by anything. Mainly when she was missing her mum.

Dot worked at the Cantrell & Cochrane Lemonade factory on the Castlereagh Road, East Belfast, and had done so for the past eight years. She was employed as a bottler. She loved her job which came with special perks – three bottles of lemonade of choice every Friday before knocking off. The bottlers were a great bunch of 40 odd girls or women, ages ranging from teenagers to grannies. Dot was popular with the gang who loved her for her steadiness and kindness. Dot was always there to pull you out of a hole. She also had a lot of bottle!

A hen night had been all the talk in work for weeks. Young Christine McKeown who was in her late teens, was getting hitched to her lifelong boyfriend Barry in a fortnight. Christine was drop dead gorgeous with a heart of corn. She was also a leggy blonde-haired stunner who blew all of the competition clear out of the water. Strangely, Christine was fond of Dot seeing her as the caring aunt she never had. Christine was determined that Dot was going to her hen night by hook or by crook.

Dot had no intentions of attending, she had way too much going on. Coronation Street had a vice-like grip on her and refused to let go. Len and Rita were getting back together again for the tenth time. The suspense was more than Dot could bear. Christine understood but was insistent that Dot at least go to the 'meet up' location at the Rosemount Inn. This watering hole was located just behind Gowdy's Store on the Woodstock Link in East Belfast. The Rosemount as it was known was a great wee boozer. Not a place frequented by the upper echelons of Belfast society. It was a left over from the bygone days of the great Belfast Shipyard era. A time when workers walking home from the yards would pop in for a pint or ten. The clientele could be a bit rough, but the booze was cheap as chips and the management took no crap. It was also super handy for the girls as Amber Taxis was right next door.

The plan was to meet there at 8.00pm and have a few swifties and then taxi it into town. There they would enjoy the rest of the night at Robinsons Bar in Great Victoria Street. The Rosemount was a leisurely ten-minute walk from Dot's house. Christine wouldn't take no for an answer and pestered Dot incessantly day after day. Dot eventually threw her hands up and surrendered, resistance was futile. As the big event approached, she slowly got caught up with all the excitement of the do. Chat about hairdressers and hairstyles began. Before Dot knew it, she had booked herself in for a hair appointment. Her stylist was the great Alexander, master stylist at 'Chique Chicks' Hair Salon, Castlereagh Street.

Dot was blessed with the thickest dark-brown hair, with maybe a few greys peeking through. It was like an abandoned garden laid waste through years of neglect, saved only by the odd hair clip. Dot attended her appointment at 'Chique Chicks' on the afternoon of the do. When she met the great Alexander, he looked at her luscious bonnet and his mouth dropped open, searching for words to fall out. He normally feigned a Lawrence Olivier tone and grandiosed a bit for effect.

(Lexi was really from Sydenham and his Da was a welder in the shipyard.) Alexander finally found voice. "Oh my… (his inner voice continued, 'God what a fucking mess!') please do come in Dorothay and take a seat over here. We'll colour that glorious hair first before we cut and wash it. Can we get you a tea or a Brazilian café con leche perhaps, while you're waiting?" Alexander struck a pose and smiled at Dorothy with his newly purchased pie edger's! (capped teeth!) Dot's poor heart was turning somersaults.

"'Café can lackey' sounds lovely," Dot replied, jumping in with both size five feet! *OMG,* thought Dot, *he's absolutely drop dead gorgeous with his jet-black wavy hair.* Ooooh and his Mediterranean tan and his tiny wee waist. To say Lexi or should I say the great Alexander had a blank canvas to work with was an understatement. It was more like an Amazonian Forest. Undeterred, he set to work, planning first the colour, then the wash and finally the cut. It was now time to choose the renaissance colour. Colour charts were presented of every hue. The pair eventually settled on Tahitian gold which by pure chance was the mix Alexander had most of, out back in his storeroom. Beads of sweat trickled down his 'alu tanned' brow as he cleared the thick hairy under growth slowly exposing a scalp that hadn't seen the light of day since Bill Hailey sang Rock around the Clock!

Alexander may have had his failings, but he did care about making people happy with his work. He spent ages colouring, styling and transforming this jungle into a delight that even the great Capability Brown would have approved of. After three labour intensive hours, it came time for the big reveal… Alexander was done in. He could barely lift the presentation mirror…

"OK, Dorothaay, you may now open your eyes."

Dot slowly opened her eyes and gasped… "Oh my God, I'm gorgeous, I mean it's lovely."

A soft wavy shoulder length bob looked back at her triumphantly! She barely recognised herself or the blonde beauty that had lay hidden for decades under the disinterested and bland old Dot! She looked up at her saviour of the scissors with eyes watering. He nodded knowing he had hit the ball clear out of the park.

"My Alexander, you are sooo great!" Dot whispered…

The transformation had cost our Dot half a week's wages, but she would happily have spent twice that. She looked and felt amazing. Say farewell to frumpy old Dot and let's welcome the delectable Dorothay.

Dot wanted not only to dazzle at the hen do but she especially wanted to make a grand entrance. It was Dot time! She laid her evening's ensemble out on her bed in her old bedroom. She wanted to be all in tune. She decided on a red satin shirt she had bought years ago but had never worn, accompanying it would be a cream woollen skirt. The shoes she anguished over but eventually went with matching cream stilettos, bought on a whim from a Littlewoods catalogue 10 years ago. Maybe a bit too racy Dot thought to herself teetering slightly? "Oh for fuck sake, Dot, get a life, we're only here the once!" She chided as she carefully put on her face.

When all was done, Dot presented herself, the finished article, in front of the mirror nailed to her bedroom wall. The blouse may have been a bit low cut because her black lacy bra was sneaking a peek. Her cream skirt may also have been an 'incy wincy' bit short with more than a hint of thigh showing. Was the lippy a little too red? Hell no, it matched her shirt and her mother's silver pendant with the letter T. Shoes a bit cheap and trollopy? Nope, it was how you walked in them that made the wearer appear cheap, and Dot didn't do that sort of walking! *Stunning girlfriend,* she thought, *we are now good to go and hot to trot!*

Just one thing more, what coat to wear? After a bit of humming and hawing Dot thought about her mother's cream woollen coat with the high collar. The beautiful coat had hung in a wardrobe in the spare bedroom untouched and unused since Tessie had passed. Feeling unnecessarily guilty, Dot retrieved it and reverentially tried it on. She loved what she was now seeing. "Perfecto!" She then eased the collar up adding to her new undeniable allure. "Who's the belle of the ball?" she said swaying back and forth smiling at the mirror.

"Why you are foxy Dotsy darling!"

Dot booked a taxi from Amber Cabs for collection at 8.15pm. She wanted to make her entrance as dramatic as possible and 'out late' any other tactical latecomer wishing to park on the yellow lines of her limelight! She stuffed £150.00 into her green plastic purse which she placed in her black shoulder bag. The goddess then went into the front room to wait. A short time later, the amber cab arrived with a beep! It was now raining lightly.

"Where to, love?" the taxi driver asked, wheezing like a busted accordion. His voice was a gravelly deep double bass which was barely audible above the bellows of his nicotine filled lungs. Her chauffeur was a man in his sixties with grey straggly shoulder length thinning hair. His scarlet eyes matched Dot's blouse. His teeth resembled a broken duck range at a funfair. His bodily odours were a raging Teutonic battle. Extreme lack of personal hygiene was just losing out to stale booze and cheap woodbines. If the old codger wasn't pissed, oh and that was another odour coming through, then he deserved a best actor award.

Dot's eyes were beginning to water. Her 'Just Because' Fragrance was fast giving ground to his stink. She tried to talk without breathing.

"The Rosemount please and don't spare the horses my good man." Dot gasped and held her breath once more. Her chauffeur turned and faced her, determined to bless her with his full range of odours all at once.

"Sure, it's only around the corner, luv." Mr Stinky wheezed. He sounded a little hard done by. Dot exhaled and sucked in a mouthful of his noxious odours.

"No shit, Sherlock, it's pissing down now, and I don't want soaked; there's a fiver in it for you. Now get a fucking move on before I die of the fumes!"

Five minutes later, Dot's cab pulled up outside the Rosemount. She slapped a fiver into the driver's hand and was released into the nearly clean air of east Belfast, there was always a slight ping coming from the river Lagan close by. It was now 8.20pm, a soft drizzle was falling and dusk was setting in. She could see the lights were on inside and judging by the silhouettes and chattering noises a fair crowd were in the bar. *It's now or never*, she thought, tentatively stepping like a baby stork in her heels towards the front door. Head back, movie star smile, tummy in and tits out. Dot gave her mother's T necklace a quick rub for luck and into the maelstrom she went.

A large choral scream erupted from the corner of the bar where 20 or so of her work mates were planted. From its midst, she could hear. "Is it her, surely not. It can't be."

Then from the centre of the group sprang young Christine gasping and smiling broadly. "Dot, I don't believe it, is it really you, you look simply stunning!" Coming from the most beautiful woman in the room, this was high praise indeed. All Dot's wildest hopes and dreams had been met and surpassed. This was maybe the happiest moment of her life!

Christine led her over to her group where more praise was lavished on her extreme transformation. Dot felt ever so glamorous. She put £20.00 into the kitty and was told she had a bit of catching up to do. Within twenty minutes, Dot had adiosed four Malibu and pineapples and had two more sitting waiting in the wings. She was having the night of her life. Her head was getting a bit fluffy, maybe her speech a tad slurred. As the evening wore on, she began to sound ever so slightly like a female John Wayne impersonator. Her friends howled at her every comment, she was now funny as well as beautiful.

A Tammy Wynette number came on over the speakers for Christine's benefit. 'Stand by your man' belted out which was followed by 'D.I.V.O.R.C.E'. The entire bar got the message and sang along. The rafters shook. Dot became the choirmaster turning one way and then the other unwittingly showing a bit too much cleavage and thigh. Her glass was never empty and not being a drinker, she never noticed. There was no nastiness to this, Dot's workmates adored her and loved the new improved Dot, and as for the male admirers, well they were like putty in Dot's hands. They had no knowledge of the plain old Dot before her amazing make over. All they could see was this 18-carat gold stunner. Their beer goggles were on double time and in perfect harmony with snatched glimpses of Dot's unwitting form.

As the clock crept towards 10.00pm, the rest of the gang were drinking up. The taxis for Robinsons were lined up outside and the second act of the hen night lay ahead. Dot was well drunk being a novice at the drinking game. Her night was over as the girlies filed out of the Rosemount singing the famous Barry Manilow classic 'Copacabana'. Christine trotted over and cozied up to Dot and sensitively said, "You're looking a wee bit tired glamour queen, (Dot's eyes blinked slowly and she nodded followed by a giggle.) shall I get you a taxi to take you home? I hear it's not too safe for us ladies around here these days." Dot finished singing the last few lines of the song as best she could and watched as the last of the gang drained out of the bar. She looked up at the lovely Christine and was grateful for her friendship and kindness towards her.

Getting a bit emotional, Dot softly spoke, "No Christine, love, you head on. It's your hen night. I'll be fine, sure I only live around the corner. I'll walk home, the air will do me good, hic." Christine smiled, nodded and patted Dot on the knee then skipped out of the bar.

Dot was now all alone. The Rosemount was empty save for a few die-hard boozers who all had one thing in common, a fascination with the bottom of their glasses! *Home time,* thought Dot. She got up unsteadily from her bar stool and headed for the door. "Bye now, I'll see yez all again." She slurred as a fart escaped from her derriere! No one took notice. The new queen from the east had left the building. Outside, it was dark but dry, the rain from earlier was gone. Dot paused swaying slightly, looking at the Amber Taxi rank yards away. "What to do, what to do. Taxi or walk girlfriend?" mumbled Dot to herself. Then she remembered 'Mr Stinky' her chauffeur from earlier and decided to walk. She didn't want to meet that drunken bum again. Dot had a simple 10-minute stagger.

Her blurry eyed journey would take her down Mount Street followed by a right up onto the Woodstock Road. A cross over on to Castlereagh Place at the end of which was Castlereagh Street and facing Dot would be Frank Street and home. The silence was now deafening apart from the thunderous click clack of her stilettos which announced her presence as she turned right onto the eerily quiet Woodstock Road and headed countrywards.

An icy breeze from the Lagan tore up the road and buffeted Dot who turned up her collar for protection. Suddenly Dot became aware of an urgent and dire need to pee. She could normally hold it in for ages but this time it was serious. If she didn't go within the next few seconds, she was going to piss herself. She had no alternative; she would do it up the entry to her left. The entry ran parallel with the Woodstock Road and still exited at Castlereagh Place. Just a slightly smellier walk. Dot's bladder was now fit to burst as her staggering pace increased. "Hurry, hurry," she whispered as she left the bright streetlights of the Woodstock Road and entered the grimy darkness of the bin lined entry.

Her eyes struggled to focus with the change of light as she opened the buttons of her coat searching, panicking for somewhere to squat. Her click clacking sounded like rifle shots echoing off the narrow entry walls. The torrential rain returned heaping misery on the now soaking helpless Dot. "Fucking great. Could it get any worse!" Dot was hanging on by the finest of threads and was now reduced to waddling like a duck. Then she spotted it, her last chance, her only chance, a yard door to a clearly derelict house. The old door was lying slightly open just ahead. "Thank you, God," Dot whispered, nearly going over on her ankle on some broken glass scattered on the rough, uneven ground.

As she entered the derelict yard, she closed the door over behind her. Filthy! She swung her handbag over her back then hurriedly rucked up her cream skirt which was agony due to its tight fit. Tights and knickers down in one go and assumed the squat position, then the glorious release. It was like a power hose. Dot threw her by now soaking head back and let out a huge sigh and smiled. She held the pose. This was better than an orgasm, not that she had experienced many of those. The yard door suddenly crashed open like an explosion. The shock and terror causing Dot to fall over onto her back like an upturned beetle. Her knickers and tights were still around her ankles as one of her shoes flew off. She struggled to get up but was viciously punched in the face breaking her nose and knocking a front tooth out. She cowered like a baby, pleading to the dark masked figure punching and kicking at her!

"Please stop, I'm begging you please."

Dot's hair was yanked by a powerful hand and forced downwards into the ground. Her attacker spoke, a local accent deep and menacing.

"Right fatso, do as I say and you might live, if you make a sound you won't live. Do I make myself clear, Miss Piggy?"

"Yes" was all Dot had in her. She felt her bladder go again as a pool of urine crept between her bloodied knees…

"Dirty fat bitch!" sneered her attacker. "Any money on you, slag?" He continued.

"In my purse in my bag, take it all please. Just let me go." Dot could just about see the lower half of her attacker. Black tracksuit bottoms and black trainers. He had set a dark green backpack down which Dot thought she heard sounds coming from. She was too terrified to look up at him.

"Good piggy, this cash will come in handy to pay for my fucking dry cleaning. You've bled all over me you selfish fat cow!" Dot's green purse was thrown on the ground beside her, and she was kicked hard to her right side cracking a rib. Then a few seconds of silence followed, her attacker was thinking. Then he spoke in a much calmer and more pleasant tone, "Well, moon pig, there's only one thing left for you to do for me. If you behave yourself, I might let you go. Do you understand?" Dot nodded, trembling. Her attacker snarled. "I'm sorry I didn't hear you say YES MASTER…" slapping her to the side of her buttock.

"Yes, master," Dot stuttered.

"It's time for your master's blow job and it better be fucking good or you'll be fucking dead fatty."

Dot was now a shivering aching mess of blood, piss and snot. She was totally compliant and broken. The BJ was a blur and Dot kept her eyes closed the entire time. She desperately wanted to live. It ended after a time when the thrusting in her mouth became more rapid and intense. She could hear him puffing, panting, rasping the words 'bitch' and 'fat whore'. His orgasm arrived in a splurge as he pulled out. Dot felt his legs shaking and then felt her tear-filled eyes dotted and her mother's T crossed with his warm sperm! Silence again and then he spoke for the final time, "Not bad, tubby, do you do that for a living! I'm away now. Stay here for a minute and then you can go. And don't report this to the fucking peelers or else!" Dot nodded as she felt her T necklace being carefully removed and taken from her.

"Noooo," she whispered. A final vicious slap on her backside culminated with the yard door opening and closing. She heard the sound of running feet splashing through puddles and then fading into the darkness and chill of the night.

Dot lay still quietly sobbing for a good three minutes. When she lifted her bloodied head, she felt defiled. Dot was filthy, sore and alone in the derelict rear yard. The rain was falling hard, and the wind had picked up. No knight in shining armour had come to her aid. No prince of the desert had come to her rescue. But Dot was alive. She comforted herself with that thought as she slowly got up and sorted herself out. She gathered her purse and checked for her house key.

"Good, at least you're there," she whispered. Absent-mindedly, she reached for her mother's T necklace for comfort. "It's gone now, silly." Fresh tears began to fall as she made her way out of the yard and began her walk of shame home. Click clack, click clack. No one was about, as this woman; hair bedraggled with blood and rain, reached Frank Street and home.

Dot was numb, she couldn't face looking at herself. Minimum lighting was used for fear of her running into her own reflection. She ran her tongue along her upper gums feeling the gap where her front tooth used to be. She then made her way upstairs and ran a bath. She would clean herself, clean him off her. Every item of clothing she had on her was stuffed into a couple of bin bags and shoved in her outside bin. As she lay wallowing in the bath thoughts ran through her head as she replayed her horrors over and over. Was it all really her fault? Should she have gone on into town with her pals? Should she have taken the taxi home? Was she asking for it? Was she dressed like a slut and then back again too was it all really her fault?

Dorothy climbed slowly out of the bath aching all over. She dried herself and put her dressing gown on. She was going to face herself in the bedroom mirror. She knew she would have to face the truth sometime. She slowly entered her bedroom and turned on the light switch. Dot was instantly dazzled by the effect of the 100-watt bulb. Her tiny bedroom was a world safe from harm. Powder puff pinks and white. Her teddy bear gazed sadly at her from her pillow. She stood before the all-seeing mirror and disrobed.

"Holy good fuck, what has he done to me!" she screamed. Clumps of hair were missing from her newly acquired blonde head. Her face was swollen and her eyes were puffed and blackening. She opened her mouth, viewing her swollen gums and the missing front tooth. Cuts and bruising revealed themselves all over the rest of her lily-white body. The left side of her chest was really tender and sore. Dot began to well up with a strange feeling. A feeling she had never had before. A deep guttural emotion began to surge from deep within and then exploded as Dot screaming raged.

"You fucking bastard, I'm going to hang your balls on a lamp post!"

Dot strangely felt much better following her outburst. She had discovered a different side of herself. A warrior if you like, a stronger better version of her already acceptable self.

Was she going to live like a mouse with the terrors for the rest of her days...?

"I think fucking not..." she said switching her bedroom light off and climbing into bed.

Dot was determined to contact the police when she woke up.

Dot made her call to the police shortly after 8.30am the following morning. She rang 999 and was eventually speaking with an officer who identified himself as Constable Sweetlove (Tweety Pie.) He was very nice, kind and patient and calmed Dot when she occasionally burst into tears. He gently steered her through a few awkward questions and informed her that a crew containing a very capable officer would be with her in five minutes. Dot thanked him for his kindness then hung up noticing her bruised hand shaking as she set the phone down. She returned to her rear living room and sat alone in silence and waited patiently for the rest of her life to begin.

The Longest Day...
Sunday 15 May 1983...

"If You Get the Name of An Early Riser, You Can Lie the Whole Day Long!"

Tony was a bit tired. He had been out last night supping with a few of his old police buddies from his Cookstown days. This now seemed like a lifetime ago. They had enjoyed a convivial evening at 'Bobby C's Bar (Bob Cratchits)' on the Lisburn Road, Belfast. Tony's alarm bleep bleeped on his watch at 5.30am. Still in snooze mode he clawed for his bedside table lamp. He couldn't feel it anywhere. Tony forced his eyes open and found he was in a strange place. Definitely not his man cave of mainly greys and blacks, it was all pinks and creams. *Yuck*, he thought trying to kick start his weary brain into recall.

He turned over and was pleasantly surprised to find a long naked olive skinned back. Long brown shoulder length hair also presented itself to him. "Think, Tony, think!" He scanned the floor, both sets of clothes were strewn all over the place. Red Louis Vuitton shoes. "Ahh, the doctor." Tony slowly remembered, she had blanked him all night long. How had it ended like this? Tony made to leave quietly in case this good doctor awoke and remembered she hated his guts. He gathered his stuff together, planning to get dressed in the hallway, and then she turned slowly exposing all her loveliness and a body to die for. "Leaving so early, gorgeous, you were amazing last night," she whispered, her eyes half closed.

"Yes pet, (Tony still couldn't remember the good doctors name) I've got to be at work for 6.30am," he said, backing out the door covering his manhood with his crumpled clothes.

"At least have a shower first, I start at 8.00am at the Royal (Royal Victoria Hospital, Belfast.). To save time we could do it together...it's an order from

Doctor Chloe," she said standing up biting her bottom lip. Tony felt something else stirring and also standing up.

"Chloe, how could I refuse, and we'd be saving water," Tony replied as he was led to the shower for a good cleaning too.

Tony had started at Mountroyal on the 3 May 1983 his first posting as a new Sergeant and he was still finding his feet. Tony was 28 years old and had seven years' service. He was the arch poacher as a Constable in Cookstown which was his first station. It was one of the larger subdivisions in the RUC where he had 140 square miles of mainly unmarked countryside to patrol and hide in. When pressed he could produce the goods and was a conscientious enough cop. But Tony in reality had more in common with the Neanderthal Man, he was a hunter gatherer and just loved the women. He loved the chase and the afters if he played his cards right. (Mrs Right was to be found in another book way down the line.) Tony was 6' 2" and a solid fourteen stone. He had jet black hair and pumped iron for the desired effect. He was born and bred in Dundonald and still lived there in a stylish two bed flat near Stormont. This allowed him to operate more freely without parental supervision. Being a good son, he still went around to mummy's for tea as often as possible and to collect his ironing once a week!

Tony attended RBAI School or the Royal Belfast Academical Institution in the heart of Belfast City Centre. He wasn't overly academic and gathered up average passes at both 'A' and 'O' levels. He was a good rugby player where he played outside centre. When he joined the RUC, he was head hunted by their rugby officials one of whom was the legendary Cliff Boomer Aka Perky. They instantly hit it off maybe because Tony reminded Cliff of himself many moons ago. Tony was blessed with looking and sounding just like a Ferrari, but in reality, he was more of a Ford Escort 1.3L. He never hid this fact. He was basically a kind and decent bloke and revelled in his unwarranted status.

It was around 6.20 a.m. as he sauntered past the Enquiry Office noting that Tweety and Vic were already in and had relieved the Night Guards. "Mornin' fellas," he whispered giving the seasoned pair a tired thumbs up.

Tweety looked up, his one green eye hidden behind dark lenses. "Morning, Sarge, the night boys are just writing off one more call. The kettles on, be with you in a couple."

As Tony approached the sergeant's office door, the top two buttons of his shirt were open. His black tie and Sergeant's epaulettes were in his pockets. On entering the office, he was initially surprised to find someone going through the stationary cupboard pilfering. Tony stood there waiting. Nonplussed, the male figure continued with his raid. When he eventually turned to face Tony, his arms were full of Mountroyal stationary. He fixed Tony with an arrogant glare looking down his nose at him. He opened his thin mouth and spoke in an officious tone. "Have you ever heard of knocking when you enter the Sergeant's Office you Cretan!" He was around 6' 1" in height. Rakishly thin with a pasty complexion and looked no more than 23 years old. His hair was mousey brown and the bum fluff resting on his upper lip was a poor excuse for a moustache. Tony noted his police attire was more 'combatty' and guessed correctly that he hailed from Strand RUC Station. This moron had Sergeants stripes on his epaulettes. His fame or infamy had preceded him. "This must be the famous Sergeant PLANK," thought Tony to himself. The office door suddenly flew open and a whistling Tweety reversed in. He was carrying the heavy C6 (Occurrence Book) and two steaming cups of coffee. Sergeant PLANK fumed.

"Not another one. How dare you enter the sergeant's office without knocking!" Tweety set the C6 down at Tony's desk along with his coffee which was in his favourite Thomas the Tank mug. His mother had bought it for him the previous Easter and it came with a Cadbury's Easter egg now long gone. Tony's Achilles heel was chocolate. Tony had by this time popped his Sergeants epaulettes and tie on. He moved casually around to his desk and plonked himself down on his swivel chair. Tony began to swivel. He loved swivelling it. Swivelling made him happy. He looked at Tweety and winked leaving Sergeant Plank hanging and fuming.

"Cheers, Tweety, you're a lifesaver." Tweety winked back but with only one eye it looked like a regular blink.

Tweety looked up at Sergeant PLANK and uttered, "Rex Placeman!" (Latin meaning King of Idiots.) Tony smiled, Tweety was having fun. Sergeant PLANK exploded! Vic in the Enquiry Office could hear it all unfolding and shaking his head chuckled.

"What did you just say to me, Constable?" Tweety now tiring of Sergeant PLANK got up and left, his parting words were, "Kia Fripono," (Esperanto meaning 'What a Moron'.) The plank was going ballistic and shouted after Tweety.

"Come right back, that's an order!" As Tweety entered the Enquiry Office beaming, he shouted back laughing in his finest Samoan, "*Kisi Lo'U Muli,*" meaning Kiss my Ass!

Pure Tweety gold, thought Tony, none the wiser, cutting Sergeant Plank off mid bluster.

"Good morning, I'm Sergeant Tony Speers, A. Section Sergeant and you are?" The pair eyed each other. It was hate at first sight! The plank spoke, "I'm Sergeant Nigel Norwood, your counterpart at Strand RUC."

Sergeant Norwood had earned his sobriquet with flying colours. He was officious, arrogant and a bully. His men despised him. He policed from a training manual and had very little service on the actual ground. A deadly cocktail that could get men killed. He had joined the RUC with an average obscure degree. His family were wealthy and well connected with ears in high places. Nigel found himself on the accelerated promotion scheme for highfliers. He was promoted after two years under protest from his then Sub Divisional Commander in Armagh. Sergeant Norwood had already attended Bramshill College for Policing in Hampshire England where he failed to impress but strangely passed his exams. The name Plank was given to him by his present Section. It evolved from Norwood to 'All Wood' and then the 'Plank'! Anyone who crossed his path felt the name was a good fit. Everyone knew of this title except Sergeant Nigel Norwood.

Tony eyed the swathe of forms under the Plank's arms and said sarcastically "Help yourself, why don't you? I can order some more from the Admin Office where you're stationed at."

The plank exploded with rage. "How dare you take that tone with me. I'm more senior in rank than you and my rise to the top will be meteoric, whereas I think you have most definitely peaked!"

Vic and Tweety chuckled from their safe domain, they liked that one. Tony really wanted to punch his lights out. The office door opened and Sergeant Tom Mills, the Night Section Sergeant, quietly entered. Tom had served 25 years on the job and had been a Sergeant for over 17 years, the last eight at Mountroyal. Tom had never married unless you could say that he had been married to the job. He lived in a nice flat in Ballynafeigh over in South Belfast. He was short, no more than 5' 8" and slightly plump with thick sandy hair. He had never left uniformed duties and was a fair and hardworking police officer who would think nothing of making an arrest or taking on a file. He was good to his troops as he called them and sucked the very marrow out of their abilities with encouragement and high praise. Many constables under his charge rose to high rank in the RUC. Tom had left his thumb print on them by way of his work ethic and his man management style. Most of these men would quote Tom as their source of inspiration.

Tom walked over to his desk and took a seat. He took his police issue notebook out of his top right-hand pocket and began to update it regarding his previous shift, this done he kept on quietly writing. Sergeant Plank continued feeling very much in the ascendancy… "Furthermore, I intend to put you and that funny one-eyed man on report. Do I make myself clear Sergeant Speers?" Tony was about to reply when Sergeant Tom Mills quietly interrupted.

"Morning, Tony, I've a couple of incidents from last night that need a wee follow up. No signs of the attacker. Just one moment please." Sergeant Mills turned towards the plank and spoke with equal softness.

"Morning, Sergeant Norwood, I was led to believe that you were stationed at Strand RUC Station and that your Section will be parading for duty in ten minutes. Am I correct in what I've just said?" The plank was flustered knowing Tom had very many more years' seniority than himself.

"Yes, but."

Tom slowly raised his hand continuing. "Sergeant Norwood, are you in a position to brief your section as to the occurrences for your station last night. Are you familiar with all the facts? Are there any areas out of bounds relating to your station? Any threats your crews should know about? Sergeant Speers here, your junior man has prudently taken the time to come in early to arm himself with all these facts. He's ready to go. The welfare and safety of his Section are at the foremost of his thoughts. Strand RUC is a seriously more dangerous station to police than Mountroyal. I believe it is factually the most attacked police station on the planet, you should be with your section now but instead I find you here stealing stationary. I heard you shouting from the Enquiry Office and your tone and manner to your fellow officers was highly unprofessional and which I consider bullying. To refer to Constable Sweetlove who lost the sight of an eye due to a terrorist incident while on duty as a 'funny one eyed' man is deplorable. So in a nutshell, we have 'Neglect of Duty' with regards to your Section who are a good bunch and deserve better, 'Bullying in the workplace' and theft or attempted theft of stationary. I have it all here in my notebook." Sergeant Plank was now like a deflated balloon. Tom had quietly dismantled the bully piece by piece.

Tweety had his ear pressed hard to the Sergeants office door, his day was already made and it hadn't even started. Tom dispassionately looked Sergeant

Plank up and down and said sighing, "Back in 1958 during one of my last days in the depot in Enniskillen (The RUC Training College.), the Commandant arranged a very small talk for us from an old constable who had done 35 years on the job. That day in fact was his last day. He had been policing in the RUC from the early 1930s. One of the things he said to us all that day never left me. He told us all that we were no better than bin men and like bin men we were servants of the public or Public Servants. Not only should we treat our public with respect, we must treat our fellow officers in the same manner. Please think on these things Sergeant Norwood. Do you have anything further you wish to say while my notebook is open because I'm rather tired and wish to get home and go to bed." Sergeant Plank shook his head avoiding all eye contact.

Tom slowly rose from his chair and placed his clenched fists on the desk. Tony noticed a subtle mood swing as Tom reddened behind the collar and then with ever increasing volume finishing with a roar he said, "Lovely, will you then please return our stationary from where you got it as we actually need it here ourselves. Once you've done that you can Fuck Away Off!" Everyone jumped all the way down to the Enquiry Office. The plank jumped the highest, but Tony was a close second. The plank exited, broken and bowed just as Tweety slipped back into the Enquiry Office.

Tom sat back down on his chair and removed his tie and epaulettes which were old and worn with the many seasons of service. He placed them in the top drawer of his desk and locked it. He then shook his head wearily. Tom looked at his new friend and said, "Sorry about losing my temper just then Tony lad. But I just hate wankers like that!" Tom got up and lifted his old brown anorak of the coat hook on the wall and smiled to Tony and on leaving said, "Beddy-byes for me. Have a quiet one chum. Catch you soon."

What a Legend, Tony thought.

Just before 6.45am, Tony breezed into the Parade Room. Under his arm was the C6, a list of relevant stolen or suspicious vehicles and the Vacant Property Register. Not forgetting the duty sheet, i.e., who was doing what that day. "Morning team," he said smiling, gazing upon their lovely smirking faces, notebooks open with pens in hand.

The Early Shift started officially at 7.00am, however the section like all the other sections would parade for duty at 6.45am. This would give Tony Speers time to brief the section of any notable events that occurred within their patch since they were last on. The briefing would also include general threats, missing or wanted persons and stolen vehicles. He would detail his crews in a fair rotation ensuring turns as the observer in the hot seat of the response vehicle AM70, was evenly spread. He also had to consider who had the most files on, i.e. the most paperwork in their In-Tray. One day, you would be the main man and nothing would stick; another day every call was a prosecution file.

His 'Call-Up register' told him the state of play, in particular, who was producing the work and who was coasting. Every Sergeant had their own Sections Call-Up Register. Every file submitted went into the register. It was given a reference number against the Investigating Officer's name and its evolving state of play recorded, basically a diary of each file. If queries surfaced these would be noted on the register with a deadline date for resolution until the file was completed to the Sergeant's satisfaction. The file was then forwarded to the Section Inspector for his or her perusal and approval.

Tony also had to take into account who was going on leave. There was no point in putting one of his gang as the 'Big O' (main observer) if they were heading to Greece the next day for a fortnight. It was a fun filled plate spinning extravaganza. But Sunday Earlies were usually a soft affair. Nothing too much ever happened in Norn Iron on 'The Lord's Day'.

News of the Sergeant Plank incident had broken in the locker room hot line. "Enough now." Tony laughed and they all joined in. When the giggling ceased, Tony briefed his Section. Calmly, he read out any noteworthy incidents from the C6 (Occurrence Book). Then any area out of bounds in their patch, missing or Wanted persons, then finally stolen or wanted vehicles. Tony leaned back in his chair.

"Everyone gets all that. Anything you missed or want me to go over again?" A sea of smiling faces shook their heads.

"Now for the Crews and in no particular order."

"AM70… (Main response crew.) The Big 'O' (Observer), Arnie Savage with Driver Gary Weaver."

"AM71 (Second response crew.) The Big 'O' Andy Lovell with Shelley McClelland Driver."

"I'm sticking out a further crew to cover the Vacant Property Register."

"AM80 The Big 'O', R. Con Stevie Uprichard with Lionel Graham Driver."

"That just leaves Pete Majury (Preacher) and Stephanie Gates (Heavenly.), Pete will fill Stevie's spot in the Box (Security Sanger) and Stephanie you're on files, it's time to put that Parkview Bar assault to bed. Troops don't forget any suspicious sightings, terrorist or otherwise. Stick them on a C.I.1 and leave them on my desk at the end of play."

The C.I.1 or Criminal Intelligence form came in pocket sized pads and fitted into any pocket. These forms were an invaluable tool for the police. Police would use them when stopping known criminals at any date, time or place. Noting what vehicles were being driven, items of clothing worn and also their associates. Police would complete a C.I.1 when driving by a known criminal thus fixing his whereabouts which often negated an alibi. Every C.I.1 was kept and stored. Many proved themselves as an invaluable piece of evidence during critical court trials.

"Any questions, queries or thoughts team?" Tony ended.

They all replied in unison as they got up and filed out, "No, Sergeant."

'The Vacant Property Register' was a register containing vacant properties in the subdivision. It was a service provided by the police. If someone was going on holidays or for whatever other reason their property was going to be empty for a period, they would contact the police giving their details as well as details of address and the period the property would be vacant, some would even leave their property keys with the police.

The police would then routinely inspect the property ensuring everything was in order. Every inspection would be recorded in the register with the inspecting officers name by it.

The VPR was kept busy during the summer months when holidays were taken. Tony had selected Reserve Con Stevie Uprichard as observer for AM80 because he was aware that Stevie had dreams of becoming a regular constable. A keen attitude and proactive time on the ground with the odd prosecution file would help his cause no end. Tony would do all he could for the likeable but slightly awkward Stevie.

Pete kicked the sanger door open gently carrying a black coffee in his old chipped blue and white metal mug. At 6' 4", he had to crouch to get in… "Morning all," he said smiling.

Pete Majury or 'The Preacher' was a quiet force of nature. He exuded calm like still, deep dark waters. He was 32 years of age and single. His parents were missionaries in Namibia, and he had basically been raised by a spinster aunt in Newtownards. He had attended Regent House Grammar School there attaining top grades at both 'O' and 'A' Levels without really breaking sweat. He played for the first fifteen at rugby where he starred at out half. No one could read a

31

game like Pete Majury. He was blessed with blistering pace, a sidestep from heaven and the softest pair of hands for passing a rugby ball. He also possessed a siege gun left boot which propelled the ball for miles. Folks didn't come to watch Regent play; they came to marvel at Majury. One of those players who would go all the way. However, when he left school, he left rugby as well. He never looked back and had no regrets. Pete only did it to help out which really summed up his outlook to everything.

He was a wild and free spirit. Pete loved to run in the wide-open spaces nature had offered. He did natural weights, lifting rocks and the like. Free rope climbing enhanced his already amazing natural strength and physique. Pete trained and excelled at karate from an early age which he balanced with his love for the discipline of yoga. As a man he loved the great outdoors, choosing solitude and the seldom trodden path. He had a charming ease and was intimidated by no one.

Pete lived alone in a very old and decrepit looking cottage on the outskirts of Killyleagh, County Down. His mode of transport was a clapped-out Citroen V2. Moss in colour. No one would ever make the connection that the driver of this car was a very special person let alone a police officer. This suited the Preacher to a tee. He just edged Tweety for the worst wheels in the section. The cottage was located at the bottom of a tiny lane just off the main Comber to Killyleagh road. It happily survived the attention of mankind by being discreetly tucked away behind a small forest. Strangford Lough and a tiny sandy beach sat yards away from his gull grey weather-beaten front door. A jetty also edged out into the lough not that any boats used it anymore. It was a remnant of a bygone age and had survived primarily because no one else knew it was there. When Pete clapped eyes on it, he was smitten. A special place to call his home. A dwelling far from the madding crowd, nestled in amongst some breath-taking scenery. Nevertheless it had the most basic of amenities. Electricity along with a telephone line had just recently been installed. The telephone was an important luxury to Pete. It was a lifeline between himself and his parents as well as a means for his work to get a hold of him should any threats arise or any changes to his shifts occur.

To say he lived alone is not entirely true. He enjoyed the companionship of his best friend, a six-year-old golden retriever called Bud. Bud came from Irish Champion parents. His official title was Golden Orient the Third but he would get embarrassed if it was ever mentioned. Bud was practically human. He understood every word Pete said and was a step ahead with most of his thoughts. Bud, like Pete, loved the great outdoors. When Pete was home, he stayed with him. When he was away, he happily lived in a tiny outhouse adjacent to the ram shack cottage. When Pete was swimming in the lough Bud swam with him. Bud had two jobs in life as well as loving Pete. He was the guard dog which entailed two things, firstly keeping Pete safe. Secondly, protecting Pete's incessantly clucking free range hens from the attentions of the hungry foxes. Oh and he had somehow taught himself to bark and bellow whenever the phone rang. For Pete was rarely in. Bud and Pete were a good fit. They didn't do walks or cuddles, but they shared in the joy of meals and quiet companionship. A peaceful togetherness shared on a tiny front porch or at the end of an old jetty on a star lit summer night. Two kindred spirits happy with their lot, together watching the ever-changing seasons pass by.

Pete was called Preacher because of his simple Christian faith which had been lovingly passed down from his parents, never trumpeting it he never hid it either.

Back in the front sangar quietly looking out at the busy Woodstock Road was 'Wee John' or John Alexander. John was 57 years old, 5' 7" with a slim fit build. He had thick dark brown hair and was married with two sons and lived in Carrick. He was a carpenter by trade and had joined the Full Time Reserve in the RUC some 12 years ago. Mountroyal was his first Station. 'Wee John' was a rock in the Section by virtue of his quiet steady nature. Like the preacher, he was a man very much at peace with himself. He looked around at Pete smiling and said, "Mornin', Preacher." He then returned his gaze to the road outside. Pete turned to another male who was standing fiddling with a portable tape recorder. He was trying to get a tape cassette inserted. Pete the Preacher spoke, "Not so fast Stevie lad, I'm you today, the Skipper has you as Observer AM80 with Lionel Graham driving. You're looking after the Vacant Property Register. With a bit of luck, you can pick up a file on your travels. Lionel will keep you right." Stevie got the cassette in and tucked the tape recorder in a plastic bag.

Stevie responded, "Cheers, Preacher. I'll pop in and see the skipper now."

Stevie Uprichard was a 28-year-old married man with two young kids. He was around 5' 9" tall. Average build, and not bad looking. He lived in a large, detached house in Bangor County Down with the not so lovely Charlene. Not that she wasn't attractive, but she was just plain ugly on the inside where it counted. They never had enough of this or that. Stevie was a bad husband and why wasn't he in the regulars. She was forever putting him down in public and would flirt with other men just to annoy him. Charlene wore the trousers. Stevie could do no right in her eyes and was on a strictly bread and water diet as far as sex was concerned. He drove an old banger while she drove a nice BMW owned by the bank. Charlene was also a leading lady of the so called 'Mummy Mafia' at her local gym which Stevie paid for. He had to work all the hours overtime just to remain in severe dire financial straits. Poor Stevie was always slightly on the outside looking in on life. He was permanently stressed.

Stevie left the sanger and headed into the main station, he was buzzed into the Enquiry Office by Vic. Sergeant Tony Speers was there having a chuckle with his driver Lionel Graham the section joker and hot head. Stevie placed his tape recorder still in its plastic bag under the counter and asked Vic to keep an eye on it for him until he got back. Sergeant Speers approached him smiling and said, "Hi, Stevie, are you happy enough taking care of the VPR (Vacant Property Register) for me today?"

Stevie straightened. "Absolutely no problems Sergeant, leave it with me." He forced a smile which came out just like that.

Tony got it. "Great Stevie, (also forcing a smile. It was becoming contagious!) One in particular needs our special attention. It's 4 Ravenhill Park Gardens, just off the upper Ravenhill Road. (a very well to do area.) It's owned by Ms Vivien Chesney, our local Official Unionist MP. The VPR shows her as being away until next Saturday the 21 May 1983. Here's the house key, have a wee look inside make sure there's no burst pipes and no burglaries. Apparently, she's a bit of a dragon. She's had the SDC's balls in a vice with the media over these sex attacks. No fuck ups with it please. Don't forget to sign it off in the VPR. I have absolutely no doubt the boss will be checking!"

Tony handed all over to Stevie who excitedly said, "No worries, Sergeant (stopping just short of saluting!), you can count on me!" Stevie and Lionel headed out with Lionel as usual cracking jokes.

Tony made his way back to the Sergeants office as the Enquiry Office slowly emptied and settled down to its sedate Sunday rhythm. Soothing classical music chilled through the office. BRC handlers (Belfast Regional Control) on the police net could be heard sounding off calls to other locations and responses crackled back. Vic was reading the salacious News of the World. Tweety, feet up and tie off was now engrossed in a book on the Byzantine Empire. Meanwhile on a lower shelf by the Enquiry Office counter a little tape recorder sat. The cassette tape turned silently. The record button was on.

Tony shuffled into his office absolutely cream crackered or knackered. He allowed himself a back cracking stretch followed by a musical yawn. A glance at the paperwork on his desk followed by a quiet whisper, "Mmm, files or Bo Bo's?" Tony came to a swift resolution. An hour's kip then the paperwork. It was the Lord's Day after all. A day of rest! He rang the lads in the Enquiry Office informing them of his cunning plan. The usual alarm would be given if anyone of note should arrive. A series of double clicks on the station intercom by the boys on security. Tony yawned and gave himself another long stretch. It had just gone 7.15am. He fiddled with the alarm on his wristwatch and set it for 8.30am. Tony was well aware that the beep beep from this alarm could raise the dead. There were three armchairs in the Sergeants office. One with arms, two without. If you shoved them all together with the one with the arms at the head, you could make yourself a reasonable bed. Tony also had the cherry for this cake, he opened the bottom drawer of his desk and whipped out a burgundy cushion saved from the bin at his mother's house. A plumpy pillow! It wasn't the Savoy but needs must. This done Tony kicked off his shoes 'footie shoving' them under his desk. He then dragged a file out from his bulging paperwork and spread it open for effect. It was then that he spotted a large hole in the big toe area of his left sock. He thought of Doctor Chloe and cringed. "Bet she noticed. You old smooth operator!" he whispered. The room was comfortingly dark as he collapsed onto his makeshift bed. Tony could have slept on a bed of nails the way he felt and was lost in deep slumber within seconds.

At 8.25am, a maroon Volvo Estate pulled up under the station barrier. Billy Porter the third of the Security Guards recognised the driver and raised the barrier. Wee John was in the kitchen frying bacon for the boys and the Preacher was in the Rec Room on back gate duties. All three were fully genned up on the double click warning system which also signalled for the Preacher to open the back gate.

Billy Porter was a flapper with honours. He had been in the Full Time Reserve for 10 years. He was 53 years old and stood at around 5' 8" tall. Billy was blessed with the thickest head of blonde hair which was never out of place. Apart from that he was quite ugly and slightly plump. He had been married to the best wee wife in the world but unfortunately his Doreen had run off with their milk man two years previously. Billy now tarred all woman with the same brush and referred to his wee Doreen as 'that fuckin bitch'! Billy spoke with a high-pitched grating voice which had the same annoying effect as screeching chalk on a wet blackboard. No matter how interesting the subject matter was, Billy would render it hopelessly and utterly boring. Doing a shift in the Box with Billy was like serving a life sentence without parole. After a few hours in his company most if given the choice would have happily opted for the electric chair. Billy loved to sweep, mop and clean which was really his true vocation in life. Wee John and Stevie were happy when he was in his sweeping mode. It gave their jangled ears a rest as well as their heads peace!

Billy in true flapper fashion flapped. He double clicked then treble clicked the intercom shrieking, "Inspector, Inspector, it's Inspector Grant."

More furious clicking followed. The boys in the Enquiry Office chuckled. Wee John smiled and threw another four rashers on. He then got the Inspectors 'Tower of London' weathered mug out. The Preacher glided out and opened the back gate to the section's popular Inspector. The Volvo Estate drove into the rear car park and on into the space marked Inspector. Out hopped Derek Grant smiling. He was wearing a beautifully tailored pale grey suit, white shirt with a dark blue and green silk tie. He wore highly polished black brogue shoes. He looked at Preacher. "A very good morning to you today, Pete, mmmm (smelling the bacon wafting) is wee John making the 'Bacon butties'?"

Pete laughed. "Guilty as charged Inspector."

Derek laughed. "Hope there's room for me at the table!"

Inspector Derek Grant was 56 years old, 6' 1" height. Rakishly thin and sinewy. He had grey receding hair which was combed over. His face was slightly too long to be considered attractive as well as possessing small dark inquisitive eyes which proved the point. His wife Miriam had passed three years previously and her death had hit him hard. They had been inseparable for 33 years and she had been his soul mate. They had a son Graham who was their pride and joy. Graham was now married with two young kids. He was teaching at a little primary school in far flung Tasmania. Derek missed them both very much. When Miriam passed, he sold their lovely traditional detached home in the coastal village of Crawfordsburn, County Down. As Derek put it, "It rattled with too many memories." In a bid to shake himself out of his doldrums, Derek bought himself a stylish third floor 2-bedroom turnkey flat in Holywood, County Down. His new gaff was in fact only a couple of miles down the road from his old place. It had amazing, elevated views out over Belfast Lough where he would sit passing time watching the ferries and passenger jets making their way in and out of Belfast. It was especially beautiful at night where a multitude of twinkling transient lights provided Derek with an amazing view. How Miriam would have loved all of this Derek would muse gazing around at all the modern furnishings of his slick chic 'des res'. Inwardly if truth be told, he felt more like a marble rolling around an empty cardboard shoe box.

Derek now realised that life or death in his case could reveal a valuable but painful lesson. A lifetime's endeavour for betterment and success did not come close to the happiness and love he had shared with Miriam for those 33 years. He would gladly trade everything he had for just one more moment with her.

Derek had served in the RUC for over 34 years. A stellar career in both uniform and CID. He had many strings to his policing bow with over 20 years as an Inspector. A prosecution file had to be tip top to get his signature of approval but when given would breeze through any court in the land. Mountroyal was to be his swan song. He was retiring this coming September and wanted no fuss made. A trip of a lifetime to Tasmania and a hug from his grandkids was in his pipeline.

Derek had been a lifelong attender at the Free Methodist Church located at lower Castlereagh Street, Belfast. It was a quaint church with a small congregation. It was a short two-minute drive from Mountroyal station. Derek could have picked safer churches to attend. His was adjacent to the dangerous Strand policing patch and actually looked directly down the Mountpottinger Road, its main thoroughfare. Derek was all too aware of this but had always held a fatalistic outlook to life. He was forever saying, "When it's your time, it's your time."

Today was all about popping in to meet and greet his new Sergeant before heading to church. He had been happy to hear from the jungle drums, namely Tweety, that he had settled in well with his new Section and that the feeling was very much mutual. What with one thing and another their paths had not yet crossed.

Tony was very, very fast asleep. He was on a golden beach on some tropical isle with beautiful native girls dancing for him. In his hand and close to his lips, a split coconut containing rum and coconut milk, it smelt and tasted amazing. A giggling creature was rubbing a soothing balm into his bronzed shoulders. Palm trees swayed easily as a soft breeze ruffled his dark hair as he watched the blue coral sea carelessly caressing the sandy shore. "Ahh this is the life, please don't stop my lovelies," Tony meekly whispered. Then from the small recesses of his mind he heard clicking noises. They were getting more frequent and louder. He felt himself getting pulled away from his sandy paradise into a black vortex with more clicking and then screeching words, "Inspector, Inspector!" powering through.

"Holy fuck, the Inspector. But it's Sunday!" Tony cried, trying with all his might and will power to open his eyes but to no avail. "Get up, get up for fuck's sake," he said spinning on his narrow makeshift bed. His twist was too violent, and Tony toppled hitting the floor hard. Chairs flew everywhere along with his dream cushion. More clicking then more screeching. "It's Inspector Grant!" Well at least the warning procedure worked. Tony's eyes were now successfully half open. The right side of his face was creased like an iceberg lettuce from the cushion. This was nothing compared to the abstract upstanding hair to the right side of his head. It looked as though a dairy cow had just licked it there. Salvador Dali would have been chuffed at this creation. He quickly rearranged the chairs, stumbling in the half light as he stuffed his dream cushion back inside the drawer. He had just taken his seat behind the desk when Derek Grant quietly knocked on his door and entered.

Derek slipping into this dark murky underworld found his eyes struggling with the near total darkness. A scene reminiscent of the movie 'Apocalypse Now'. With a searching outstretched hand, he spoke, "A very good morning to you. I'm Derek, Derek Grant, your Inspector. It's Tony Speers, isn't it? I've heard a great many good things about you. May I call you, Tony?" Tony met his hand and feebly shook it. He smiled a smile which looked as though his face was set in plaster of Paris. Derek inwardly marvelled at the specimen before him noting that he liked to read his files in the dark and upside down. As for his hair style, quite remarkable what the young ones were sporting these days. His wrinkled face, premature ageing perhaps. *Poor chap,* he thought. Then the penny dropped with a clang. The young Sergeant had been having forty winks, something he had done many a time over the years. Time for a bit of harmless fun. Derek shot a glance across at the three chairs and then gave an airy look around at the low light. He sighed and tut tutted before fixing Tony with his fiercest glare as he slowly turned the file on the desk the correct way around. Leaning forward over the desk Derek glared at Tony's besockled feet especially his left foot where his big toe had broken free and was triumphantly staring up at him. Poor Tony was sweating bullets, his life flashing before his very eyes. Derek then pulled himself up to his full height and filled his lungs trying hard not to laugh and in feigned trembling rage shouted out, "I put it to you Sergeant Speers that you have been sleeping on duty. What do you have to say for yourself man!"

Tony spluttered, "I can assure you Inspector I've done no such th..." BEEP BEEP BEEP BEEP BEEP BEEP BEEP! Tony leapt with shock as the alarm on his watch howled faithfully and repeatedly stabbing him in the back responding to its 8.30am setting. The game was up. A sergeant for only a couple of weeks Tony thought as he turned his alarm off looking crest fallen at Inspector Derek Grant. There was nothing more to say. Derek's deadly gaze softened as memories of his own younger mishaps flooded in. Tony watched in amazement as Derek's scowl began to change before erupting into a howl of unbridled laughter.

"Aww, Tony lad, I just couldn't resist it, and then when your alarm went off, pure gold. Thank you sooo much! I haven't laughed this hard in ages!" Tony, hugely relieved, allowed himself a chuckle while still none the wiser as the colour slowly returned to his cheeks. Derek looked earnestly at Tony and said, "Please forgive me, Tony. I only have a couple of months left before I retire and I want to enjoy it as much as I can. I also want to help you all I can as you take control of your first section. Your service will fly by in a heartbeat. The jobs are the best but the friendships you make are even better. Get your clogs on big toe, Wee Johns made us bacon butties and a mug of tea!" The pair sauntered down to the Rec Room where the craic was mighty. Stephanie Gates, Pete, Wee John, Derek and Tony himself howled as Tony described Derek's windup in all its glory. All this and bacon butties with sauce of your choice. Life was good!

Tony and Derek would form a professional bond and friendship as tight as any mortise lock. A relationship that would extend far beyond the vagaries of the job. A tale of two kindred spirits. Not exactly the same but a lovely ham and egg combo. They would always have each other's back.

The Rec Room door opened and a solemn-faced Tweety entered. "Sorry folks, there's just been another attack reported!" He held a sheet of paper with all of Dorothy Walker's details on it including a summary of the attack. Derek reached up for it and whilst reading it tutted, "Poor, poor woman. We'll have to let the boys from CID know. Who's in?"

Tweety replied, "Pinky and Perky, sir. BRC have also been informed and a C.6. entry has been completed. We need a crew to attend!"

Derek nodded. "I'll pop upstairs and deliver the bad news to the boys, they'll be gutted." And with the sheet of paper and his mug of tea, he left shouting from halfway up the stairs, "Thanks for the butties, Wee John." Tony was raging. Poor Dorothy Walker. Another attack and more pressure on the subdivision. The best crew for the job was sitting in front of him.

"OK, Tweety, would you put a call sign AM72 on the system. Make them aware they're attending Dorothy Walker's home to record a written statement of complaint and not available for calls."

"On it, Skipper," Tweety said, leaving for the Enquiry Office.

Tony looked at Stephanie and said, "Would you do the needful?"

She nodded, taking a deep breath preparing herself for the stressful and emotional task. Now looking at Pete, he said, "Driver please and lend a hand."

Pete nodded. "Absolutely, Skipper."

They were gone within a minute taking with them all they would need.

Five minutes later, their red Cortina vehicle, (AM72) turned into Frank Street and stopped outside the front of Dot's house. Both officers got out of the vehicle and made their way to the front door. Dot on hearing the doorbell ring wearily got up and opened the front door to meet them.

"Come in, come in, constables," Dot spoke looking downwards embarrassed by her wounds and grotesque appearance. She led them into her rear living room before sitting herself down on her favourite armchair and looked up for the first time at her guests.

Two young officers stood before her and had they not been in police uniform Dot thought she must have died and gone to heaven. The female officer was mid to late twenties. She was tall and slender at around 5' 7" in height. She had the most beautiful face with stunning blue eyes which hid just a trace of sadness. She was immaculate in her uniform in spite of her cumbersome flak jacket. She was holding a black clipboard and an elegant looking classic parker pen. She smiled at Dot and placed her hand on her arm and spoke, "Good morning, Miss Walker, I'm Woman Constable Stephanie Gates. Constable Sweetlove has explained to me about your ordeal last night and my Sergeant has sent me to speak with you and record a written formal complaint. Can I call you by your first name?"

Dot felt completely at ease with this angel in green as she suppressed tears of relief. "My name's Dorothy but everyone calls me Dot," Dot answered, covering her mouth with her hand. Stephanie spoke again looking over her shoulder at the male officer who stood softly smiling stooped at the doorway.

"Oh and this is Constable Peter Majury (Preacher), he's here to give me a hand if that's all right with you, Dot!" Dot who swore to herself last night never to like another bastarding man again gazed upon this male specimen. In her mind's eye if ever she imagined what the Angel Gabriel looked like it was like this! He stood there before her. Early thirties. 6' 4" of power oozing from beneath his uniform. His flak jacket resembled a tea bag on him. He had soft brown curly hair which looked slightly uncontrollable, his eyes were dark and brooding, eyes capable of reaching into the depths of any soul. He smiled at her, oblivious to her shattered looks and said, "Morning, Dot!" Her battered and bruised heart exploded. Like a fireworks display. Those were the loveliest words anyone had ever said to her. Dot was in love. "Fuck you, Sheik, in shining armour," she mumbled to herself.

Stephanie then listened as Dot gave recollections of the previous night's events, initially taking only notes patiently filling in missing gaps. Pete had several sized evidence bags and labels and retrieved Dot's clothing from the outside bin. These were required for Forensic examination by the boys at the Forensic labs at Beechill. (DNA was not available until 1986 so the evidence sought for then was hair, blood or fingerprints!)

When all the facts were assembled in date time and place order with no stone left unturned Stephanie began to record Dot's formal statement of complaint. This was painstaking and thorough. When it was completed, Stephanie read it out aloud to Dot who garnered growing strength as the words of her new defiance and fight back lifted her to a place of tomorrows. Dot agreed with the contents of her statement and signed it as being a true and accurate account.

Stephanie stressed the urgency of a medical examination by her own doctor or an A&E doctor who were both well versed with recording injuries for police investigations to which Dot agreed. Dot then signed a permission statement for police to access her medical records. She was also made aware that CID would be dealing with her case and that several other similar attacks had occurred in the area in the recent past. Dot took comfort that she was no longer alone in this matter and that the CID and all the police at Mountroyal were taking care of things for her. When all was done, Dot looked at the clock on her mantelpiece. Two hours had gone by in a flash.

As the constables were leaving by the front door, with Pete leading and Stephanie close behind, Pete suddenly spun around causing Stephanie to collide into him. "Ooops!" she went. Pete fixed Dot with his eyes now deadly serious.

Like those of an avenging angel and spoke, "Don't worry, Dot, we'll get the man that did this to you!" And somehow, Dot knew that they would. Dot thanked both officers for everything they'd done for her, and to her dying day would never hear a bad word said about the police.

...Pinky and Perky...

It took just three minutes to get from Frank Street back to Mountroyal Station. The pair parked their vehicle up at the side. Mountroyal Station was not visible due to a twenty-foot-high brick fronted blast wall. A security sanger was built into the front right-hand corner and was manned by three full time reserve constables known as the security guards. Their job was to cover access and security of both the front and back station gates and the general security of the station itself. Security cameras were placed strategically around the outer perimeter walls of the station and the viewing monitors were in the sanger. These monitors were viewed every second of every day. Van bombs and mortars fired from the rear of improvised lorries was a popular weapon of the Provisional IRA (Provos). There were only two ways into the station, through the main pedestrian gate at the front, and through the rear large back gate. A secure car park for officers and staff was to be found there.

Stephanie and Pete hopped out of their vehicle and climbed up the three steps to the pedestrian gate, manned by the guys in security. The release buzzer sounded, and the door freed. Stephanie peeked into the sanger seeing that it had been Stevie Uprichard who had let them in. 'Cheers Stevie'. As she approached the heavy metal front door of the station. Pete nodded as he followed carrying several evidence bags containing Dot's soiled clothing. The main front door was too heavy for the average person to open, it was in fact a blast door and could withstand a serious explosion. A large metal button the size of a saucer opened the huge door when pressed. This done, the pair entered the main public reception area. To the right was the Enquiry Office manned by two permanent Guards. Constables Victor Snape and Harry Sweetlove aka 'Vic the' and 'Tweety Pie'.

The Enquiry Office was the hub of the station. Complaints were recorded there from members of the public either in person or over the phone. Depending on the type and urgency of the call the guards would task either a response vehicle, a neighbourhood call-sign or in very serious matters the CID. All tasked calls were recorded in the C6 or the OCCURRENCE Book as it was otherwise known. Each call was given a unique reference number. At the end of every day the guard, usually the night guard, would do a return sheet of all the notable occurrences encountered by Mountroyal Station during the previous 24 hours. These returns were sent to the RUC Headquarters at Knock along with all the other RUC Stations in the province.

The Enquiry Office was separated from the reception area by way of a wall with a counter and a large reinforced security glass window which ran the width of the wall. A small sliding hatch was located at the centre of the counter. This was used for inspection of documents and payment of fines etc. There was a door located to the right-hand side of the wall which accessed the office by way of a security buzzer from within. On entering the reception area and looking straight ahead was another door which led to the rest of the station. Access was gained by a buzzer release controlled by the guards. Downstairs was the domain of the uniformed personnel in both response and neighbourhood. A parade room which doubled as the constable's work room. Two prisoner cells. A recreation room and a kitchen with all the usual appliances and a couple of vending machines.

Upstairs was the domain of the CID General Office, the Collator and the typing pool.

It had just gone 11.00am and Stephanie was drained emotionally and mentally. "Hi, Tweety, could you let me into your office, I need to update the C6 on Dot or should I say Dorothy Walker."

Tweety hit the buzzer and both Stephanie and the Preacher trundled in.

"Well, Heavenly. (her nickname due to her stunning looks and her surname as in 'Heavenly Gates.') Do we have another victim?" asked Tweety anxiously. Stephanie slid Dot's statement over to Tweety who had taken the initial call while she updated the C6 entry. Tweety read the statement with his one good eye and fumed, sliding it over to Vic, his partner.

"Fucking Dirty Bastard," growled Vic. Tweety nodded.

"And so say all of us," said the Preacher.

"Indeed," said Heavenly.

This had been the fourth attack on a female in their patch since 29 January 1983. All the attacks followed a similar pattern. The victim was viciously assaulted and robbed in an entry adjacent to a pub and the victims were forced to perform oral sex. The assailant always took a trophy, in Dot's case her mother's T necklace. A green backpack was always mentioned, and the brute spoke with a local accent.

Tweety rang BRC (Belfast Regional Control) who updated their log. He also informed them that AM72 call sign would be unavailable for calls for twenty minutes or so as they had to brief the boys at CID. Stephanie and Pete headed upstairs to see Pinky and Perky, two of the top Detectives in the RUC.

As they approached the door to the main CID Office, they heard shouting and roaring. On entering the office, they became aware that the heated exchange was coming from the D.I.'s Office (Detective Inspector). A high-pitched staccato voice was hurling abuse at a deep booming voice who was returning fire in equal measure. "You're one fat useless bastard!" said the high-pitched voice. "Go fuck yourself with bells on you, skinny wee bollocks," came the reply. Stephanie and Pete stood in the middle of the office smirking. Enjoying the performance. Pinky and Perky were in! They had been briefed shortly after 8.30am that morning by Inspector Derek Grant as to the attack on Dorothy Walker and the pair were very much expected.

Out from the rear, CID kitchen breezed their office manager Mrs Catherine Mercer. Catherine was 62 years old and a happily married grandmother. She was just over 5' in height with greying hair with a modest application of make-up. Catherine was always beautifully dressed, classically elegant without fuss. She lived in the Braniel Estate surrounded by her large family circle. Catherine was blessed with a sweet nature, but all knew never to mistake her kindness for weakness, cross her at your peril irrespective of who you were or what rank you held. She possessed the tongue and mind of a guillotine. Her job was to maintain all aspects of administration in the office freeing the detectives to do their jobs. "Aww, it's wee Stephanie and young Peter. Don't you pair make a lovely couple? (Pete blushed.) It's a terrible business all these attacks on those poor women. When will it ever end? There's tea freshly made in the pot, and I've got a lovely fruit cake looking sorted… Boys, we have visitors."

The door to the D.I.'s office opened and out popped the two characters, both besuited and that's where the similarities ended. Leading the pair was Detective Inspector Archie Brown, 57 years old, a happily married grandfather from a working-class background who resided in Carryduff. Archie was around 5' 8" on his tip toes and nine stone ringing wet. There was more meat on a butcher's pencil. He was bald as a billiard ball save for the sides and wore thick glasses which made him look as though he was always amazed at something or another.

Archie had been on the job 33 years and was a DI when the troubles kicked off in 1969. His dress sense was the colour brown, everything from suit to shoes and in between. Archie was warm and kind and took time with people. He knew everyone by their first name from the station cleaner up. He spoke with a slightly high-pitched broad Belfast accent and spoke very fast. Apart from his wife, the love of his life was his pipe 'Woody'. Woody helped him think, Woody helped him to relax. Woody and Archie had solved more cases than you've had hot dinners.

Ambling behind Archie as he usually did was Detective Sergeant Clifford Boomer or 'Cliff'. When the good lord created Archie, he must have been low on supplies. The day he created Cliff he obviously had won the pools and invested it all in creating this impressive specimen. Cliff was 53 years old. A massive 6' 6" tall. He weighed in at around 20 stone and was built like a brick shithouse. Cliff had a full head of grey hair stylishly cut. He had glacier blue eyes and was swarthy all year around. His nose had been broken a few times but that just added to his charm. A handsome beast who was once a ladies man but marriage 20 years ago to the lovely constance or 'Connie' put an end to his bad old ways. Together they had a son, Finn who was the spit of his dad. Cliff was born and raised in Bangor where he still lived. Both his parents were teachers and were super sporty which rubbed off on Cliff. Cliff had attended Bangor Grammar School where he excelled at rugby. Due to his God given attributes, he was a natural Lock in the forwards pack. Cliff had great hands and feet and a quick brain to boot. He was selected to play rugby for Ulster in his early twenties and was hard as nails. He became the team enforcer, not that he was a dirty player but if you started it, he would finish it.

His claim to fame amongst the Ulster Rugby faithful happened on the hallowed turf at Ravenhill in the autumn of 1955. A touring Wallaby side (Australian Test team) pitched up looking to roll Ulster over. They arrived that day unbeaten, and Ulster was their last game. The game itself was close and the young Ulster scrum half was playing a blinder behind a huge Ulster pack. Out of the blue and off the ball, he was punched by an 'Aussie' open side flanker famed more for his nastiness on the pitch than the quality of his game. The scrum half went down in a heap and the medics were called on. Everyone on the pitch missed it including the ref but not the 13000 Ulster fans who went ballistic. As the Aussie thug ran off, he foolishly ran his shoulder into Cliff. His tour ended right there, or should I say at the Belfast City Hospital where the lovely nurses took care of him. When he woke up, he discovered that his jaw had been broken. He was to enjoy the rest of Ulster's culinary delights through a straw.

Cliff sent him a bunch of flowers, a box of toffees and a 'Get well soon' card. Cliff never held a grudge. He was nice that way. No one in the crowd saw anything! Cliff became a rugby legend and played for the RUC first fifteen well into his forties. He hung his boots up some 10 years ago but was still very active in the RUC rugby circles and was a committee member at Newforge RUC Sports Club.

Cliff was a stylish dresser favouring blue woollen sports jackets with silver buttons and silk ties. Usually correctly contrasting trousers and brogue shoes which were always polished. Cliff in contrast to Archie spoke with a low deep North Down drawl. Every word he spoke, came out carefully phrased and in precise fashion. Cliff had been in the RUC for 28 years and had been attached to CID since 1965. He became a DS or Detective Sergeant in 1968.

These two behemoths though poles apart on paper were as deadly as a team of investigators. Watching them interview was a master class. No egos or rank ever entered into it, results and clearances is what they were all about. They had worked together at Mountroyal for over 10 years. Although work colleagues they were also the very best of friends.

Archie spoke from between his pipe clenched teeth slowly releasing a lovely Saint Bruno tobacco aroma. "Aww it's the lovely Constable Gates and the handsome Constable Majury... Catherine, where's the tea and cake woman?" He chuckled, giving them a wink.

Cliff blurted, "Braver man than me Gunga Din!" cringing as Catherine entered stern faced with a tray of tea and cake. Cliff was afraid of no man and only one woman... Catherine! Stephanie broke the bad news over tea as the two senior detectives listened without interruption. Pete had now grabbed three exhibit labels from the CID Store and had attached them to the three evidence bags from Dot's incident as PM1, PM2 and PM3. He signed and dated the back of each label and Archie took them off him also signing and dating the labels. Both Archie and Pete made notebook entries of the handling of the exhibits, proving continuity. The exhibits were now legally in Archie's possession.

Archie then read Dot's statement of complaint, Woody was on overdrive as he sucked and blew. A faint humming sound started, low barely audible. Pete looked up and around for the bee or wasp. Catherine smiled and suppressed a giggle. Cliff rolled his eyes. Archie made this noise when he was deeply engrossed in something. Pete caught on and grinned. He handed the statement over to Cliff for his perusal. "It's a bad business so it is. This is the fourth attack. Judging by the M.O.'s (modus operandi) it's the same fella, and we're no closer to catching the bastard, pardon for my French Stephanie!" Stephanie smiled. Catherine raised a rebuking eyebrow. Cliff noticed.

"Great work, kids. Get your statements written up before you leave, good work or good luck will get him and I don't give a flying f... (Catherine coughed loudly for effect.)... fiddle which," Archie recovered.

Stephanie and Pete rattled off their continuity statements and their job as far as Dot's complaint was done. It had rolled on to 12.00pm. Their break wasn't until 1.00pm. Pete gave BRC a call and placed them back on the ground and available for any incoming calls. Pete took them out on a scenic drive to get their heads showered and to kill the hour before their break. Out around the Ormeau Embankment with the River Lagan to their right. On into the Ormeau Park where he parked up beside the bandstand and watched normal life go by for 15 minutes or so. Stephanie went over this morning's events with poor Dot. How horrible it must have been for her. Nobody deserved that. The hour passed uneventfully, and our two reluctant heroes returned to base for their bravo or break.

...The Vacant Property Patrol...

Lionel just loved Sunday earlies. Life was good. He was out with Stevie Uprichard doing the old VPR soft shoe shuffle. You pitched up at an address in the register, checked the front door then the back followed by all the windows. If there was a garage it would be looked at as well. It worked even better when a nosey neighbour spotted you. Then you would turn on the professional peeler act feigning genuine concern. A reassuring chat always went down well as no one could deny your having been there. Sometimes a house key was left for a more thorough inspection of both inside and out. They had one of those today and they had agreed it was to be the last call on their to do list.

Lionel Graham was born to be a policeman. He was 42 years old and had been raised in Portrush in the beautiful north coast of the province. He was 5' 9" with a medium but athletic build. He had a full head of sandy hair just stopping short of ginger. He had blue mischievous eyes and a joke or a prank was never too far off his horizon. A temper also lurked under the surface which had to be triggered. Injustice or unfairness would usually awaken this particular monster. To coin a phrase 'Light the blue touch paper and stand well back', Lionel would fight his or anyone's corner if he felt he was in the right or something was wrong.

He was happily married to Charlotte or Lottie. She was a partner in a Solicitors Practice in Ballygowan. They had been happily married for twenty years. They had tried to have children, but none were forthcoming. When they finally went to have the issue looked at, they were told that as Lionel would phrase it 'My heads have got no tails'! They lived in a beautiful home in Massey Avenue, Belfast and money was not in short supply. Lionel, being an only child, had been left a huge dairy farm when his parents died. The proceeds of which set him up for life. In reality, he didn't need to work but he enjoyed it. He had no ambition to be anything other than a constable but he was a very good one. When a call came Lionel's way it was in the very best of hands. He was thoroughly professional but also kind-hearted and fair. But just be wary of the blue touch paper.

Lionel had done 20 years on the job. His first 10 years were spent at Ballymoney where he learnt his craft and the following 10 were at Mountroyal where he was happily settled.

As a crew that morning on the surface they were much of a muchness, but a little bit of light digging would reveal major differences. On one hand Lionel a well-respected experienced cop who was happily married with absolutely no money worries, on the other hand, Stevie a wannabe cop. Being in the Full Time Reserve was good money but it came with a three-year contract. One slip or the wrong boss writing on you could leave you booted out on your shell pink ear. Stevie was very unhappily married to a money grabbing gold digging social climbing wife who constantly put him down. His very high sex drive was parked very much up the drive. Charlene, his hateful wife was literally bleeding him dry. His Bank Manager wanted a word, and he was or should I say she was maxed out on all the credit cards.

On leaving the station that lovely Sunday morning, they cruised up the Woodstock, Cregagh Road to Castlereagh RUC Canteen which was open 24 hours a day. Crews from other satellite stations would appear there and over the years' friendships were made. In modern day lingo, a source of networking occurred. Each being made familiar with the nitty gritty in each other's patch and sometimes a crumb of casual information would result in a collar. Everyone knew Lionel, the Canteen Staff loved him. He ordered an Ulster fry, soda bread, potato bread, mushrooms, sausages and bacon, with red and brown sauce and a mug of tea. He flirted outrageously but all in jest and they loved him for it. He usually got a bit extra on his plate. Lionel was just Lionel no matter what rank was around. Stevie wasn't at all hungry. Lionel nevertheless bought him a sausage sarnie and a mug of tea which he demolished in an instant.

Stevie was secretly in awe of Lionel, who had never noticed, and basked in the afterglow of his charming personality, especially with the ladies. The girls in the canteen came in all ages, shapes and sizes. Some loud and lardy, some quiet and demure. Married, single or divorced never mattered. Stevie watched as they went about their business, and some enjoyed a wee flirt and a chase. He caught the eye of a young server and lingered for a second longer. She spotted this and visibly returned the look, a smile playing in her eyes, and then she looked directly at him and smiled. *Result*, thought Stevie imagining doing the deed with this young maiden in all manner of ways. Lionel broke into his palace of perverted thoughts. "Let's go, Stevie, we'll do a couple of houses on the list then go to the Ormeau Park and read the Sunday rags. I'll get the mail on Sunday."

Stevie replied, "I'll get the News of the World to see who's shagging who." Stevie looked over his shoulder as they left the canteen and was excited to find the young server watching him and smiling happily. If only she knew!

By this time, news of the attack on Dorothy Walker had been transmitted over the radio.

"That's the fourth one I think; what sort of bastard would do that sort of thing?" said Lionel winding his window down as their vehicle slowly entered the main entrance of the Ormeau Park. "I mean can he not just watch a porno or read a mucky mag like the rest of us pervs." As their soft skinned vehicle passed two elderly female dog walkers, one of the dears smiled in at them and said, "Lovely day for a walk, Constable, I'm sure you're sweating in all that clobber!"

Lionel nodded. "Indeed, ladies, indeed."

Their day was made as the vehicle pulled up at the bandstand. Time for the Sunday papers. After a while Lionel broke the birdsong and the rustling of the rags. "Also, it's the violence I don't get. All that effort for a blow job. There must be more to it than that, after all it's a hell of a risk to take just to have your flute played!" Stevie shook his head. "Search me if I know, maybe he's not getting his fair share at home unlike us two palomino stallions. Maybe he just hates the bitches or maybe he just needs a bit of rough to get himself off! Who knows what goes on behind closed doors in good old Belfast? I knew a girl who used to like it rough, you know her ass slapped and all, foul language the works, (Lionel raised his eyebrows in amazement and listened on.) She loved to do it in the great outdoors where there was a chance of getting caught. There were two sides to her. One side was a sweet butter wouldn't melt in her mouth, a bank clerk who tut tutted at dirty jokes on the other side was this amazing whore of Babylon who liked it any which way but definitely rough!" Stevie was practically frothing at the mouth as his fantasy took life.

Lionel shook his head and said smiling, "Don't suppose you have her phone number handy? Let's go, we'll do a couple more before lunch."

The VPR crew were doing a smashing job; all properties thus far had been inspected and found to be in order. It was approaching 2.00pm as their vehicle drove into the tree lined and affluent Ravenhill Park Gardens. These Victorian properties exuded grandeur with large front gardens and driveways cramped with the latest and most expensive run-arounds. No nosey neighbours brushing down

51

and mopping their doorsteps here. "Last one Stevie then that's us," Lionel said bringing their rather tatty soft skin vehicle to a halt outside number 4 the home of Ms Vivien Chesney, 45-year-old Official Unionist MP and tormentor of the Sub Divisional Commander. Lionel reached into the back and grabbed the 'News of the screws' for some salacious reading as Stevie hopped out. What a residence this was. The front garden was beautifully laid out in shrubs and plants, the pink, purple and white petunias were in all their glory dancing lightly with the African marigolds in the spring breeze. The ornate granite front porch was framed with two delightful wicker hanging baskets each burgeoned with deep purple fuchsia plants which gave off the faintest aroma.

Stevie walked up the gravel driveway and edged himself past a dark blue Mercedes car which had a white leather interior.

"Money, money, money. It's a rich man's world," hummed Stevie checking for the right key as he stood on the porch. The second key did the job as he opened the heavy wooden black door and entered. The hallway oozed of expensive period detail. The floor was graced with its original black and white tiles. A beautiful sweeping mahogany staircase led the eye upstairs. The walls were tastefully adorned with original artwork which depicted scenes from a rural era long past. Not quite Stevie's cup of tea. He entered the front living room which was no less grand. The walls were a pale lemon leading to a large bay window, light cream satin curtains hung heavily to each side. The carpet was a thick shag pile of dark green.

Stevie felt guilty momentarily and considered taking his grubby boots off. A large three-seater Italian leather settee, cream in colour was backed against the main living room wall. A matching recliner faced the front window with a small coffee table to its right. On the table sat a well-thumbed paperback novel by D H Lawrence. "Well, well well. What have we got here, Lady Chatterley's lover!" smirked Stevie opening its pages to where a bookmark was? A quick skim over the pages and he smiled. "Dark little secrets have we, matron." He looked up at a large, framed photograph which was hanging above the fireplace. It must have been taken some time ago. The photograph displayed a beautiful smiling twenty something female in her graduation gown. She was holding a parchment. She had lovely chestnut coloured hair draped over her shoulders and stunning hazel-coloured eyes. The smile itself was radiant, a smile of hope, a smile for her future, filled full of promise. This was surely the young Miss Vivien Chesney. Another smaller framed photograph sat on top of the fireplace. This was a more up to date image. It was the same female taken some time in the present. She was standing outside the front of the Official Unionist Party Offices at Strandtown Hall on the Belmont Road, Belfast. The smile was long gone. An arrogant superior glare looked back. Her hair was now greying and pulled tight back in a formal bun. Her face was still attractive, and makeup had been carefully applied by a woman who liked to look good. She was wearing a dark blue pencil suit and a white silk blouse which maybe opened a button too far. The slightest suggestion of cleavage was showing. A pearl necklace and matching earrings were also on display. All of this finished off with sheer stockings and dark blue stiletto shoes which met with Stevie's approval. "A real cock tease if ever I saw one!" He smiled.

Stevie quickly checked the windows, all good. A quick glance into the rear living room all greys and stately looking. The kitchen was thoroughly modern with all the latest appliances though nothing looked much used. "All show and no-go Princess," Stevie murmured as he exited the rear kitchen door and stepped out onto the patio. A huge garden with some apple trees revealed itself which was equally as well laid out as the front. South facing as well which had Stevie blinking from the afternoon sun. He quickly gained entry to the garage, much like the kitchen. It had everything a gardener would need but never looked used. "She must have a gardener on tow, lucky socks." Stevie then locked the garage door and re-entered the kitchen door locking it behind him. Downstairs was done.

Curious, he quickly bounced up the plushily carpeted stairs and ran a lazy eye around two spare bedrooms which were all very nice but clearly spare. Musty, fusty and dusty. "Shame on you, princess." He tutted. "And now for the piece de resistance!" What dark secrets lay in store thought Stevie as he entered her boudoir with ensuite bathroom. The bedroom was to the rear of the house and was classically furnished. A large king-sized bed was the dominant feature which faced a large bay window. The duvet and pillows were of a rich purple satin. The bed sheets a crisp white. The walls were painted a deep red and the silk curtains were a dark purple. The carpet was a flecked mix of both those colours. Large built in mahogany wardrobes revealed numerous suits all dark and austere. Blouses also hung which looked expensive to Stevie's eye. To the base of the wardrobe were a vast collection of stylish dress shoes which would have been the envy of Imelda Marcos. A lonely pair of Adidas trainers which looked straight out of the box sat looking out of place amongst its illustrious wardrobe counterparts.

Stevie couldn't resist a peek and eased across to the bedside dressing table. This had a classically framed mirror fitted to its back. It was of a dark mahogany and its handles resembled cut glass crystal. A woman's makeup bag and hairbrush rested on its top. He knew he was way out of line as he carefully opened the drawers which revealed the usual intimate treasures. Stevie frowned holding up a beautiful pair of scarlet silk panties to his cheek and thinking of the cotton bloomers his nagging wife wore which were all discoloured and out of shape just like her big wobbly self. A final stretch to the back of the final drawer and he felt something hard wrapped in a plastic bag. He quickly pulled it out and laughed out loud. "Bingo!" he shouted pressing the on switch as the instrument of pleasure began to hum and vibrate. "I'll never watch you on the UTV News in the same light with your Christian morals and values you old slut. Let's just keep this our little secret." Stevie then replaced everything as he found it covering his pervy tracks. When all was good, he left by the front door locking it securely behind him.

As he climbed back into the front passenger seat, Lionel looked up to him and said, "For fuck's sake, I thought you'd fallen asleep in there. Anything strange to report?"

Stevie replied smirking, "Nope just the usual handcuffs, whips and lesbian videos."

Lionel laughed out loud saying, "Home time, partner, our duties are done."

...Perfecting Records...

Back at Mountroyal, the daily flurry and buzz was taking place in the Enquiry Office as the early section signed off and the late section signed on. The usual throwaway banter and slagging took place as radios were being signed in and out. Sergeant Speers shook his head laughing as he gave the C6 one final check before the handover to the late section Sergeant. Stevie followed Lionel and enjoyed this handover time. Lionel took over the show leaving everyone in stitches as Stevie returned the VPR to its allocated spot on the shelf. Tony shouted over to him, "Did you do a proper job on Chesney's place?"

Stevie smiled back. "Yes, skipper, all good." He then reached for his tape recorder which had been left there since morning time and headed upstairs for the changing room. As he climbed the stairs, he looked into the bag and pressed rewind. Three hours recording done. "Mission accomplished!" he said to himself smiling. "I can't wait to get into the regulars and leave those dickheads in the box behind. I could have me some real fun on manoeuvres." Stevie then entered the main changing room and arrived at his locker located at the end of a line of lockers. His locker was secured with a four-numbered combination padlock which only he knew. He deftly feathered the four numbers, 1,9, 2 and 8 and carefully placed the tape recorder on the top shelf beside a small gents washing bag where he kept some music tapes and a few private items. He quickly got changed out of his uniform and back into his civvies. He closed his locker door and locked it tight, scrambling the combination numbers. He threw his dirty police shirt over his shoulder and trotted down the back stairwell to his car and headed home to see his kids and the soup dragon.

Tony Speers was done in more ways than one. It had been a long and eventful day. From his morning wake up and 'refreshing' shower. His encounter with Sergeant Plank, then Sergeant Tom Mills and finally the lovely Inspector Grant. A true gentleman. Tony wouldn't let this man down. Now for Sunday din-dins at mummy's. He turned and headed for the Sergeants office wearily taking off his tie and epaulettes his head thumping. As he approached the door, he heard the light clatter of footsteps behind him and then a female voice, "Excuse me, sorry excuse me Sergeant Speers."

Tony turned to be greeted with a sight for his very tired and sore eyes. "Yes Heavenly, sorry Stephanie, what's up?"

Stephanie looked up at him looking as fresh and as radiant as she had been since she paraded for duty at 7.00am. She too had endured a long day carefully dealing with Dot Walker both in personal and professional terms. She rolled her blue eyes at him and laughed. "I suppose you may as well call me 'Heavenly' as in 'Heavenly Gates', everybody else does. Here's the Parkview Bar assault file you asked me for this morning." She placed it in his arms releasing herself from one more file in her In-Tray.

Tony shook his head and said, "Heavenly, I really wasn't expecting this after the day you've had. But cheers, I'll check it out and fire it on to Inspector Grant tomorrow, I'm sure it's a sparkly wonderful file!" She laughed out loud this time and punched him in the ribs. This was the first time Tony had seen the normally demure Stephanie break out from her slightly sad demeanour. It was a wonderful sight to see the joy in her eyes. "I'll 'sparkly wonderful' you Sergeant Speers. My files are usually tip top and squeaky clean." Now it was Tony's turn to laugh, still rubbing his ribs.

"Of that I have no doubt, no offence meant Heavenly," he said smiling.

"None taken," Stephanie replied, cocking an eyebrow at him as she turned and left. Tony's eyes followed her down the corridor until she disappeared upstairs.

A formidable woman, an intelligent woman, a beautiful woman, a woman to be loved, a woman to marry, have children with and to grow old with. A woman to bring home to mummy! In short, way way too good for you, she's out of your league loser. Know your station in life Tony lad.

His shift was done.

So much for his quiet and peaceful Sunday!

...The Legend of Tweety Pie!...

Once in a very very long time, nature throws up an exceptional freak. An individual blessed with all of the gifts and secrets that the Universe has to offer. An individual who is cognisant of all these gifts, who doesn't abuse their power for self-advancement, greatness or adulation. A genius who is true to himself and to others and who is also kind!

Harold Sweetlove aka Tweety Pie was born 38 years ago in Dromore, County Down. His parents ran a bookshop there and had him late in life. His doting parents were kind giving people, maybe that's where Tweety got his kindness from. His mum and dad were also very clever. Tweety however had been blessed with a huge intelligence and an intellect that only a few have ever possessed. It was unique and unquantifiable. We all of us in life have a beginning of something and then an end which marks our place. Stuff like hard earned degrees and educational qualifications which define us and set us apart. Tweety was not bound by these fences of norm. No fence was high enough or ran far enough to contain his brilliance. The rules of man simply did not apply to him.

Tweety was aware of his special gift from a very early age. It never bothered him unduly; it was more like water off a duck's back as opposed to a yoke around his neck. He knew he had to be extra careful around people and that the light of his brilliance could affect folks in many different ways. He was a caring soul and never wanted to make people feel small or embarrassed when they were with him. He also didn't want to be labelled as an intellectual freak or find himself in the position of being used or abused by unscrupulous types. One thing was for sure, his loving parents were extremely proud of him. Tweety growing up attended his local schools and was very popular. He was sports mad but alas sports bad. Coming near last at most sporting events fazed him little. In true Kipling fashion he met both triumph and disaster on the sporting field with the same embrace.

He achieved As in all of his 'O' and 'A' levels and breezed into Cambridge

University when he was 18. There he studied the Classics for something to do, and really enjoyed the Latin aspect of the course. Needless to say, Tweety gained his degree with first class honours.

He was blessed with a photographic memory. Allied with his huge intelligence and the ability to understand and practically apply all he read made him appear almost superhuman. Anything he read or studied stuck. He spoke as many languages fluently as he had read or listened to. It would take Tweety a couple of minutes to read a daily rag. From there, he could recite every page verbatim, from world news to the latest sports as well as the classified ads.

He enjoyed a little flutter on the horses which naturally involved the legendary Racing Post. This racing rag provided Tweety with all the details of the horses, their owners, trainers and jockeys. He would pour over their most recent form including any past histories of illnesses or injuries. He devoured the going on the ground and also the forecasted weather conditions of the day. He lapped up the cloak and dagger of it all and in particular the subtleties of horses being brought on for a specific race as well as horses being held back for handicap purposes. All in all, he loved the horse racing riddle. If truth be told, he just adored the physical specimen of the thoroughbred racehorse, an animal bred purely for speed.

Tweety was a good punter and won way more than he lost. Luck, good or bad, had nothing to do with any of it. He kept a separate account for his betting which had many thousands in it. He called it his 'play dough'. Tweety wasn't into betting heavily, for him it was all a bit of mental fun. His valued opinion was always sought by his fellow punters about the Station. These golden nuggets were always free but only to those he liked. He would often say, "A horse race is like life, nothing is certain."

Naturally with all these immeasurable gifts on tap Tweety could have chosen any calling or profession. He could have made millions on the stock exchange. Had he applied himself to the medical field, maybe an innovative surgeon. Had he admired the heavens, a rocket scientist or a champion of rights, a barrister at law.

Greatness was never on his radar for that would have been too simple. As for money, he would say, "Sure it's only a thing to get a message with!" After some serious thought, Tweety felt rather surprisingly that the best place for him to use his amazing talents and be happy was in the police. There he could use his gifts quietly in the background. He would be a member of a large policing family and make friends. Primarily though his life's goals were simple. He wanted to help people that were in need of it, and he wanted to be happy. He was a lifelong explorer, an adventurer, a seeker of happiness.

Harold Sweetlove joined the RUC in 1969 just as the troubles were really getting started. He was 24 years old, 5' 11" with a slim build. His hair was fine and black in colour but there was plenty of it. He kept it combed tight back. He had a swarthy complexion due to his love of walking in the great outdoors and had piercing green eyes which held the key to this brilliant mind. You couldn't describe him as drop dead gorgeous but the more time you spent in his company you became ever more drawn to him without really knowing why. Maybe it was because everything came easy to him, maybe because he was without fear in intimidating company? Who knows, but he was a good laugh, very kind, great company and a loyal friend.

Tweety sailed through the RUC Training Depot at Enniskillen, County Fermanagh where he was awarded the baton of honour for getting the best grades.

His first posting was Kesh RUC Station which was only a few miles away from the Depot. The station was built in the 1930s and was full of old worldly charm and character. Its location was stunning resting on the beautiful shores of Lough Erne and the famous Fermanagh landscape. It possessed a personality all of its own. When the winds and rain hammered on its windows and heavy doors everything rattled and whined. The radiators were never off, and you were always either faint with the heat or just plain sweltered.

Tweety was given his own bedroom on the second floor which gave him a glorious view of the lake which he loved. Within no time, he had settled in and had made it his own.

A few other guys had rooms there. These guys were townies as the locals called them hailing from Belfast or thereabouts. The station was a curious mix of both young and old coppers which gave it a happy lively vibe and buzzing 24 hours a day. Parties were known to start at strange hours but made sense when you knew who had just finished a stint and when they were next on. A siege mentality existed because it was too dangerous to venture out socially so a strange type of norm prevailed with few questions asked. Safe to say lifelong friendships were formed. A couple of the old timers had been stationed there since the mid-fifties and lived locally. Their local knowledge was second to none and had saved countless lives. The full-time reservists there were all local men from different walks of life who were an amazing source of information.

Tweety loved being stationed there and fell under the wing of Sergeant Sean O'Brien, his Section Sergeant. Sean was relatively local and hailed from Ballinamallard where he still lived a dangerous 9-mile drive away. He was 43 years old and single and lived with his parents on their working dairy farm. He was never quite sure whether he was a full-time policeman and a part time farmer or the other way around. But whichever way around it was, he gave both jobs his all. He was a strapping 5' 10" of natural muscle developed from a lifetime's heavy lifting. He had thick untrainable straw-coloured curly hair which always looked a day short of a haircut. His eyes were large and blue in colour and always looked a tad sad or was it just plain tired. In his lifetime, he had shifted hundreds of hay bales and dug many ditches and built many a stone wall with his huge bare hands.

Sean was a man of few words but when he spoke his soft Fermanagh lilt was a pleasure to take in by the open station fire, smouldering under fresh peat logs. He policed fairly but firmly. He knew the difference between a body fallen upon hard times and the out and out chancers or career criminals. One would get 'Advice and warning', the other would get their day at Enniskillen Magistrates Court. Sean was popular with both sides of the community. He was a Roman Catholic by faith as well as a serving Police Officer. All of these factors combined frustrated the hell out of the Provos.

Several attempts had been made on his life over the past eight years whilst at Kesh RUC Station. Fortunately for Sean, he had unseen guardian angels watching over him. Paid Touts would contact their Special Branch masters and Sean was moved out of harm's way until the storms blew over. The free Confidential HotLine had also come to his rescue on an occasion which ultimately saved his life from an ambush at his farm. Such was life in the beautiful Lakeland County of Fermanagh. Sean knew they would get him one day, but he would enjoy his time while he had it. He had a very philosophical Fermanagh attitude to life, a gentle and easy going one.

Tweety in policing terms grew up fast. He knew the law inside out and was planning to sit his Sergeants and Inspectors exams as soon as he could. After this he would sit his Legal Bar Exams. He did this for no other reason than why not! He had read all the books, knew all the powers and could recite stated cases ad nauseam. Sean marvelled at this gifted prodigy who intellectually came from another planet. His section grew to lean on him for advice and occasionally had him sit in on interviews when certain arrogant barristers were present looking to humiliate a young constable or a seasoned Sergeant. Tweety would play with them very much as a cat would toy with a ball of wool. First one way then the other, from the legal frying pan he would have them dancing with thanks into the fire. It got to the stage when they would contact the station ahead of an interview just to ascertain if Constable Sweetlove would be present.

Sean wasted no time in letting the young Tweety oversee his paperwork and write on submitted files. He argued that he was helping his young tyro in gaining experience for his future stellar role within the force. In reality Sean knew that Tweety was infallible on paper and would make him look good. It also freed his mind to worry more about the farm, his family and the cattle. Tweety hero worshipped Sean and loved his simplicity. Here was a man who was as you found him. He had no bad traits, no moods and was always the same whatever whenever. He had taught Tweety how to stay alive in this beautiful bandit country. A picture postcard setting for ambushes and death.

Sean was fully aware that book knowledge in Tweety's case only took him so far. He lifted Tweety out of his books and into the killing fields to teach him his craft and to appreciate the guile of his unseen adversary. Sean taught Tweety the best and safest practices of tactical Vehicle Check Points or road stops. He had shown him how to safely perform route clearances when out on all day patrols.

Culvert clearances were also an essential task for the security forces in these times. A Culvert of itself is a man-made structure that allows water to flow under a road or railroad from one side to another. They were constructed in pipe or cement form and were sized according to requirement. Some were large enough for an individual to stand up in, others so small and narrow that a person could barely squeeze into and crawl through. These culverts were typically embedded in and surrounded by soil. They proved to be a deadly ally for the terrorist who adapted them into an explosive killing device. When packed full of explosives and tripped by a command wire from a safe distance they claimed many lives throughout the troubles.

The following are tragic examples of their deadly use. On 19 May 1981 near the town of Bessbrook in South Armagh, five British soldiers travelling in an army personnel carrier died as a result of a 1000 lb culvert bomb. On 13 July 1983, four Ulster Defence Regiment soldiers died as a result of a 500 lb culvert explosion whilst travelling on the Ballygawley Road near Dungannon in County

Tyrone.

These clearances were a deadly exercise of cat and mouse with the terrorist trying to plant the explosives and the security forces trying to locate them while all the while trying not to get caught by booby trap devices in and around their routes to the culverts. Sadly, a culvert clearance was only as good as the day it was cleared, and this routine had to be repeated in all weathers and under all conditions time and time again stretching the nerves of those involved to the limits.

The young Tweety had to learn fast and hit the ground running. But there were moments out there when he could lift his head and simply marvel at the scenery about him. *How weird is all of this,* he would muse sitting on an old tree stump at the edge of a field. Re focusing his mind as the sun set on the shores of the breath-taking Lough Erne. Here he was armed to the teeth with a Ruger Rifle and three fully loaded magazines. By his side was his personal issue Ruger revolver capable of firing magnum 357 rounds each with a lead tip for maximum damage. A map and compass to guide him sat in his lap. Tweety was well aware that the safety of his group was entirely in his young but very capable hands. With death all around him, he realised he never felt more alive. Every sense in his body was working at 100% and he would need every ounce of it.

Life for the young Tweety just couldn't get any better. He was in a job he loved. It was dangerous yet exciting. He was part of a team who were all in it together. He was in the great and beautiful outdoors most of the time which he really loved and yet there was the primal challenge of staying alive. The ability to see the traps or ambushes ahead, the bogus calls, looking for anything out of the norm, a footprint where it shouldn't be, a snapped twig or a broken branch, a car, trailer or horsebox somewhere out of context. With every foot patrol Tweety realised there was something he had missed or had not factored in, things that were not to be learned from books. With every passing shift, Tweety vowed to get better.

One morning, Tweety paraded for duty for the early shift. Country stations started at 8.00am. He already knew that he was down for a route clearance with the army which were the Gloucester's, a fine regiment and a great bunch of lads. It was 7.45am and Tweety was dressed well for the occasion. He was wearing his RUC shirt (no tie), his NATO jumper and his Dartex water resistant coat. For his bottom half firstly, he wore combat leggings and finally on his feet were his commando boots. He had obtained these mysteriously from his mates in the army. These boots were a must have, they were amazingly comfortable and could be walked in all day and in all weathers. He was chilling out having a hot sweet mug of tea along with the rest of the gang parading for duty. He was already aware he was down to do his shift with old Rex McKane, a Full Time Reserve man. Rex was a local and knew the area well but more importantly the terrorist players like the back of his hand. Between them, they had proven to be a good fit.

A route clearance was an all-day affair. It involved a joint police army patrol being transported to a designated location from where they would make their way back to base by foot. During this 'dangerous dander', they would check the hated culverts, bridges, behind walls and derelict properties for explosive devices. Snap VCPs (Vehicle Check Points.) were also carried out and anything suspicious was logged and forwarded to the Collator at Enniskillen RUC. There was always something about these mornings. These were very dangerous times, a kind of pre match jitters existed where banter and light hearted quips broke the fear and anxiety bubbling just beneath the surface. RUC Officers were dying on a daily basis throughout the province. Singularly or in groups, they were being shot, blown up or severely injured. There was always that sneaking fear amongst its members, was today's shift going to be the one? Graveyards were littered with RUC Headstones carved with names from quickly forgotten tragedies.

Rex nudged Tweety's knee and nodded at the window, from their elevated view they could see across wheat fields and beyond to the Lough. Thick grey clouds were scudding in as heavy dollops of rain began to splatter against the Parade Room window. Tweety rolled his eyes heavenward 'Perfect day for a dander I think not Rex old bean'! Just then, the Parade Room door opened and Sergeant Sean O'Brien reversed in holding the C6 under his armpit whilst balancing a mug of tea on top of the stolen vehicles and areas out of bounds clipboard. He turned and faced his chuckling section attempting a smile. A round of heavily buttered burnt toast was wedged beneath his teeth.

A young female constable quietly followed him in. Sean carefully placed all the bumph on the Parade Room desk and removed the round of toast from his crumby mouth. He quickly finished chewing then swallowed, clearing his throat. "Good morning, everyone, it's not looking too pleasant out today (sniffing over at the window), make sure you have everything you need before you venture forth and don't get caught out in the rain. It's a wetter rain here than anywhere else in the province so my townie friends tell me. (Winking over at the laughing

Belfast contingent.) Without further ado, I want to introduce you to the newest member of the section. This is her first posting from the depot and I'm sure she's a bit nervous so let's all give a big Kesh welcome to Woman Constable April Spence."

April stepped forward from behind Sean O'Brien with her hands nervously clasped in front of her. She smiled at a sea of strange faces wondering why some were dressed like policemen and others more like soldiers.

"Good morning, everyone. I'm April. I'm new to all of this but I'm here to do my best. I'd appreciate any help you can give me. (Tweety gulped not realising he was spilling his tea on his lap. He was convinced that she was talking directly to him.) I'll try not to let anybody down. It's nice to meet you all."

April Spence was 21 years old. She was just over 5' 3" in height and could best be described as pleasantly plump. Definitely not fat. She had a beautiful face with searching deep green eyes, a pale complexion and outrageously ginger hair which was thick and wavy. She had it tied back in a ponytail that particular morning. She didn't wear any makeup, there was no need for it. This particular rose required no gilding. April hailed from Augher which was at the far end of Fermanagh roughly 30 miles from Kesh. Her parents worked at the Ulster Bank in Ballygawley along with her elder sister. They were shocked when April bucked the trend and joined the RUC after having endured a short stint at the Halifax Building Society in Fivemiletown. Banking was not for her. She felt trapped like a bird in a cage. April was clever and had the 'O' s and 'A' s to prove it, but as far as her new job in the police was concerned April wanted to be judged on ability and attitude and here, she was starting from a very lowly scratch.

The mornings briefing had come to an end as notebooks were being tucked away into favourite pockets and mugs of tea or coffee drained. It had happened, the day had finally arrived. Tweety was in a state of gobsmacked rapture. This beautiful creature standing before him was the one, of that he had no doubt. His powerful mind ran through major calculations of compatibility, but he received no feedback! Why, he didn't even know her! He inwardly flapped like a pigeon stuck up a chimney breast! She might be stupid or even worse bossy. Or worst of all boring or worst of worst of all not the slightest bit interested in him.

"Excuse me…" April was speaking in Tweety's direction as Section members began to file past and leave the Parade Room.

"Excuse me please." Tweety was petrified, she actually wanted to speak with him. How could she know? Tweety pulled himself together in what seemed to take a lifetime.

"Well hello, April, welcome to Kesh, you'll love it here. I'm Harold Sweetlove but everyone calls me Tweety or Tweety Pie, take your pick I really don't mind at all." April gazed upon Tweety's flummoxed features, her green eyes examining his young anxious face. There was something about this one. He was different but in a good way. She was becoming strangely fascinated by him. She returned to planet earth with a bump and could feel herself going red with embarrassment. She laughed saying, "Sorry, Tweety, it's just that you were spilling your tea all over your lap, I didn't realise I had such power over you men!" Tweety did all he could to regain any lost ground and rested his hands on his gun belt in a somewhat jaunty fashion. He struck a mighty warrior pose for effect and laughed casually much like John Wayne in 'True Grit'. Tweety was now hopelessly lost in her green eyes realising they were the same colour as his own. "If you look up clumsy in the dictionary, it describes the word as Harold Tweety Pie." April laughed and touched Tweety lightly on his left arm. Tweety exploded or it felt that way.

"I'll not keep you back, Tweety, the boys are waiting on you. I'm in the Enquiry Office for my sins 'the day'. Hopefully, we'll see more of each other?" She raised both eyebrows and flashed her fullest smile. April inwardly admonished her brazen self. This was totally out of character.

"Absolutely, April, '*Sans aucun doute*!' (French for 'without doubt') as Tweety floated out of the Parade Room door."

April surprised responded, "*J'ai hate* (French for 'I can't wait'.)"

Tweety was in seventh heaven as he clattered down the stairs much like Old Ned the carthorse trotting over cobblestones on the way 't'it market'. April was gorgeous, intelligent and funny and just maybe she was interested in him!

If Tweety had been trying to hide his brilliant mind and intellect from her, he had done a stellar job. He would have romped any 'Village Idiot' prize. Sean O'Brien had witnessed the sparks flying between the young pair and was quietly pleased. Amidst all the hate and violence that surrounded them, tiny shoots of love could flourish. He crossed his fingers.

Tweety bounded out across the Station Courtyard and hopped into the front passenger seat of the lead land rover of four. He was in overall charge of this dangerous foot patrol.

The vehicles were army land rovers containing two bricks of soldiers usually

16 in number. This patrol contained their senior officer, a very young lieutenant and two seasoned sergeants to keep him right. The rest of the Gloucester's consisted of privates. For most, it was their first tour in the province, and they would find it a steep learning curve. Wills were already written, and final letters of goodbyes lay waiting should the need ever arise. They had a 3-month tour to endure then hopefully a safer posting. Their primary role that day was to support the RUC officers and keep them safe. A helicopter hovered high above, keeping watch, its blades drowning out the pastoral birdsong that damp grey morning. It was lashing down as the army land rovers sped out of the station gates, all four engines screeching and burping acrid fumes as they headed for their designated drop off point. Their location was somewhere near the southern border less than five miles away. These trips were always twitchy bottom affairs.

The 'Provos' had eyes on the Station 24/7 and any element of surprise always lay with them. When their traps were set, they had the shooters and bomb makers to do the killing but working tirelessly in the background were their other fanatical foot soldiers. They came in many forms and guises. A friendly shopkeeper, a bank employee, postmen, nurses, doctors, priests, pensioners and children. All these volunteers were wrapped up in the deadly struggle of the republican cause and the aspirational dream of a united Ireland.

A form of ethnic cleansing and demographic change was systematically being carried out by these Volunteers and their Provo ASU's (Active Service Units). This came in the form of murdering Ulster Protestant farmers whose properties fronted the border.

Many of these farms had land spanning on both sides and had been in protestant possession for many generations. However, once a farmer was murdered and his property became vacant, it would take a very brave Protestant to take on the land exposing himself and his family to the same fate as his predecessor. A Provo ASU would carry out a murder then quickly slip back over the border to anonymity and safety. With the brutal deed done they would return to their loving families and daytime jobs, leaving devastation and heartbreak behind. Areas of borderland Fermanagh that were once Protestant enclaves were being auctioned off and sold cheaply to farmers who had no such fears of death by assassination. A 'Legitimate Target' was a wide-ranging metaphor.

Rex, who was sitting directly behind the army driver leaned forward and spoke above the heavy engine clatter and the heavy rain and windscreen wiper thrashing. Smiling, he said to the young Tweety, "Morning, Doctor Love, I trust your mind is fully on the job today. We need your 'A' game." Tweety needed that and pulled his mind into gear. He was responsible for the lives of everyone on that patrol and steeling himself pushed thoughts of April to the back of his mind. He looked back over his right shoulder and smiled at his sage wise partner, "Absolutely Merv, 100% (in truth 99.8%)."

They were dropped off at a narrow country road within yards of the lough shore. There were no road markings and precious few signposts to guide their way back to Kesh. What they had were a map and compass and all day to get back. It was lashing down as the sounds of the land rovers and helicopter above faded into the relentless tympanic downpour. They were on their own and getting drenched. Merv saddled up beside Tweety and chuckled. "Only the most dedicated Provo would be out on a shitty day like this, Tweety lad." The lonely call of a curlew drifted across the damp lough shore like a warning siren exposing their presence. Tweety smiling nodded looking down at his waterproofed map as the rainwater drip dripped off his forage cap onto his cold hands then blobbed across the map's plastic surface. A quick look about him confirmed the army personnel had already adopted a safety cordon all looking outwards and well-spaced giving an excellent field of cover. These adopted positions were born from many hours of extensive training in a safer place and were now second nature.

Tweety gave a thumbs up to the young lieutenant whose grim face showed intense concentration and no little anxiety. That's the attitude and mind-set Tweety wanted to see, this was no place for 'Hooray Henrys' unless you wanted to be a dead one! Tweety placed his hand on top of his forage cap signalling for attention. Twenty yards ahead, there was a very narrow hole in a hedge whose field bordered the shore. He then placed his fingers up to his eyes and then pointed to the hole in the hedge repeating this move several times. He was indicating his wishes for them to enter the field that way. They would skirt past a large metal gate with a cattle grid accessing the field. This gateway was a much easier option but also the deadlier option. Valuable lessons had been learnt from the past. You avoided the obvious way at all costs. The Gloucesters quickly got into their rhythm. No words were required as they struggled initially through the hole in the hedge and then spread out advancing using cover and movement.

A cool stiff breeze picked up of the lough blending in with the steady downpour creating a cocktail of soaked bodies. The patrol carefully moved as one like a concert orchestra with Tweety carefully waving the baton. Dry walls were examined. Culverts specifically marked on the map were checked as safe as the group slowly and methodically made their way back towards Kesh. Tweety coordinated the manoeuvres of this novice group with a high level of efficiency and grim determination. Yes, everyone was tense and on edge but there was also a level of Zen amongst them. Every member of the patrol was totally focussed on their role and the job in hand. Even when they stopped at a safe woodland clearing for lunch there was no idle chit chat. A few whispered comments or a quick fag for stress relief. All eyes skinned and ears pricked to their adrenaline saturated limits. All of this is among the most beautiful breath-taking scenery. The Ying and Yang of the killing fields of Northern Ireland.

When they eventually returned to the safety of the barracks and the huge metal gates clanged comfortingly behind them, a state of euphoria occurred very much like a collective sigh of release, a *'joie de vie'* where they could become human beings again as opposed to the survival automans of their previous strained hours. A brief period of high jinks often occurred followed maybe with a can of beer and some heavy music. This was usually short lived as physical and nervous exhaustion steamrollered in and then to bed and deep sleep.

Tweety slapped Rex on the back who had kept a watchful eye on the young constable. He had a dangerous 14-mile drive back to his home in Enniskillen. This would take Rex some 20 minutes with his handgun in his lap. Twenty minutes of travel along lonely roads in a car his killers knew only too well. "Ta awfully Rex old bean, you toddle off home. I'll throw the returns in." Rex smiled at his young colleague; this one would go far. "Cheers Tweety, toodle pip."

As Tweety made his way past a group of the young soldiers, they stopped mid horseplay and shouted over at him in their Gloucester drawl. "Cheers Tweety, nice one mate." Tweety gave a quick thumbs up then trundled into the Enquiry Office, he was 'dawg' tired. The responsibility of people's lives was exhausting. His eyes fell upon April whose back was to him. She was updating a call on the Occurrence Book (C6). His knackered heart skipped a weary beat. She turned and faced him and spoke, "Aww, the mighty warrior has 'retoined', give me those," as she took his returns from him.

"I'm on till 7pm and it's dead as Hector in here." She could see he was shattered and gently took hold of him and walked him out of the Office.

"Go get some rest, your day's work is done. C'ya themarra, Tweety." She squeezed his arms ever so slightly just as she'd done that morning and eased him forward. The end to a perfect day!

Such was life in rural Kesh. In the rest of the province the slaughter continued unabated. Security force murders. Sectarian murders. Tit for tat murders and just plain old murders continued ad nausea. The grim reaper enjoyed his fine dining courtesy of the provinces all you can kill buffet. Belfast City Centre was being crippled with bombs and hoax bomb calls. The clergy pleaded for restraint and quoted love from their bibles. Alas their pleading fell on stony ground as the Pale Green horseman from Armageddon whose name was Death had already bolted. Death and destruction was everywhere.

Unable to cope with this explosion of violence and hate, the RUC who in 1969 were a peacetime force of some 3000 strong had to go into a recruitment overdrive eventually levelling out to some 13000 men and women. It was during this shortfall when the province was on its knees and at breaking point that the British Army was brought onto the streets to assist with maintaining law and order.

Back at Kesh, RUC station life went on as abnormal. Joint Police and Army foot patrols continued, changing only slightly for the police personnel when a new regiment moved in. Then the learning curve of survival began anew. Different seasons brought different challenges. Attacks from across the border continued along with the genocide but to the untrained eye everything appeared picture postcard normal.

Tweety and April were now very much an item. They would have liked to have taken things a bit slower but love had a very firm grip of their reins. Tweety had met April's family at their home in Augher. Her parents were a bit taken aback as their youngest daughter had never shown any inclination towards the opposite sex before. They were gobsmacked when out of the blue a handsome Tweety was paraded before them. April's father was quite an imposing figure and well used to making an individual squirm. All his efforts at subjugation were futile as Tweety being Tweety shone through. In a short space of time, they were besotted and totally got what their daughter had seen in him. It was here that April introduced Tweety to horses and where his lifelong love affair with them began. She had been a junior show jumping champion and her tiny bedroom was adorned with photographs and rosettes. She also opened Tweety's eyes to the love of home-grown vegetables and tomatoes grown from the greenhouse. From seed to your plate and the journey in between, very much like life itself mused the ever-pondering Tweety. This was something to get into, a lifelong hobby requiring minimum effort, maximum thought and a modicum of patience.

The more time the pair spent together the deeper and dearer their love grew. By now, they were having full blown conversations in a gathering with as little as a cough, sniff or the raise of an eyebrow. Tweety wallowed in delight as April shone softly in a crowd never shirking from a firmly held opinion but careful not to put anyone's nose out of joint.

It was a no brainer, Tweety would bring April down to Dromore to meet his parents at the end of this next early shift and propose straight afterwards. How lucky could a man be?

It was a lovely summer's day in August and Sergeant Sean O'Brien was hot, bothered and bored stiff from his morning admin on the second day of that particular 'Early Shift'. He fancied a wee break. An ice lolly is what he wanted, no, craved for, a 'Porky Pear' to be exact. A Porky Pear, a bit of fresh air and escape. He had paperwork to leave off to the Process Office in Enniskillen and that would do as his excuse. He was aware that Tweety was in the 'Cons Workroom' doing files or someone else's files as he could hear ghastly classical music drifting through the draughty gaps in the stations-tired walls. Sean dandered down to the Enquiry Office where April was the SDO. She was lounging on an armchair which was older than herself, it was busted, torn and full of stains but was the most comfortable seat in the house.

April was engrossed in a Reader's Digest, an article on organically grown tomatoes in Tibet had tickled her fancy. She didn't stir as Sean lifted the station's Tannoy microphone, "Tweety to the Enquiry Office, Tweety to the Enquiry Office please." April looked up, her curiosity now peeked, abandoning her tomatoes dangling on the slopes of the Himalayas.

After several seconds Tweety breezed in and was told of his skipper's cunning plan, "I need you to ride shotgun with me Tweety, there's a papa papa in it for you! I've got stuff to drop off at Enniskillen and besides I'm bored titless, I need a bit of fresh air about me."

Tweety's eyes lit up. "Mmmm a papa papa, just what the doctor ordered, I'll go get my kit on. With you in two shakes, skipper." Tweety scurried off to the locker room for his forage cap, rig and flacker. Sean signed out two radios and a long arm.

April huffed. "Well, Sergeant, what the fuck is a 'Papa Papa', they didn't teach me that one in the depot?"

Sean chuckled. "April pet, it's the one code the Provo's haven't cracked."

Tweety returned and lifted one of the radios and clipped it onto his gun belt.

He then lifted the Ruger rifle and popped out into the front yard of the station. Tweety proved the weapon at the loading bay before placing a live magazine in it. All this was done in a jiffy as Tweety bounced back into the Enquiry Office. Sean winked over at Tweety.

"Well, shall we tell her, Tweety?"

Tweety chuckled. "Well I suppose she's signed the Official Secrets Act skipper."

Sean let out one of his infectious laughs. "OK, April, you've broken me, a Papa Papa is a Porky Pear ice lolly and in this weather resistance is futile." A beaming Sean looked at April's bewildered face and then noticed her having a light bulb moment as her eyes widened breaking into a smile.

"Can I have one? I'm on my break in five minutes and we'll be back within the hour. Pleeaassee, Sarge, it's such a lovely day." April gave Sean her best pout which rendered Sean's resistance futile.

He shook his head slowly and said, "Oh all right, woman, go get your hat and flaker, but you're buying."

Sean had the keys to an orange soft skin Ford Escort signed out and when April's relief arrived, they all climbed aboard. Sean would be driving, April the front seat passenger and Tweety in the back with the long arm. It was a scorcher as the three friends laughed and bantered on what was truly a beautiful summer day. After 10 minutes' leisurely travel by way of the scenic route, Sean pulled up outside a small garage with only two pumps, one for diesel and one for petrol. Clintons Garage had been there forever and had always that 'On its last legs' look about it. Rumours abounded about dodgy cross border petrol fraud and vehicles coming and going at strange hours of the night, but no one seemed bothered, any day now the place would close for good surely. Though it never did close as a matter of fact it was rarely closed. Its dull petrol pump lights flickered morning, noon and night. It really was a shabby affair. April turned to Sean with questioning eyes, "Here!" Sean smiled. "The most important fact is that it sells Papa Papas woman and we're but five minutes from the Devenish jetty where we'll enjoy them. Scurry along, we haven't got all day."

April slipped out of their vehicle and entered the garage shop. A doorbell chimed as she entered. The shop was sparse and fusty and low on supplies unless you were after pot noodles, baked beans peas or carrots. It was in dire need of a good clean, its shelves were covered in dust and the floor looked as though it hadn't seen a mop in years. It had that cold sweaty air about it. However true to his word a large fridge freezer burred in the corner containing a supply of Porky Pears amongst other questionable things. April lifted the large heavy glass lid and gathered three of the frosted delights and approached the counter as a middle-aged woman by the name of Rosa Clinton appeared from the back. She was in her late forties, scrawny with dark mincing eyes and pale as a goose down. Her hair was a shoulder length bottle black and was in dire need of shampoo. Her ragged teeth were an off-cream colour, and her bony hands were stained with nicotine. She was draped in a light black cardigan which looked about as worn as herself. She had been part of the fixture and fittings for years. A radio was playing 'fiddle de Dee' music in the background. You could see by her features if you dared to stare hard enough that she had been good looking in her day but a bitterness of soul and 40 fags a day had hastened her aging process. Two poles apart met at the counter.

April smiled warmly at the woman who from behind cold dark eyes nodded back, then a forced smile. "Will that be all you're wanting on this lovely day. Sure there's nowhere like here when the suns got its bonnet on." April was slightly disarmed by the sudden apparent warmth and friendliness, sometimes looks could deceive. She decided to make the effort and returned the smile.

"You're right there, the boss wants to have these down at the Devenish jetty, I better go before these lolly's melt." April quickly paid and left with a 'Thanks now'. The woman's eyes followed her as she returned to the orange Escort. A yellowed 'Clintons' biro pen worn and chewed at the end was now in her hand as she scribbled the vehicle registration down on yesterday's copy of 'An Phoblacht'. She smiled coldly as she spotted the driver. "Sergeant O'Brien, how are we this fine day." She returned to the back of the premises and made an urgent phone call.

A few minutes later, the three musketeers were down at the Devenish jetty. It was used by foreign tourists as a mooring point following a day's cruising on luxury five or seven berth cruisers hired out by local operators. Not that there was much tourism going on in those days. The road taking you down to the jetty became narrower as you neared its location with the final quarter of a mile offering width for only one vehicle. It was a place and location only a few could find and get to from the road. Because of this it was a haven for wildlife. Sean and April had their asses parked on the front bonnet gazing out at the beautiful lough sucking away at their lollies. Tweety was leaning against the rear boot, both he and his Ruger rifle facing country wards. If there was any danger coming, it would be coming from that direction. His view was equally as nice as he gazed over pastures, forests and fields. Mother nature was bursting at the seams as all manner of wildlife sang their songs of joy to that spectacular summer's day. Sean finished his lolly and fired the wooden stick into the lough watching it bob in the richly organic peaty blackness. "Sure, where would you get a job like this? No Bank work here April. No classics here, Tweety lad. I wouldn't trade it for the world." A mother duck appeared from behind a cluster of reeds followed by six little ducklings tweeting impervious to any dangers.

"Why can't we all just get along without trying to fucking kill each other." Sean sighed and kicked at a pebble watching as it plopped into the blackness never more to see the light of day.

"Right kids, back to the real world. Let's go." Sean and April had taken off their flak jackets and thrown them in the boot down at the jetty. Tweety hadn't bothered, the heat never annoyed him.

Enniskillen was an easy 10-minute drive, and the troubles seemed a million miles away as Sean cruised back up the narrow country road. "Oh look, guys!" April excitedly pointed heavenwards as a male skylark rose vertically from the ground and then high into the air hovering stationary in full song flight. Sean looked up and smiled, his spirits lifted. Tweety spotted a tricolour flag hanging limp attached to a stone gate post. It hadn't been there before as the orange Escort trundled up towards it.

Sean and April's eyes were still cast heavenwards when it happened. A huge roadside bomb was detonated by way of a command wire. The flag had been positioned beside beer kegs packed with explosives and acted as a sighter for the terrorist who flicked the deadly switch. The vehicle took the full force of the explosion and was ripped in two. The front half was thrown 20 yards down the narrow country road. The back half of the vehicle containing Tweety was hurled backwards ending up in a wheat field on its roof. Sean and April died instantly; their bodies vaporised by the blast. Two masked terrorists hugged each other from the crest of a hill some 200 yards away their ears ringing as clouds of smoke and dirt fell all around them. They quickly gathered up their murderous gear and made of across the border on a motorbike. The tiny skylark lay dead in the crater created from the blast its last song sung.

Tweety had survived but only just. When the explosion was reported, a helicopter was dispatched from Enniskillen to ascertain its location. Then a recovery operation was quickly put in place to recover the bodies and gather any evidence. This was always a case of more haste and less speed. The Provo's were masters at killing two birds with the one stone and had used secondary devices in the past on police or army attending such scenes of devastation.

The media arrived as they always did, and the television cameras captured footage of the aftermath for global consumption. Reports were filmed against the heavy drone of overhead helicopters. Snatch interviews were held with local members of the public.

One such interview was recorded by the BBC whose reporter spoke with Ms Rosa Clinton. Ms Clinton related serving the young female officer earlier that day at her place of work and how shocked she had been at the sound of the explosion. Ms Clinton offered her heartfelt sympathies from behind charcoal dead eyes while inside her heart burned with pride at the part, she had played in the death of the two officers. Her role now elevated amongst her fellow freedom fighters in their struggle for Irish freedom.

After several painstaking hours, the scene was preserved and a joint police and army cordon was installed. All of the officers maintaining the cordon were devastated, most with tears in their eyes. A brilliant sergeant and a father figure to his section was gone. His desk would have to be cleared along with his locker containing his personal belongings. A beautiful caring female colleague was also gone. She had started the day on desk duty, but fate would take her on a quiet country road along with her Sergeant. Both had so much more to offer. The Sub Divisional Commander of Enniskillen had two heart breaking visits to perform that day. Firstly, to Sean's parents and then to April's.

CID and forensic staff worked grimly through the wreckage as fragments of Sean and April were gathered up. An emergency services helicopter landed in the wheat field and whisked Tweety off to the Royal Victoria Hospital in Belfast. He was in very bad shape but by the finest of margins he had survived. Wearing his flak jacket and being in the back of the vehicle proved to be the difference. Tweety had suffered massive internal injuries both his legs and arms were shattered and he had lost his right eye. Many gallons of blood were used to keep him alive. He lay in a coma for several weeks under the watchful care of all the very experienced trauma staff at the R.V.H.

During this time, the funerals of Sean and April took place. Both funerals were formal at the request of both families. Kesh section members bore their colleagues in full dress uniform to their final resting places. They did so with immense dignity as tears of pain and grief flowed. They had to perform this act twice and the loss of two colleagues who were also dear friends was hard to bear. Their coffins were draped with the union jack flag along with their respective forage caps. The RUC Pipe Band played a lament of solemn respect as Sean was interred in the Chapel at Ballinamallard and April at Enniskillen Methodist Church.

After nearly a month, Tweety opened his eye and looked around his hospital bed. A specialist Intensive Care nurse was at his bedside. It was 3.30am and the month was September. His summer had gone along with his hopes and dreams. The nurse leaned quietly over to him and whispered gently, "Welcome back, Mr Sweetlove. We weren't sure you would make it." What was left of Tweety with his body so terribly broken and what of his brilliant mind? Tweety slowly closed his single green eye then fell into the safety net of his dreams. Happy dreams where he was back at Kesh Station laughing and joking with April and Sean. Then singing folk songs with the rest of the gang as the open fire crackled and flames danced in the grate.

It would take a further six months and a lot of rehabilitation before Tweety was up and about. He had learned to live with a replacement glass eye. He had light facial scarring but all in all, he was better though he would never be fit enough for 'Ordinary Duties'. When he was deemed strong enough, he was told the news of Sean and April's deaths and the effect it had on his colleagues at Kesh station and the subdivision. He was told that morale at Kesh had hit rock bottom and that the station personnel had all but for a few locals been broken up and moved on to pastures new. Kesh RUC Station as he knew it was no more.

Tweety was now in a quandary, take a medical retirement or spend the rest of his working life in the police on restricted and light duties. Money was never an issue; he could print it on the stock exchange and his needs were few. Whilst mulling over his future he sat the sergeant and inspector's exams at the same time just to see if the old grey matter was working. He knew the law inside out and with a quick swish through the RUC Code he felt ready. He came top in both exams and feigned shock and surprise when he was told the news. He was immediately offered specialist posts but declined and amazed his superiors when he jumped at the offer of Station Duty Officer Constable at Mountroyal RUC Station, East Belfast, a million emotional miles away from lake shores of wild Fermanagh.

It was time to move on, time to start a new chapter.

Tweety found himself a nice but neglected thirties semi just off the Sandown

Road of east Belfast. Its previous residents had passed on via a slight detour for several years to a residential home. The semi was located in a quiet tree lined Cul de Sac. It was south facing and had a long private overgrown back garden. The property was tired to say the least but retained all of its original features. Elegant stained-glass windows had survived in their original wooden paint flaked frames. These light reflecting windows cast an ambience from a bygone age and were in keeping with the spirit and demeanour of the house. A deep green coloured front door sat smugly on a beautiful terracotta tiled porch. On it was a brass door number four. April was the fourth month and Tweety took this to be a sign. He then discovered a thirty-foot long glass greenhouse with more panes out than in. It had hidden, shattered and broken for several seasons in the wilderness of the back garden. Tweety's heart skipped a beat. Here was a place where he could grow fruit and vegetables and be with April again. His heart would always ache for her, but he knew April wouldn't want him to stop living or merely exist. He made her a promise to live a full and productive life and leave no stone unturned in what would be his lifelong pursuit, the pursuit of happiness.

Tweety paid the asking price for the place and quickly got it knocked back into shape.

The original furniture had been abandoned there and was Georgian in style which was very much to Tweety's liking. A capable French polisher was hired and soon had fresh life breathed into many of the pieces. Bookshelves in keeping with the style were installed in both the front and back living rooms. Soon they were filled with all manner of eclectic reads befitting of their owner's avaricious mind. A state of the art hi fi system was purchased with a high-end turntable and speakers. This was placed in the rear living room which afforded a glorious view down the back garden. Here he would sit of an evening with a glass of vintage port in his hand. His green eye closed, lost in a far-off world whilst listening to his beloved Mozart, Brahms or Bach according to his mood. Here he would think and plan, here his memories washed in and then out again like the autumn tide. He kept as many of the house's original features as he could. He loved the old white and green tiles in the bathroom. The bath itself was restored as was the toilet complete with original chain. Tweety's bedroom located at the rear of the house was a Spartan affair. The original wooden framed bed was kept and polished. An expensive orthopaedic mattress was purchased. This greatly helped with the aches he would quietly endure for the rest of his days. His wardrobes and drawers were basically empty. A simple 'four of everything', was his rule of thumb. This for all his winter and summer 'clobber' as he described them.

Beside his bed was an original reading lamp which cast a yellow glow and an art deco period radio which hissed and crackled as it presented Tweety with his beloved classical music. The rest of the unoccupied rooms remained empty and closed.

A celebrated garden landscaper pulled up in an expensive Landover outside Tweety's house one day. You know, the one with his gardening show on the telly. Inquisitive neighbours gawped from behind net curtains as Tweety and the celeb paced the rear gardens. Ideas were expressed and challenged, and a notebook was furiously scribbled upon. A fortnight later builder's skips appeared along with diggers and workers. The rear garden was transformed from the ugly jungle to a freshly laid lawn with raised beds containing stunning shrubs and annuals. The greenhouse was completely restored with the latest temperature management and watering systems fitted. 'Their' beloved tomatoes and the like were planted and an amazing workstation for potting and seeding with shelves and drawers to hand was created.

To the front of the house, the old tarmac driveway was replaced by the latest brick pavers. Its flower beds restored and special areas created in sunny aspects for a mass of beautiful daisies the flower for April. The following summer, Tweety's new home was stunningly beautiful. It was transformed from the worst house in the best street to the best house in the best street. He had made new friends along the way amongst his elderly neighbours who fell hopelessly into Tweety's charms. Tea and cakes were a regular occurrence on his back patio surrounded by all manner of blooms and scents as butterflies danced among the daisies. Tweety loved listening to their life stories realising they were the same as him except they were in deep disguise hiding behind elderly masks.

He became particularly fond of Hilary Grimason, a spritely 72-year-old retired Physics Lecturer. Hilary lived two doors down and like himself loved the 'classics' and the growing of tomatoes. She would make him think and more importantly laugh. He told them all his story and from that day Tweety had his own very tight private security firm. Nothing moved that they didn't know about. The only thing they frowned upon was Tweety's knackered rust bucket, his beloved brown Vauxhall Viva which he called 'Our Vera'. Vera was 11 years old and for all her visible failings never failed to start or transport its master from A to B.

For Tweety, the experience had been cathartic. He had given the old house a complete restoration, a new life and a future. He now had one thing left to do. One more trip before he returned to work.

Rain splattered hard against the mud-stained window of Clintons Garage as the dark coloured vehicle pulled up and stopped outside. The air was hot, muggy and wet with the torrential downpour. A male figure entered the store accompanied by the chiming door and the howling rain. He carried a plastic shopping bag which was full. Rosa Clinton appeared as if by magic eyeing the male with her usual cold suspicion. The male had on a dark blue overcoat with the collar turned up against the weather, dark trousers, a flat cap and driving gloves. He also wore heavy dark blue tinted glasses. Rosa spoke first, "Jaysus, have you no home to go to, what brings you out on a day like this?" The male laughed. "Sure you're right there, it's a dirty one all right. I've just popped over from Donegal. A wee bit of business to do with my northern comm…friends if you know what I mean. Today is a good day to travel for the likes of me." He leaned back and turned his head to the side and viewed Rosa before laughing out loud. "Sure, weren't you on the tele when those three black bastards were blown to fuck down at Devenish last summer?"

Rosa smiled coldly. "Sadly, only two out of the three died, one survived but I think he's a vegetable or something. A great result for the 'RA', jaysus the whole station at Kesh was cleared out after it. Sure one of them, a wee fat ginger haired bitch was in that morning buying ice lollies. She told me where they were heading and a quick phone call from me done the rest!"

The male laughed. "Good for you, girl…Tiocfaidh ar la ('our day will come', The Irish Republican Slogan.)."

Rosa swelled with pride. "Aye and the sooner the better."

"Tell me this comrade, what sort of ice lollies were they last sucking on?" His back was now to her as he rummaged through the old vibrating chest freezer.

"Porky Pears comrade, I've taken a liking to them myself." She cackled. Rosa watched on as the male continued his search while outside the rain continued its freefall clawing and grabbing away at the shop window.

"No siree, no fuckin Porky Pear bastards in here missus," shouted the male, his head buried deep inside the freezer.

Rosa sighed. "Fuckin men, can't see fuck all unless its staring them in the face, move over let me take a look." The male stood up and stepped back allowing Rosa to stoop over into the freezer. Rosa laughed up from the freezer, "They're in here somewhere, I calls them my Lucky Lollies!"

The male walked quietly over to the shop front door and gazed out at the deluge. Not a sinner about. He reached to the sign hanging from the door and turned the open side to closed. He placed his hand into his shopping bag and pulled out a large wrapped frozen leg of lamb. He then moved back to the freezer and quickly held Rosa's head down into the frozen trough. She began to scream and plead for mercy. Leaning over into the freezer he whispered the last words she would hear, "Ta do la tagtha soith! Your day has come bitch!" One blow from the frozen leg ended Rosa's struggle and her war. Three Porky Pears were then removed. The male then calmly flipped the corpse into the freezer and closed the lid tight.

Quietly, he rounded the shop counter and removed the security tape from its dated recorder. Stepping back out into the isolation and fury of the squall, he flicked the lock snib of Clintons Garage and shut its door behind him. Clintons Garage had finally closed. Several minutes later, the dark vehicle stopped at the Devenish jetty. The male got out and walked its length as the wind and rain howled hard into him. The lake was a furious mass of swell and battering waves. The male stood there for a minute absorbing the fury of the weather and at the same time releasing his own fury back to the pain of his past. Suddenly, the storm stopped. The wind ceased raging and the rain softened to a quiet drizzle. The lake flopped back to a black mirror and birdsong slowly returned. The male quietly wept as he listened again to the beautiful strains of a lark. It was finished now. The male threw the security tape out into the lake's blackness, never more to be seen and then a melted Porky Pear ice lolly. He returned to the vehicle unnoticed, unseen and was gone.

That night, Tweety had company for dinner. He collected Hilary from hers and walked her down to his. Mozart was playing softly in the candle lit back living room and a bottle of French red was breathing ready for their arrival. The table was beautifully set with the finest silver sitting upon a beautiful Belfast linen tablecloth with matching napkins. A Tyrone crystal vase took centre stage containing the most fragrant pink and white hybrid tea roses freshly cut from his garden that evening. Hilary stopped and smiled. "Tweety, how beautiful, those roses are stunning and what a delightful smell, what are they called?"

Tweety smiled at Hilary. "They're called April in Paris, my favourite. We're having roast lamb tonight, your favourite I believe. A glass of wine before we start?"

"Oh Tweety, what a wonderful host you are…" Hilary laughed as they sat for a while in front of the open fire, two friends alone with their thoughts.

Many miles away in the graveyard at Enniskillen Methodist Church a plot had been freshly tended. A glass vase was festooned with daisies and hybrid pink and white roses and strangely a melted Porky Pear ice lolly wrapper and stick. A small handwritten note was scribbled saying the following. "Thought you would like these from our garden pet. I've left a similar bunch and a lolly with Sean as well. How I miss you both. The tomatoes will be ready next week. See you then. Love always, your Tweety. XX."

A few days later, Tweety returned to his new workplace as a Station Guard or Station Duty Officer at Mountroyal RUC Station. It was a short 10-minute drive from his new home. There he was welcomed by his new partner Victor Snape, and they ran a happy ship for the next few years to present.

A Bollocking From The Sdc
Monday 16 May 1983...

It was a bleak Monday evening on the 16 May as the two old codgers Pinky and Perky wearily climbed the heavy metal fire escape steps taking them to the top floor of Strand RUC Station and their meeting with the Sub Divisional Commander a Superintendent George Sewell. D/I Archie Brown (Pinky) and D/S Cliff Boomer (Perky) chose this route as they weren't in any mood for socialising. A special meeting of all the heads had been called for by the boss. They were all aware it was to do with the ongoing spate of attacks, robberies and sexual assaults on females within the subdivision. These attacks had occurred over the past few months and showed no signs of abating. The metallic steps clanged like a bell tolling and for the two men it felt as though it was tolling for them. This was not going to be pleasant. Four attacks to date and not a crumb of information.

As they reached the top, they swung open a heavily fortified metal door revealing a magnolia corridor and made their way to the bosses' function room. Cliff spoke first, "Well cunty bollocks have you your National Geographical stuffed down the back of your wee brown trousers?"

Archie replied without breaking stride, "November '82, otters in Ottawa."

Cliff returned, "February '83, hamsters up the Hudson." Both allowed themselves a nervous chuckle. They were met by the ever-smiling Debbie Dean, the bosses' personal secretary. Debbie was as stylish as ever and was once big Cliff's type. She approached the pair as though she was gliding down a catwalk. Debbie Dean would not have looked out of place in a Marks and Spencer's catalogue. Everything about her from her dress sense to her make-up was the finished article. She was excellent at her job and very protective of her boss. Debbie was not smiling. The omens were not good. She pointed them in the direction of the boss's function room and mimed that he was on the phone and mouthed, "Not good chaps, not good at all."

Cliff suppressed a giggle. More nerves than anything at the sound of Archie's squeaking brothel creepers as they approached the function room door. They gave each other a final nod of support and swung the door open and purposefully strode in. Inside, they found a sea of grey and that wasn't the walls. Grey faces looked up at them in an 'All is lost' fashion. It was like the waiting room for Valhalla. They both took a seat, their pallor also turning grey in true chameleon fashion. Looking about them, they could see a familiar cast, two neighbourhood inspectors and the section inspectors from both Mountroyal and Strand. Archie was sat next to Derek Grant the A. Section inspector at Mountroyal. They had been friends and colleagues for many years. Archie whispered into Derek's ear, "National Geographical time chum!"

Derek smirked and leaned back to Archie and whispered, "July 81, meerkats in Mongolia."

The Function Room door opened, and a heavy-set female entered in plain clothes. She had a binder folder under her arm. It was Janet O'Loan the subdivisional collator. Janet was a constable with 14 years' service, she was blessed with an eye for detail and patterns of behaviour. She found her niche in the job and her calling in life in the role of a collator. The collators' role was to monitor the crime occurring in their patch as well as studying the criminal types. She logged their movements, where they lived, who they associated with and what vehicles they drove or had access to. A lot of her valuable information came from the officers on the ground who would submit C.I.1's (Criminal Intelligence Report Forms, a small pad which could fit in a back pocket.) These intelligence slips were being submitted 24 hours a day province wide.

A good collator studied Crime Pattern Analysis as well as all the terrorist related intelligence. A collator would brief a section on any relevant comings or goings once a week. A good collator's office door was always open with information passing both ways for the greater good. Every main station had a collator and all were vital in the war against crime and terrorism. Janet was a very pleasant hard working 35-year-old. Quite plain to look at, perhaps a bit shy and a few stones on the wrong side of the scales. Because of this a few of the smart arses called her 'Planet O'Blong' which was a cruel and nasty jibe. When they got to know her and appreciate all about her, they inevitably ate humble pie. Janet nodded and gave a quiet 'Evening all' to everyone there but to no one in particular. She took a seat at a small desk beside the boss's large table and green leather swivel chair. There they waited listening to the tick tocking of a small Vienna Regulator wall clock which was quite relaxing.

Suddenly, the door burst open and in stormed the SDC, Superintendent George Sewell. He was slight in frame and in good shape for 62. He had a good head of well-groomed grey hair and was a bachelor. He had done his 30 years and had been a senior officer for over half of them. He looked as though he had just stepped off a 'Man at C&A' commercial in his dark grey three-piece suit and pink silk tie. His black brogues were polished to a mirror standard. George Sewell made the normally sartorial Cliff look like 'Stig of the Dump!' George nodded to all in general, his face set in stone. He approached a pine coat stand and hung his jacket on one of its hooks. His jacket slipped off and fell in a heap on the thick pink carpet. Sighing, he tried again with the same result. He gathered his jacket up and hung it precisely on the back of his swivel chair. He then quietly opened one of the huge reinforced security glass windows and leaned far out into the damp evening air. Pinky and Perky looked at each other, was the boss going to jump? George returned to the pine coat stand and swiftly lifted it up and carried it to the open window. A final glance and then it was gone crashing into a yellow builders skip in the station yard below.

George closed the huge window and returned to his swivel chair smiling from beneath clenched teeth. He then roared, "Debbie," and waited, seconds later Debbie entered with a notebook in hand smiling.

George had visibly calmed and smiling up at Debbie spoke, "Two things Debbie, could you sort us out with tea or coffee, a show of hands please!" Hands were raised according to preference. "Secondly, could you order me a new coat stand, one that you can actually hang a coat on? Our last one committed suicide and jumped out of the window. Poor thing's lying dead in the skip below." Everyone laughed which cut the ice. George clasped his well-groomed hands and began wringing them anxiously. Looking around at the gathered faces, he expelled a stressed lung full of air and spoke.

"There's no point beating about the bush, we're in the spotlight, under the cosh. Up shit creek without a paddle and basically Daffy Ducked. The press is on my back. UTV and BBC are looking for me for interviews and the Chief Constable is calling me daily. I'm just off the phone with that dreadful Official Unionist MP Ms Vivien Chesney. If she had her way, I'd be hung, drawn and quartered. HELP ME… Somebody please!!"

George exasperated looked over at Janet just as Debbie entered quietly handing out the teas and coffees leaving a selection of assorted biscuits in plates within stretching distance of those gathered.

"Janet, would you run us through with what we've got to date?"

Janet cleared her throat and began the briefing in her usual concise and analytical fashion.

1. First victim, a Mrs Sarah Prentice; 50 years a married woman with two children. She resides at 14 Imperial Street. The incident occurred on Saturday 26 February at 9.45pm. She had been drinking with mates at the Cosy Bar in Omeath Street. She was attacked in an entry off Roslyn Street and forced to perform oral sex. Her attacker took her pearl earrings.

2. Second victim, a Ms Rachel McKnight; 39 years divorced. She resides at 23 Florida Drive. The incident occurred on Thursday the 24 March at 10.40pm. She had been drinking at the My Lady's Inn on the My Lady's Road. She was dragged into an entry off Canada Street beaten and forced to perform oral sex. The attacker took her purple head scarf.

3. Third victim, a Miss Tracey Armstrong; 24 years single. She lives with her parents at 9 Channing Street. Her incident occurred on Friday the 8 April at 11.10pm. She was at a friend's Hen Party at the Eastenders Bar on the Woodstock Road. She was attacked in an entry in Ardgowan Street. Reading the statements to this point the attacker appeared to be getting more confident and much more violent. He began to speak with the victims and a more sinister and degrading side to him came to the fore. He was now taking his time with them and forcing them to undress and then perform oral sex while slapping and beating them. With Tracey, he took her charm bracelet.

The final victim to date was Miss Dorothy Walker; 41 years single. Dorothy lives alone at 14 Frank Street. Dot's incident occurred on Saturday the 14 May at 10.45pm. Funnily, Dot was also at a hen party. Hers was held at the Rosemount Bar, Mount Street. She was attacked while having a pee in an entry backing off the country bound side of the Woodstock Road just below the Beersbridge Road junction. Hers was the most violent and degrading to date. Her attacker broke her nose, punched a front tooth out and cracked a couple of ribs. All the while verbally abusing her. All ending with oral sex. He took with him a necklace bearing the letter T. This was Miss Walker's deceased mothers. T as in her name Tessie.

The room was silent as Janet blue tacked a large map of the Subdivision on a white board. On the map, she had given each victim a colour which highlighted their address, the bar they drank on the night in question and the location of the attack. Janet stood back and paused for a moment allowing those present to absorb the topography before continuing.

"Similarities with each attack are as follows. The male is described as being of slim build. Fit at around 5' 9" or 10". He speaks with a Belfast accent. He wears dark clothes and a baseball cap. A mention of him carrying a backpack maybe green in colour. Oh and finally two of the victims mentioned a crackling sound maybe from a radio type device coming from the back pack. I've released these details to the local press and to Crimestoppers but as yet no responses." With that, Janet was finished, she sat down and took a sip of cold tea.

George looked around at the sea of drawn faces. "Section and neighbourhood inspectors, what have you got for me?"

He was met with sad shakes of the head, no 'Nell Mangles' from 'Neighbours' fame had come forward with any doorstep pearls of wisdom. Overtime had been dished out for increased beat and mobile patrols with entries and alleyways under constant vigil but to date nada, nothing.

"Pinky and Perky, give me something, anything for fuck sake!" George pleaded.

Pinky or Archie Brown slowly shook his head. "Sorry, boss, we've put out to our touts but no one has the slightest notion who this bastard is. He's like the fucking Scarlet Pimpernel. He's either very lucky or has some sixth sense as to where we are. We'll keep trying."

George wrung his hands further. "Right, pubs and clubs. I've made out a list of pubs and clubs in the subdivision. Each section has two to cover. Call with them and give them a squeeze when deemed safe to do so. I want full reports made out and forwarded to Janet who will keep me briefed, and for fuck sake have back up on standby. These places can go up like a powder keg."

Derek Grant, the A section Inspector was given his two. The Cosy Bar in Omeath Street, a UVF run bar, and the Blades Club on the Beersbridge Road. A Sheffield United supporter's bar. George Sewell then gave a warm smile to all around. "That's about it, folks. Let's gird our 'lions' and catch this pervy son of a bitch!" As the room was clearing, George waved over to Pinky, Perky and

Derek who shuffled wearily over to him. George was slipping back into his jacket as Debbie was tidying the cups and saucers away. He looked at his three friends and said, "Who's up for a confab at the HOP House? I'm buying!"

Cliff blurted in, "Count me in. The last time you bought a drink, Queen Victoria was in nappies." George laughed as the other two nodded.

"Oh and by the way, see if Tweety is free, I know he's busy with his harem and tomatoes et al but we can only hope." Archie suppressed a laugh whilst smoking up Woody his pipe.

"I'll give him a bell. Mines a pint by the way."

The HOP House was an abbreviation for the 'House of Pain' a place where stressed out peelers would go for a pint, solve the world's problems and make plans. Sometimes the plans bit was forgotten about along with their worldly worries. The HOP House was in fact the Rosetta Bar located just below the Upper Knockbreda Road not far from the magnificent Chapel. Aesthetically, it wasn't too pleasing, a 1970s brick and cement box with large windows. It was a safe haven for police. A small secure back bar located upstairs was set aside for their use at a drop of a hat. Its owners, staff and clientele were all very pro police. It was situated in a 'safe' location and had excellent security cameras.

Some 30 minutes later, the four amigos were sat in a corner snug facing a large open window. The first pint usually went down without much chatter or brain interference as jets were slowly cooled. A view of the Castlereagh hills also helped. Cliff was contemplating getting the next one in when Paddy the barman buzzed the security door open. Tweety glided in wearing his favourite green woollen overcoat, dark trousers and outrageously loud lime green socks. He was wearing his usual heavily tinted dark blue glasses which masked his missing eye. A tanned fedora hat was propped in a jaunty fashion on his head. The look shouldn't have worked but for Tweety it did. He spotted that another round was needed.

"Evening, Paddy, same again and the usual for me. A wee banker for you, Harvest Gold 10/1, it's running at 2.30pm tomorrow at Newmarket. A tenner on the nose should do the trick." Pinky and Perky gave each other a knowing wink.

"Evening all," Tweety said to the four men taking a seat that had been dragged over for him. Paddy brought the next round over. Four pints and a white coffee and a soberano brandy with ice for Tweety.

Paddy fidgeted for a while then spoke, "Tweety, ya see this? Harvest Gold horse, themarra, there's 15 other runners and he's not even favourite. Should I not just go each way on him?"

Tweety seeing the worry on the old barman's face smiled up at him. "Paddy old son, if our horse doesn't romp it tomorrow, I'll give you a tenner."

Paddy laughed. "Fair 'nuff, Tweety." A comfortable silence followed for five pleasurable minutes as batteries recharged for another shove at the problem. George the SDC spoke, breaking the karma as sweet Saint Bruno smoke filled the air. "Tweety old bean, we're in a bit of a pickle with these attacks. Derek tells me you're up to speed with it all. (Derek smiled.) Any ideas, comments or observations you'd care to share with us mere mortals?" Tweety took a sip of coffee quickly followed by a nip of the brandy.

He sat back and sighing, spoke, "A lot of work has gone into this with as yet zip results. The attacker is male. Around 5' 10" in height with a slim to medium build. He speaks with a Belfast accent. He wears the same gear in each attack and has always had a rucksack or backpack maybe green in his possession. Two of the victims thought they heard what sounded like the crackling of a radio during their ordeal. The attacks take place in entries close to pubs. The victims are forced to perform blow jobs and the attacker always takes a memento which is probably a trophy of sorts."

Cliff piped in, "Yeah we've got all that Tweety but we're no further on."

Tweety nodded and spoke, "I hears ya, Cliff, but maybe you are further on than you think. Hear me out and correct me if I'm wrong anywhere. The attacks have all occurred within a small area in the 'Prod' side of East Belfast. Our man appears to have a superior knowledge of and is comfortable in the area. With every opportunity presented to him he has been successful. Appeals to the press and media have been fruitless. The natives, the good, the bad and the ugly have no information whatsoever. Increased patrolling both covert and overt have also drawn blanks. So there you are then." Tweety sat back and took further sips from his coffee and brandy and looked up at the Castlereagh Hills contented.

George shook his head looking over at the rest of the gang totally bewildered. Was the master losing his touch? They all leaned forward, and Woody was now in full flow. One more puff and the smoke alarms were going off! Cliff broke rank shaking his head like a punter short changed at a strip joint. "No shit, Sherlock, but again we're still no further on!"

Tweety startled, looked over at his four friends and laughed. "Ha, Sherlock you say, Cliff. Never a truer word." Pinky and Perky looked at each other shrugging much like 'Dumb and Dumber'.

Tweety continued, "Have any of you read the Sherlock Holmes novel *The Sign of Four*?"

Tweety gazed upon the four blank canvases. Smiling, he continued, "In the book, and much like our situation here, all I's had been dotted and all T's crossed. All avenues of enquiries exhausted, and the sleuths flummoxed. Holmes then came off with this fabulous quote (which Tweety's photographic mind produced verbatim)...

"How often have I said to you that when you eliminate the impossible, whatever remains, however improbable, must be the truth?"

Archie went, "Eh!" George sat grim faced.

Tweety went again. "I'm curious about the nature of this beast. Why the green rucksack, what's he got in it? Two of the victims say they heard a radio type crackling sound. How is it we've had no luck with him? He knows the area, but no one seems to know him. Maybe the answers staring us in the face or maybe we stare at his face quite regularly. Could he be more than plain lucky?"

Derek spoke, "If I'm hearing you right Tweety are you saying the bastard could be one of us? You mean he knows our movements because he's listening out on a police radio!" Pinky and Perky looked at each other and shrugged.

George looked at Tweety and said, "I hope you're wrong my old son but do the work on it. Find out what sections were on when the attacks were occurring. My reasoning being if he's one of us he can't be at work and attacking the women at the same time. Double check who was on leave or on training courses or at court or the like. Establish where every man was relating to that particular section on the nights of each attack. Do the same with the Neighbourhood Sections that were on and the full package again with the Strand Station members. If a different section was on during a different attack, go through the same procedure as the first. We might get lucky and find that there was one section that was never on at the time of the attacks. And that would prove very interesting. Go through the radio logbooks and again check who had radios signed out, were any radios for whatever reason not signed back in. And for God's sake, keep this all under your hats."

Tweety smiled. "I think it's worth a try boss, leave it with me."

The team had one more for the road and howls of laughter ensued as banter flowed among these friends as their night at the HOP House ended. As they were having their last swallows George leaned over to Derek and whispered loud enough for all to hear.

"Derek, my old son, you've hit the jackpot. I've arranged for a beautiful female MP to visit you at Mountroyal tomorrow at 2.30pm. She wants to discuss all aspects of these attacks with you and find out what the Police are doing about it. I could think of no finer man for the job." Derek looked at his boss and shook his head. He had been done up like a kipper. He groaned and looking at the four men smiling at him he said…

"Please God let it be anybody other than Vivien Chesney. With friends like you lot, who needs enemies."

The Not So Cosy Bar Incident
Tuesday 17 May

Tony Speers was really getting used to this being a Sergeant malarkey. Keep the paperwork moving and your call up registers up to date. Administer the odd judicial kick up the backside to the troops for motivation. Advice when required on tricky files from Tweety. Hot coffee and buns in the Guard Room followed by the odd supervisory patrol. This in essence was a talent spotting exercise whilst out and about cruising the subdivision. He was also spoiled for choice with regards to the eye candy issues. He could always fall back on either of the two lovelies in his section, the angelic Stephanie aka 'Heavenly' or her firecracker pal the burlesque, Shelley. Yes, life indeed was good. He was happily swivelling away at his chair behind his desk this particular day. He hadn't told any lies when he mentioned urgent paperwork which is what he was hard at. Tony was totally engrossed in the Sun newspaper when he was rudely interrupted by the station tannoy blaring. "Sergeant Speers to the Inspector's Office. Sergeant Speers to the Inspector's office pleeaasee." Tony disgruntled raised his head from the tit bits from page three. *Quack oops,* he thought, wondering what cluster he had unwittingly got himself into.

He left the safety of his lair and sauntered out into the corridor with a confident swagger, feeling anything but. Shelley passed him carrying paperwork under her arms. She was on files. The top two buttons of her blouse were open. She caught him ogling and he had no time to recover. She gave him her special smile and that lingering glance reserved for those lucky few who stood any chance. "Morning, Sergeant, we were just wondering if you were up for a quick toot at the Eastenders Bar today at close of play. It's a Tuesday earlies thing we do. We only have a couple. Even the non-drinkers go like the Preacher and Wee John. It will give you a chance to see us all with our clothes off. Oops out of our uniforms I mean."

Tony laughed. "Lovely, Shelley, I would love to (in more ways than one), what time?"

Shelley laughed. "We're all usually there by 4.15pm and gone before 6pm." Tony smiled and gave her a thumbs up. Then pointed at the inspector's door rolling his eyes as he knocked twice and entered.

Inspector Derek Grant was at his desk which was in immaculate order. He was perusing through a serious assault file, his beady eyes fixed in concentration. He motioned Tony to take a seat and continued reading, making notes on a scrap sheet of paper with a beautiful gold ink fountain pen. Derek was truly a class act. Tony realised that he was merely acting class, he had a way to go yet. A minute later, Derek placed the lid on his Parker pen and smiling looked up at Tony. "Fucking paperwork. I'm knackered. Was at the HOP House last night with the boss, Tweety and the dynamic duo Pinky and Perky. We had a few, or should I say a few too many. I can't do it anymore, honestly Tony I really can't." Derek rubbed his temples and then his bloodshot eyes.

Tony laughed. "Yes Tweety mentioned it, the House of Pain. What a hoot."

Derek looked blank for a moment. "What did I page you for? Ah that's right I remember now. It's regarding the attacks on the women in the patch. We're no further on. The boss has given each section a couple of watering holes to call with and see what they know. Ours are the Blades Club and the Cosy Bar. Call in with them and see what's what. Stick a few lines on a report when you've done. Win, lose or draw, keep ourselves right, eh? Mark it for my attention and I'll fire it up to Janet the Collator. Take Arnie Savage with you. He's a frequent caller to these locales enforcing licensing laws if you get my drift (Derek raised an eyebrow). The boss wants you to call when things are quiet, and he insists on backup." Derek frowned. "I wish I was going with you. The boss has shafted me with a visit from the delectable Unionist MP Mrs Vivian Chesney this afternoon. I have to field questions with regards to these ongoing attacks while at the same time trying to blow smoke up her 'Londonderry Air!'. You couldn't cut that woman with a diamond. One slip of the tongue and the boss will have me in the meat grinder. Lucky Derek, anyhow, are you happy enough?" Tony smiled as he reversed out of the Inspector's Office door and back out into the corridor.

"No worries. We're having a quiet one today. I'll get cracking, Inspector."

Derek shouted after him, "Good luck, Tony."

Tony headed towards the Enquiry Office plans forming in his head. As he neared, he could hear singing filtering through the walls. Walking through the partition door and into the public waiting area he was stopped dead in his tracks. Looking in through the Enquiry Office window he could see that Tweety was waltzing with Agnes Patterson or Aggie the station cleaner. Her mop and steaming bucket were resting in the corner. Her tiny portable radio was blasting that 'Ashford and Simpson' classic 'Solid'. Aggie being a tad deaf was belting out her own version ably assisted by her crooning partner Tweety. They were a sight for sore eyes. Tony roared with laughter as they arrived at the chorus. Aggie spinning chanted in her finest broad Belfast soprano 'Salad in Iraq'. Vic Tweety's partner was struggling to breathe such was his laughter. Aggie was out of puff and screaming, "Stap it, Tweety, enough nae!" One final burl of the office ended with Tweety on bended knee singing up to Aggie the words. "Our Aggie let's have ourselves some Salad in Iraq."

Aggie was a Mountroyal institution and shared the cleaning of the station with the much quieter Malcolm. No one could remember a time when she wasn't there. She would have been in her early seventies. Aggie was of average height and build with grey thinning hair. She wore a modicum of make-up and was slightly bandy legged which drew the eyes to her mass of varicose veins or as she called them 'my horrible various veins'. She was a 'widow woman" having lost her husband to the Second World War. Her Alec never returned from the Burma Campaign. She had been pregnant when he left and had a daughter Evelyn who sadly died at two years of age. Life can be cruel and to none more than Aggie. In spite of the cruel cards that life had dealt her, she was always upbeat and happy. She could see the light in the darkest corner and was an encouragement to all who knew her. If ever the parable of the widow's mite was written for any woman, then it was surely written for our Aggie. She lived in her marital terrace house in Pearl Street alone which she kept like a new pin. She never missed a day's work and was in on time in all weathers. Aggie was forever bringing in cakes and buns for her beloved crews at Mountroyal. Every Christmas for the past few years Aggie would receive a beautiful unsigned Christmas card. It carried the same message 'Merry Christmas Aggie, for the light and love you give 'X'. It also contained ten twenty-pound notes in a smaller envelope which also carried the same message. 'Sure, it's a good thing to go a message with'. Aggie would never know who her kind benefactor was. If you didn't love Aggie, you were incapable of love.

Tony dandered across to Tweety's desk which was a mess. Assorted duty sheets relating to specific dates were sprawled out and pinned down by the

Mountroyal Radio logbook. A large sheet full of Tweety's jottings was half hanging over the desk. It was all double Dutch to Tony. Tony looked up to Tweety who was smiling broadly and returning to the devastation of his desk. "Don't ask skipper, a wee job for the SDC." Tony gave a quick thumbs up. If it had nothing to do with him, he didn't care. Tony found a spare sheet of paper and began scribbling. When finished, he looked over to the lovely Aggie who was recovering by her mop and bucket. "Careful there, Aggie, Tweety's a bit of a wolf in sheep's clothing."

Aggie gasped and puffed for air, "Dear Lord, preserve us. I'm telling ye, you'll be the death of me Mr Tweety Pie."

Tweety laughed. "Marry me, Aggie, I've had my eye on you for some time, only the one mind. They say love is blind but in my case it's only half true!"

Aggie screamed with laughter as she shuffled out of the Enquiry Office and was buzzed through the partition door, "You're a tarrible case, Tweety, so you are nae give over."

Calm resumed and the soft tones of Tweety's classical music returned. Tony, seeing Tweety was occupied, handed Vic the sheet. "Could you sort this for me Vic. A wee change of runners and riders for this afternoon. Me and Arnie Savage are going out on a wee pub crawl."

Vic chuckled. "No finer man there, skipper!" Tony had rejigged the crews so that he would have himself and Arnie Savage out doing the calls in AM80 in the red Escort unarmoured supervisors' vehicle. Their back up crew AM72 was the 'Preacher' Pete Majury and Gary Weaver, both popular members of the section. Both were young fit six-foot plussers who were handy in a tight squeeze.

They met in the Enquiry Office at 2.00pm for an Ad hoc briefing. Tony looked around at his assembled team and felt safe enough. "Right team. Each section has been given a couple of pubs to call with. We've been given the Blades Club and the Cosy Bar. The SDC wants us in there to see if they know any more than we do re these attacks on the women in our patch. Whether they want to play with us is another matter though one of the victims had been drinking in the Cosy on the night of her attack so they might give a slight fuck. Inspector Grant recommended you as my wingman for this tasking Arnie. He tells me you're a stickler for enforcing the licensing hours." Tony smiling looked over at Arnie while the Preacher and Gary suppressed a giggle. Arnie Savage wriggled a bit uncomfortably in his space. He was sweating profusely, and it felt to him that every pore in his body was expressing stale booze. A noxious mixture of cheap whisky and beer. Tony went on, "We'll play it this way, our call sign will be AM2O, you pair will be AM72. You will be our back up in case anything kicks off. We'll call with the Blades first and then the Cosy."

Arnie's stomach flipped, could his day get any worse. Tony continued, "On each occasion we'll let you know when we're going in and then when we're out again. One of you set your hand-held radio to channel 8 and we'll work off that. The other of you listen out on our normal channel in case something big goes down in the city that we need to be aware of. Are we all carrying timber and raring to go chaps? This could take five minutes or an hour. But our safety comes first. Vic, have you made BRC (Belfast Regional Control) aware of our wee 'Op' and what channels we're working on?"

Vic nodded. "Yep, skipper, I rang the Controller Wes Lamont 10 minutes ago. He's all over it. You're all good to 'rock n roll'."

Just then, Tweety appeared from the radio store waving his arms shouting, "Data! Data! Data! I can't make bricks without clay." Then realising he had interrupted Tony mid briefing. "Oh, I'm terribly sorry skipper. I thought me and Vic were on our lonesome." He then swivelled through 180% and disappeared back into the radio store mumbling and shouting.

Vic, the straight man of the pair shook his head from side to side and looking around at the group said, "See what I have to put up with?"

Arnie Savage retrieved the keys to the red unarmoured Escort. He would be driving, and he had a skin full the night before. He had also had a few tinnies on the way into work. He would repeat this regime on the way home as well. The traffic had been light that morning so it had only been a three-tin journey. When Arnie had downed a can, he would throw the empty over his shoulder and it joined the rest of the dead 'tinnies'. By the end of the week, his little cream Austin Metro sounded like a Caribbean calypso every time he applied the brakes or hit the accelerator. He had up to this point steered clear of the new sergeant but he was now trapped and in the sergeant's full glare. He also had the prospect of being further exposed when they trucked up at the two bars. Arnie had been a frequent caller over the past seven years at both of these locations during his time at Mountroyal.

Arnold Savage was the Senior Constable in 'A' Section. He was an unhealthy 47 years old who deluded himself, but no one else, that he was in good shape. He had served for 22 years and had spells at Carrick, Musgrave Street, Belfast and finally the last very happy seven years at Mountroyal. Arnold or Arnie was

5' 9" tall. His slowly receding hairline was dyed crudely from a cheap bottle. Arnie kept his hair as black as a raven's wing, he was actually pure ginger all over. Valuable drinking time was wasted on this constant dyeing of ginger hair which included wild and untamed eyebrows as well as his walrus 'tash'. Arnie lived in his own delusional world that he was the Stag in the forest. The main man, the head honcho. The man every woman wanted to be with and every man wanted to be like. He was threatened by the male specimens in the section like the Preacher, Gary Weaver and now the new Sergeant Tony Speers who unwittingly threatened his place as the king of his jungle.

He was married and lived with Molly, the love of his life in Whitehead. There were no kids. Nobody had ever seen Molly but to put up with Arnie and his heavy boozing which appeared to be morning noon and night whilst on and off duty had to be the perfect argument that love actually must be blind. Arnie had survived in the job by staying under the radar. He submitted a plethora of average files such as no insurance or faulty headlights and such. Enough to get by allied with his feigned likeability which enabled his drinking. In reality, the section put up with him, and eight hours patrolling with Arnie in Arnie's world was hard going. Arnie detested Tweety though he didn't know why. Tweety knew and would have told him if he had ever asked!

Gary hopped into the front passenger seat of the red Escort and gave a thumbs up to the vehicle behind containing Gary and the Preacher. Stevie Upritchard was at hand to open the huge metal Station Security gates as the two vehicles eased out onto the Woodstock Road heading for their first port of call the Blades Club on the Beersbridge Road. The smell of stale booze hit Tony with full force, you could have cut it with a knife. He opened his passenger side window and subtly breathed from his left. Arnie spoke trying to break the ice but with every word he was forcing Tony into a corner which he would later have to act on. The stench of alcohol was nearly making Tony wretch. "It's a terrible thing so it is skipper these attacks on those poor women. I've been stopping everyone that looks to fit the bill and firing the Criminal intelligence report forms in like confetti, not like some in the section naming no names. Care for a polo mint?" Arnie held over a pack which was half empty. The other half was being sucked and crunched in Arnie's mouth. The minty fragrance lay slaughtered by the stench of alcohol bathing in Arnie's potted belly. Tony, struggling for breath, replied, "Er no thanks, I'm not long after me lunch." Just as their car came to a halt outside the Blades Club.

95

It was now 2.30pm in the afternoon and three notable things were happening at the same time. Firstly, and most importantly Harvest Gold at 10/1 had just begun his race at Newmarket against 14 other nags. Important to Paddy the barman of Hop House fame who had a tenner on the nose riding on the result. Not quite so important to Tweety who had £200 smackers riding on that same nose. Actually, it had slipped his mind what with his radios research and an absorbing conversation with Vic as to who was the greatest heavyweight of all times, Cassius Clay or Rocky Marciano!

Secondly, back at Mountroyal Billy Porter was out in the back yard sweeping and clearing. It was a fresh day and he had to chase after the leaves a bit. Billy had clean forgotten to pass on an important message to his two security colleagues given to him by Inspector Derek Grant that morning when he opened the back gate for him. The important message that Wee John and Stevie Uprichard should have been aware of was that Vivien Chesney the Official Unionist MP was arriving at 2.30pm and the lads in the 'Box' or Security Sanger were to give her the five-star treatment she expected and was used to.

Thirdly, Ms Vivien Chesney was in particularly bad twist. UTV had just contacted her, cancelling a televised interview relating to her hard work and service to the single parents in East Belfast. Not that she had ever worked hard at anything. She had staff who performed those duties. She was the Press image at the other end of it all. She had however laboured hard that morning in her own service. She had her hair done and a full facial and Vivien was now wearing her favourite deep plum two-piece suit. A champagne-coloured silk blouse contrasted from beneath. Smokey grey stockings with suspenders and no knickers (her little secret, it gave her a sense of power).

Vivien clip clopped up the steps to the pedestrian gate with a superior air and hit the buzzer, the back of her bouffant hair facing the sanger window making identification impossible. Inside the sanger, Wee John and Stevie Uprichard were none the wiser and totally unprepared. Wee John who was in his usual stool leaned across to the pedestrian window and observed the back of the stylish woman. Stevie was standing just behind his shoulder. Vivien screeched haughtily, "Wakey wakey, would one of you let me in. Do you not know who I am?" Wee John, unflappable as usual, adopted his formal but friendly tone.

"Good morning, madam, how can I help you?" A strong gust of wind blew up from out of nowhere and hurled Vivien's £80.00 hairdo all over the place. It was also trying hard to lift her skirt up over her wobbly backside and expose her modesty as well as her little secret. She was incandescent with rage as she was now twisted like a piece of fusilli pasta. One hand holding onto her 'medusa' like flailing hair while the other was holding her misbehaving skirt firmly down.

The merciless gusts were unrepentant and continued to do its worst. Vivien was going to explode. "Little man, I cannot believe you don't know who I am. I am Ms Vivien Chesney, Official Unionist MP for East Belfast. I have an appointment with Inspector Derek Grant at 2.30pm and I was assured that I would be expected. What is your name, you incompetent little man, I'll have you transferred to Rathlin Island for this!" Wee John had heard worse and smiled. A quick buzz through to Vic on the intercom confirmed her story.

"Ms Chesney, many apologies. My name is Reserve Constable Alexander. Letting you in now." Wee John smiled as Ms Chesney stormed onwards towards the main station whose huge metal door opened as she approached. Stevie Upritchard was secretly raging. What a vile horrible woman. A stuck up her own ass snobby superior bitch. He looked at wee John and marvelled. He seemed totally unperturbed. Flabbergasted, he said, "Wee John, are you not totally pissed at her?"

Wee John smiled. "Stevie, Stevie worse things happen at sea. Don't fret yourself man." The Sanger door opened and in shuffled the ruddy skinned Billy Porter fresh in from his leaf sweeping duties. Wee John turned to him and said, "Billy, Vivien Chesney??" Billy froze, his jaw dropped open.

"Holy fuck lads, Inspector Grant told me this morning. I totally forgot. I'm fucked!" Wee John laughed.

"No Billy, I'm the one whose fucked thanks." Stevie seethed for the rest of the shift.

Ms Chesney rearranged herself in the reception area. She gathered a semblance of composure and approached the Enquiry Office counter. Heads were going to roll. Vic was on the phone taking a call. Tweety's back was to her. He was engrossed in his radio project, a hint of a pattern was maybe emerging. She furiously slammed her fist hard against the partition window positively frothing at the mouth. More police morons. Monkeys and peanuts sprang to her twisted mind. She would have a strong word with their Chief Constable at the Ulster Unionist May Ball in a few days. Vic was still on the phone intently writing. More impatient slamming followed. Tweety paused and slowly straightened up and turned to face her. Before her was a tall slender man in his mid-thirties. Dark hair, dark skinned with a slightly marked face. He was wearing glasses with the darkest blue lenses, but they still couldn't disguise the fact that he only had one eye. He then calmly approached the counter and looked down at her and simply said, "Yes." All the cruel things that she had preloaded to say tried to come out. But his presence, the brute force of the eye in his storm made her begin to babble incoherently. His slowly blinking green eye was drawing all the bad out of her and she began to feel weak. She was going to faint. She softly spoke and offered him a smile, "I'm sorry, Constable. I'm here to see Inspector Grant." Tweety smiled back.

"Ah Vivien, we've been expecting you. I'll take you through to him now."

The partition door buzzed and Tweety ushered her through. She couldn't feel her feet moving and the next thing she was sitting in Derek Grant's office feeling a sense of euphoria. Derek had met Vivien before and she had kept him on his tippy toes but today she was pleasant, polite and most supportive. Their meeting went without the slightest bit of rancour. And they parted on the best of terms. As she left the main building through the reception area escorted by Derek Grant, she kept looking across into the Enquiry Office. Trying to snatch another glimpse of that man. Vic waved over, Tweety was nowhere to be seen. She ached. Derek was bewildered.

Tony and Arnie entered the Blades Club giving the Preacher and Gary who were parked up out front the thumbs up as they entered. The Blades Club was unique as it was non-sectarian in the main. It was an homage and watering hole for Sheffield United fans, not that there were many. Its walls were a subtle blend of the team colours which were red, white and black. Framed pictures of teams and players past and present hung from each wall. It was kept spick and span. Gary and Arnie entered the main lounge. One old codger was sitting in the corner nursing a pint. He and the barman were glued to the tele. The horse racing was on and the 2.30pm from Newmarket was on its final furlong. Fifteen magnificent horses came careering around the final bend and were sprinting for home. The old codger leaned forward coming to life. "Come on, 'Ennis Flyer', run ya bastard run."

The barman who hadn't noticed their entrance had a fiver each way on the 5/1 favourite 'Lucky Beaver'. "Come on, 'Beaver', run like fuck!" It was making all the running and leading the rest of the field home. The 'Flyer' was second and pressing hard with 'Harvest Gold' at 10/1 sitting third. Tony and Arnie watched on. With 100 yards left, Frankie Silvano the "Gold's" jockey showed him the whip. A turbo button was tripped and the horse eased out and raced past the Flyer and the Beaver leaving them in his wake and winning easily by three lengths. "Fuck ye harvest fucking gold," said the barman who turned and was suddenly aware of the two policemen. One of them he knew very well, "Ach hello Arnie, fer fuck sake you're never out of this place. Brought a new friend with ye? The usual, a pint and a whisky chaser me old son?" Arnie wanted to die. Impervious, the barman smiled at Tony. "What's yer poison mate?"

Tony smiled back, "Hi, I'm Sergeant Tony Speers. Thanks but no thanks, not while we're on duty." The barman howled with laughter, shaking his head and looking at Arnie.

The old codger joined in, "Arnie yer mate's a hoot."

Tony smiled. "No speriously but I'll have a quick coffee if you don't mind, milk and sugar please."

The barman smiled. "Nat a problem Sergeant, coffee for youuu Arnie?" Like the drink inside him Arnie was dying.

He smiled with that, "I'll get you for that," and said, matter of factly, "White coffee for me Fred (oops), no sugar, I'm watching my weight." More ribald laughter followed.

Tony was introduced to Fred who lived around the corner in Clara Street. Fred had done 20 years in the navy and never touched a drop himself. His appearance was immaculate, and he was a fit mid-forties. He was a mine of information and Tony, and he got on like a house on fire. The coffee was good too. Fred as well as the old codger were aware of the attacks but had no information to offer. An enjoyable half an hour passed, and Tony was assured by Fred and the old codger that if they heard anything they would pass it on. As they left the 'Blades' they gave the thumbs up again to the bored-titless Preacher and Gary. Five minutes later, they stepped into the Cosy Bar.

In contrast to the Blades, this place was a pit. Its muddy coloured carpets were threadbare. The walls were a filthy cream, stained by nicotine and seasons of smoke. Fruit machines rhymed annoying hook-in tunes and flashed and flickered in the corner. A television was on with the sound turned down, but no one was watching. The bar itself was half full of both young and old has-beens or would-bes. This was a UVF bar. If you supped here, you were part of an organisation. You belonged. You were important and you had some serious heavy-handed backing. Tony noted a group of four males playing pool in the corner. They were heavily muscled courtesy of the Maze Prison and grotesquely tattooed. All things Ulster, King Billy, 1690 and fuck the pope. They were loud, gorilla loud and if looks could kill Tony and Arnie would have died on the spot. Tony smiled as he made his way up to the counter, his stomach in knots. "Fuckin black bastard!" came from the area of the pool table.

"Let's just get this over with Arnie," he whispered as a bar man appeared from a rear yard carrying a fresh keg. Here was another of Ulster's finest thought Tony. Male mid-fifties sporting a shiny oiled shaved head. He was pot-bellied and wore a Glasgow Rangers football top. When he spoke, his teeth dazzled like the poker machines in the corner as his gaudy gold fillings sparkled. "Arnie, my man, thought we were going out of business. We haven't seen you since yesterday. Same again, a pint and a whisky chaser?" Arnie cringed.

Tony introduced himself and spoke of the attacks. The barman who was called Glen turned out to be spot on. Surprisingly articulate and if you didn't know better, he would have passed as a teacher going to a 'Thugs Themed' fancy dress party. With his UVF mask off, Glen was in Northern Ireland terms 'Dead on'. Sadly, just like Fred everyone knew of the attacks but nothing else was known. Glen whispered in Tony's ear, "Just catch the bastard before we do if you know what I mean."

Arnie had remained silent during the chat. His nerves were jangling and he was aware of the four thugs at the pool table giving them the evils. He was eyeing the Black Bush whisky optic and gasping for a hit and a fag. Suddenly, he was shoved from behind the force knocking him into a bar stool and on to his knees. He was being prevented from getting up. One of the goons, Gary Caskey from Dundonald was holding Arnie down with ease with one needle pitted arm. Gary Caskey was an up-and-coming hawk within the UVF ranks. Mid-twenties. He had three kids to three different women and had forgotten them all. He was an enforcer, drug dealer and pimp. Tony spun around to face the threat noting that two of the thugs had blocked the door. The third had snapped a pool cue across his thigh and was making his way to the counter in support of Caskey. Glen tried to calm the situation. "Calm down, fellas, the Peelers are just after any information about the women that's been attacked for fuck sake."

Caskey snarled. "Are you fucking touting to those black bastards you fenian loving whore bag?"

Caskey's eyes were large and dancing in his head. He was high on something and it sure wasn't life. He leaned across the counter and head-butted Glen as quick as a blink. Glen screamed blood and gore spraying from his face. Arnie had struggled free and placed his hand on Caskey's shoulder. "Caskey, I'm arresting you for assault and…" Mid-sentence, Arnie was grabbed by the scruff by Caskey's mate and frog marched to a large black plastic bin located by the toilet doors. There poor Arnie was lifted up and shoved ass down into it. His head, hands and the top of his feet were the only things visible. He looked like an upturned Hermit crab. Glen tried again to restore order and pleaded for calm from behind a blood-stained bar cloth. Tony weighed the situation up. Yep, he was fucked. With a bit of luck, these goons mightn't kill him. The rest of the bar was frozen with fear. Tony contemplated his gun but if he went for it and failed, he was in tomorrow's obituaries. Caskey growled, "Me and you, Peeler. I'm going to make you beg."

Caskey threw an overhead right which Tony easily blocked and followed through with a knee to the chest. Caskey stumbled back and was momentarily winded but more shocked. He was used to quick finishes and the Peeler was quick and strong. Outside and oblivious, the Preacher and Gary were chilling. "Preacher, when you're marching, you're not fighting. Easy money." Gary chuckled. The Preacher smiled. The radio came to life; it was from Arnie who had managed to free one of his arms from the bin. He was still terribly stuck, "AM72 from AM20 urgent assistance required, urgent assistance required Cosy Bar!"

Gary shouted, "Fuck!"

The Preacher replied, "And so say all of us." Wes Lamont the Controller at Belfast Regional Control, quick as a flash, tasked a further two crews to their aid. Back inside Caskey weighed up his odds as adrenalin and other substances went rampaging through his body. He couldn't be seen to take another dig from the black bastard and lose face.

Screaming with anger, he shouted, "Right lads, grab him and hold him down. I'm going to give him a beating so that even his mother won't recognise him."

Tony knew it was only a matter of time but if he was going to go out, he would go out fighting. He sprung forward and slapped Caskey hard on the right side of his face bursting an eardrum. Caskey squealed in pain. Tony was then struck to the side of the head with the broken pool cue. He staggered back dazed, his vision out of focus. Two of the goons grabbed him by the arms and held him while he struggled. Caskey licked his lips and said, "Right Peeler, it's my turn."

The main front doors flung open and in bounced Gary and the Preacher batons in hand. The Preacher looked about him and weighed up the situation. Arnie was stuffed in a bin but otherwise all right. The skipper was another matter.

He was getting it tight, there were three men all over him. Arnie from the comfort of his bin croaked, "Gary son, there's one behind you." Gary spun instinctively swinging his baton. His 14 stone of power-driven timber ploughed into a fleshy collar bone smashing it resulting in howls of pain. One attacker out of the picture, three to go. The Preacher glided up towards the counter where his Sergeant was fighting a losing battle. Passing by two elderly dears sitting terrified at a table he smiled reassuringly and said, "Afternoon, ladies, we'll have this sorted in a jiffy." Gary was now tight on his shoulder. Tony was by now spent. He had given his all and was blacking out. All three goons were oblivious to the two oncoming policemen. Glen the barman should have given them a shout but didn't feel the slightest inclination. Caskey was loading up a punch ready to spread Tony's features all over his face when he felt a tap on his shoulder. He turned around yelling, "What the fuck!"

The Preacher was smiling at him, "Now now, sir, three against one isn't a fair fight."

'Thwack' Gary buried his baton into the knee of the goon holding the broken pool cue. He went down like a ton of bricks his knee shattered screaming, "Me fucking legs broke you bastards." He was in deepest darkest agony. Caskey's jaw dropped as the Preacher threw a razor-sharp punch striking the last of the henchmen square in the Adam's apple. His arms dropped instantly freeing Tony from his grasp. He then fell to his knees before blacking out.

Gary then grabbed hold of his Sergeant for support until Glen brought him a chair to recover on. The silence was deafening in the Cosy Bar as the two men faced each other. One a thug and a bully the other his worst ever nightmare. Glen chimed in, "Well Caskey, not quite the big man now without yer goons about ye!" Caskey was panting and breathing hard while the Peeler appeared serene. Whispers began to circulate among those there.

The Preacher spoke, "All done are we, sir. I'm now going to arrest you for assault on police, namely my Sergeant over there and disorderly behaviour." The Preacher was about to formally caution Caskey when he exploded in a fit of rage. He leapt at the Preacher kicking and flailing but couldn't hit the target. The Preacher barely moving avoided all contact and then with the faintest of exertion kicked at the side of Caskey's left knee which resulted in a total loss of balance. He stumbled forwards and into the most excruciating arm lock. Caskey begged for mercy as a small, suppressed cheer went up from the crowd. The Preacher smiled at the crowd who were now putty in his hands. He leaned over to the squealing bully and twisting the hold a notch tighter said, "Now are we sure you're all done Mr, Caskey?"

The bully from Dundonald screeched with pain, "I'm begging ye please stop. You're going to break my fucking arm!" Just then, the back-up crews arrived, and the resultant arrests were made.

Caskey and his crew looked a sorry sight as they were cuffed and led away. Excited babble among the patrons followed as an air of relief and normality returned. Glen the barman declined to make any formal complaints regarding his injuries. That would be viewed as a twisted betrayal. He did however assure Tony that if the cosy clientele got any information with regards to the attacker they would pass it on. The preacher, seeing Arnie still wedged in the bin, nipped over and helped him out. The preacher couldn't have been kinder. Arnie had witnessed the heroics of his three colleagues, especially the fighting skills of the Preacher which left him speechless. It began to dawn on him he was no longer the Stag of the forest but a delusional old fool.

After a few minutes, Tony felt much more like himself as the team left the Cosy Bar and headed back to Mountroyal for a debrief. The four men trudged wearily back into the station and stopped off at the Enquiry Office. The Preacher made a C6 entry in the Occurrence Book detailing the incident and subsequent arrests. Tweety and Vic listened intently as he rang Wes Lamont at BRC and had the incident closed off on the system. The Preacher did everything without fanfare or fuss. That was his way. Back in Tony's office, the four updated their notebooks which would be the first thing requested at Court. Tony's head ached a little but all in all he was good.

The office door knocked and in came Tweety with four mugs of hot steaming tea and a fresh apple pie brought in by Aggie who had heard of their dust up. "Tea and tart gents, you look as though you could use it. Well done one and all. And as for you Preacher (Pete looked up smiling.), to quote Byron from Don Juan, 'The mildest mannered man that ever scuttled a ship or cut a throat.' Sums you up perfectly!" They all laughed. The preacher blushed. Tweety left them mouthing a well done to Gary and the Preacher.

Tony finished with the debrief spoke, "Lads, I'm not here long but I think I've got to know you all quite well. Thanks for the big effort at the Cosy today. Well done, Arnie, for getting the call for assistance out. You remained composed throughout. And as for you two brutes, Preacher and Gary, thanks for saving our bacon. I owe you both a pint. We've only half an hour of our shift left. Go write up your statements and get into your civvies (plain clothes), I take it we're all good for a couple of swifties at the Eastenders at close of play?"

Gary spoke up, "Preacher doesn't drink, can I have his pint?"

Tony laughed. "If the Origami Master doesn't mind." The preacher shook his head smiling.

As the three were trailing out of the office, Tony called Arnie back for a quiet word. Arnie's heart sank into his boots. He took a seat before the young Sergeant with the swollen face and awaited his fate.

Tony spoke, "Arnie there are two ways we can go regarding your drinking habits, the official way or the unofficial way. You choose?" Arnie wasn't stupid. He was caught bang to rights. To protest would be an insult to the sergeant. Arnie swallowed hard.

"The unofficial way, skipper. I'm sorry about today, I was a laughing stock, a big fat drunken bum and a joke. I let you down and the uniform. Seeing the three of you in action made me realise how far I've fallen."

Tony saw how crestfallen the normally chirpy Arnie was and spoke. "Arnie, there's a big drinking culture in the job. We're trapped, our lives are under daily threat. You've done twenty years plus and picked up a few lumps and scars along the way. I don't know what bedtime terrors visit you every night and I don't want to know, but if you need help get it. I'll back you 100%. However, if I catch a whiff of booze from you starting from tomorrow, I'll report you for neglect of duty and a few more. The upshot of it all will be the sack for you which means no police pension which by my calculations you're eight years shy of. Do we understand each other?" Arnie nodded, the skipper could have ended his career then and there, but he had been given a golden ticket. One last chance.

Tony snatched a peek at his watch. It was 4.00pm and their shift was over. B. Section had now taken over. His office door burst open and in flew Shelley looking gorgeous. Her jet-black curly hair framing her full and beautiful face. She was wearing a low-cut white blouse and tight fitting dark blue jeans. A heady musk perfume slapped them hard in the face. Smiling at the pair, she giggled, "Are you both still on for the Eastenders, the rest of the gang are already away?"

Tony smiled at the vision of loveliness, "Absolutely, Shelley, I'll be there in five." Shelley pinned Tony down with her gaze releasing him as she spun around and headed out the door singing, "Alrighty then, see youse pair of hunks there then." Arnie was in a pickle, damned if he does and damned if he doesn't.

Tony laughed. throwing his tie and epaulettes in his drawer, "Come on Senior

Man I'll buy you a pint." Arnie laughed for the first time that day.

Five minutes later, Tony was perched on a bar stool on the first floor of the Eastenders Bar. They were all gathered in the corner of the bar by a large full-length window offering a view down the busy Woodstock Road. Tony thought to himself, *What a bunch*. Tweety, Arnie and Wee John were in a huddle talking music. Billy Porter was on their fringes and quite surprisingly knew his stuff. Stevie Upritchard, Lionel and Gary Weaver were full on football, Liverpool, Man U and dirty Leeds. The two lovelies were on the wine. Shelley was slurping a red and Heavenly was nursing a white. Shelley was a natural upper and had Heavenly in stitches with her impersonations of the lads in the section. Her Pinky and Perky had Tony, Preacher and Vic in convulsions as she puffed away on her imaginary Woody. It had been some day.

Tony supped at a smooth pint of Carlsberg. Vic was on the stout and the Preacher was on a pint of orange cordial. Seeing the two girls together reminded Tony of a question he was meaning to ask. He leaned across the din and asked the smiling Vic, "What is it with Heavenly. At times, I look at her and she appears very sad. I don't want to bring it up or anything, but I also don't want to bite the elephant on the bum if you get me?" Vic and Preacher looked at each other, inviting the other to speak. Neither wanted to.

Vic began, "Heavenly was engaged to be married to a great guy called Ozzie Gordon three years ago. He was also in the job. They were a golden couple. Both were flying high and had their sergeant's exams. They bought a stunning house in Groomsport overlooking the harbour. They had it all lovely." Vic took a sip of stout and looked across at the beautiful Stephanie. The Preacher carried on, "Yeah, Ozzie was acting up as a Sergeant in Crossmaglen. The real bandit country. Three weeks before they were due to be married, he was out on a routine foot patrol with the 'Paras'. If you can call anything routine in that neck of the woods. He was taken out by a sniper with one high velocity round. A head shot. One second Stephanie had it all the next second she had worse than nothing. She's a class act, though she won't talk about it so never bring it up!" Tony looked across at Heavenly, his heart heavy. She looked over at him and gave him a full-on brilliant smile. He waved back smiling but felt himself filling up. Vic noticed and patted his new skipper on the shoulder. Its OK Tony, she's got us. We're her family." Tony nodded. "True true Vic, she's got us."

Tony was tired but very happy as another pint of Carlsberg appeared in front of him. He was loving his new station and loving his new section. They were a rag tag mob all very different and at different seasons in their career, but they were teak tough and tight and very loyal to each other. Preacher nudged Tony who was staring into a pleasant melancholy. "You all right, Skipper, how's the noggin?" Tony stirred from his frothy repose and took a smooth sup wallowing in his happiness. "Never better Preacher, the saviour of my life today. Oh and by the way, how much are we putting into the 'kitty'?" Vic and Preacher looked over at each other and laughed.

Vic replied, "Nada, Tweety is covering it. He had a win on the gee gees today. His horse came in at 10/1." Tony laughed and remembered the race. He pinged his pint glass several times and stood up calling for a smidge of silence from his troops.

"Ladies and gents. A wee toast firstly to us. Here's to us and who's like us. (A jovial cheer followed). Secondly to the benefactor of today's session and his brilliant nag. To Tweety and the wonderful Harvest Gold."

Tweety laughed and shouted in his bestest broad Belfast accent, "Yez are more than welcome…"

The Good Shepherd:
20 May 1983: Friday 10.20am.

Occurrence Am 3410/83

The mustard-coloured mark 2 Cortina harrumphed its way wearily along the Roseberry Road of East Belfast. Its 2-litre engine groaned at being in third gear pleading for a slip to second.

It had also been subjected to a furious downpour which had lasted five torrid minutes.

This had cleared the mug in the air. Early spring sunshine arrived lifting the palate of the working class terraced houses. Its occupants and crew members were Gary Weaver and Shelley McCann. Their call sign was Alpha Mike 70 and they were the main response vehicle for the Mountroyal Police Station that day. Gary and Shelley were performing the Early Shift which was normally from 7am to 3pm. Unfortunately, that particular day both were held on to 7pm on further security duties. A routine 12-hour shift come slog lay ahead of them. Shelley was detailed as the designated driver. Gary was the Big O… The Observer. The catcher and stopper of the buck. The First line responder.

Gary had served in the RUC for six years and Mountroyal was his first station. Gary at 33 years old was a strapping six feet one fourteen stone figure. He had been a top-class footballer, a central defender in the Amateur League. Sadly, for Gary a nasty tackle and a wrecked knee put an abrupt end to his footballing dreams. When time permitted, he jogged several days a week. He was chuffed to have run two Belfast Marathons. Not having had the required 5 O levels to walk into the job he had sat the written exam. No one was happier or more surprised than Gary when he passed. He always felt a tad guilty at getting in via the backdoor. A part of him worried that he would one day get a call saying there had been a mix up in the test papers and in fact another bloke should be in his place. He was a worrier by nature, spending a lot of his day brooding on the "What ifs…" in life.

Gary was very much a family man with a gorgeous wife, the lovely Irene. They had a beautiful 4-year-old daughter Maddie who was the apple of his eye. The Weavers lived in a nice semi-detached home on the outskirts of Comber. The area was considered a safe place for police officers and their families to live. A community within a community. They watched out for each other every second of the day. This is how normal life was for police families in those dangerous times. Their home had good sized gardens and was private at the rear. From the back garden, you stared into a farmer's wheat field with Scrabo Tower and the rolling hills of County Down beyond. There was nothing Gary liked more than a barbeque with friends around the back with a tinny in hand!

Gary could enjoy the female form as well as any man, but his mantra was… "Pork sausages, steak at home!" Gary Weaver was unaware that he was considered one of the top constables in the subdivision. He was totally dependable and would be the top pick partner for most of his colleagues. As a man, he was highly regarded by his bosses. If only someone had told Gary!

Gary had successfully whipped his In-tray into reasonable shape and a quiet day today would leave him soaring like an eagle and looking good in front of his new skipper, Tony Speers. Gary liked his new Sergeant, a man he respected and looked up to. Tony was straightforward, decent and fair. He also enjoyed a laugh. They had recently done battle together at the Cosy Bar along with Arnie Savage and the Preacher. There he had proven himself handy in a dust up. He was also a sociable critter having enjoyed a tipple together with the rest of the gang at the 'Tuesday Club' in the Eastenders Bar a few days ago.

"Well, I think he's hot… You can tell he works out and the rest. Fond of the old sun lamp methinks. What do you think, Gary?" Shelley had blurted in right out of the blue, smiling, her attention half focussed on the road ahead. Gary had zoned out. He was presently cavorting in the land of Zob, dancing with the fling flangs and singing with the jube jubes. Shelley gazed across at her partner or pard for the day. He was clearly in a land far far away. Exasperated she screamed, "Gary, what the fuck, pay attention for fuck sake!!! Fuckin men!!"

Shelley had been in the RUC for three years and like Gary, Mountroyal was her first station. She was a more than capable officer. A team player and no shrinking violet. She could dish it out and she could take it all day long. She was an excellent communicator and reader of people.

There she excelled and was fluent in the commonest talk speak of the Broad Belfast guttural tongue. She had a rosy future in the RUC except for one tiny thing. She wanted a man, marriage and babies.

Shelley wanted the treble, the Holy Trinity or to the male species. "The Holy fucking Trinity!"

Shelley had the face of a snow white, with hair black as a raven's wing. However, the mirror tended to crack when she opened her sweet cherry lips! She had been blessed with a jaw dropping Rubenesque form and knew how to wiggle her bits to get her way through the day. Nevertheless, however, you swayed with Shelley, no one could ever deny that she had a heart of corn. She had no problems getting men. But her Mr Right generally turned out to be Mr Wrong. She seemed to have the uncanny knack of landing the married or alcoholic types interested in only one thing or maybe two, depending upon which part of her form they were taking in. Shelley lived with her widowed mum in Newtownbreda located just on the outskirts of the Big Smoke as Belfast is known by its natives.

Gary returned to planet Earth with a bump. "Sorry, our Shell. I'm pure 'Daffy Ducked' today. A tad too much of the devil's vomit last night. My head is banging like a flute band on steroids... Tread softly petal." Their vehicle slowed at the Roseberry Road/Ravenhill Avenue junction. The vehicle's Motorola radio crackled into life.

"AM70 from Uniform..." (BRC... Belfast Regional Control.)

Gary's stomach churned; he recognised the slightly effeminate voice from BRC as Wesley Lamont aka Wes. Wes was a legend amongst the Belfast rank and file. A Call Handler or Controller of the highest order. Wes looked after the crews, ('His babies') when they were on the ground. He considered every possible outcome when dealing with incoming calls. Their safety was always his primary concern. Wes was characteristically smooth on the radio or RT. A velvety soft transmission would flow barely above a whisper. This exuded a calming effect on his babies. Wes would task a crew into the fiery pits of Hell with all the softness of a library attendant singing a lullaby to a butterfly during quiet hour.

"Uniform from AM70 send over."

"Roger AM70. Got a wee call from worried neighbours regarding 10 Woodlee Street. The old gent that lives there hasn't been seen in a day or so. They tell me the milk bottles are gathering up on his doorstep which they say is way out of character for him. So all in all not looking too promising! They tell me his name is Mr Gilbert Jenkins, believed to be in his seventies." Gary scribbled the details in his trusty notebook. "Uniform from AM70, Roger on your last. OUT." A warm inner glow filled Gary's dickey tummy as his vehicle grumbled left onto Ravenhill Avenue. Then heading city wards towards the Beersbridge Road and further onwards to Woodlee Street. He couldn't contain himself any longer, "Yabadaba effin dooooo, A Code 37, A Suddenly Deaf..." Gary spooned joyously.

Shelley glared, "Gary love, I really worry 'bout you. you're far too sensitive for this job." Gary rolled his eyes and reached for his fake black leather briefcase sitting in the back seat. A quick search come rummage located his lucky clipboard and the two forms he may need. The P1 for the Pathologist and the Form 19 for the coroner.

Sudden deaths were a straightforward matter for a constable to deal with. Most crucial funnily enough or not funnily enough was a DEAD Body. Following this, a doctor is required to attend the scene to pronounce Life Extinct. If the deceased had not been seen by a doctor within the last 28 days of their life a Death Certificate could not be issued by law. At this point, the attending police officer is acting on behalf of the coroner. The police officer will attempt to have the deceased identified to him from a next of kin at the scene or failing that at the mortuary prior to a post mortem.

He would carry out all relevant enquiries regarding the deceased. He would seize all medications taken by the deceased which would ultimately be of help to both the pathologist and the coroner. At this time, the Coroner's Office will be informed, who then request a post mortem. A post mortem carried out by a State Pathologist would then be held in order to ascertain the cause of death. When the resultant cause of death has been found, the pathologist informs the coroner and a death certificate would be issued. The deceased body would then be released to the family for burial.

Several minutes later, Gary and Shelley's car pulled up outside 10 Woodlee Street. Gary noted three hardened looking old dears standing out front. These three ladies were living Oracles, Encyclopaedia Britannica's of all things East Belfast. Their combined age of around 300 years awaited him. Unbeknown to Gary, these three were lifelong friends. They were born and bred within a stone's throw from each other. They had attended the same schools and had started work in the Linen Mill on the Beersbridge Road Belfast on the very same day. A job that was hard and demanding physically. These were tough women with a love forged through hard times and even harder work. They were known to the outside world as the MILLIES.

Their use of the English language could be described as colourful to say the least. During those times, they had married and had children. They watched their partners go off to two World Wars. Many of whom never returned. When they could, they returned to work earning a pittance while their masters made a fortune. A large proportion of Belfast City's finest architecture was created off the backs of these tough women, and in the Mills they remained. "From the cradle to the grave." At one time, Belfast was the linen capital of the entire world. As a consequence of exposure to the continuous clacking of the heavy weaving machinery over many years the majority of the Millie's suffered from hearing damage in later life. A Millie would stand out in a group because of her raised voice caused by her poor hearing.

It was this collective heritage that awaited Gary. Green coat, black coat and a ridiculous ginger wig approached their front passenger door. All smiling gummily as their vehicle stopped beside them. "Hubble bubble toil and trouble." swished through Gary's mind. "Uniform. AM70, Arrival 10 Woodlee Street. AM70... Uniform. Roger out." Gary, sighing and opening his passenger door turned to Shelley.

"Care to tag along pard?" Shelley turned to him offering her sweetest smile framed against her cute 23-year-old face. The only thing missing was the seven dwarves.!

"Gary, you know these calls creep me out!! Don't I always buy you a bottle of wine to do my 'Suddenly Deaths' for me. I'll stay here and listen out pard..." Shelley flashed a grown-up smile at the old dears as Gary disembarked. Speaking at the group but to no one in particular Gary assumed his serious professional peeler demeanour, sometimes he even surprised himself at how convincing he was. Clipboard in hand, Gary began his searching enquiries with his new besties, the old dears, the Covenly three.

It transpired that Gilbert had been born in Woodlee Street. This had been his lifelong home and he had outlived his family. Gilbert was the last of the Jenkins! A postman all his working life. A quiet soul. He had very much kept himself to himself. With gentle prodding and probing, Gary was able to piece together Gilbert's life and routines. A picture of the person of Gilbert was forming.

Gilbert left the house each morning at around 8.30am, rain, hail, sleet or shine. He dandered around to the BP Spar on the Beersbridge Road for his daily messages and his Newsletter newspaper. He was usually back home by 9am. Apart from the odd night out at the Blades Club on the Beersbridge Road that was all there was to Gilbert or Gibby as he was known. After a bit of humming and haa-ing, the old dears agreed that Gibby hadn't been seen in a couple of days, noting the accumulation of milk bottles on the doorstep was their clincher. A unanimous coven vote resulted in a call to the police and Gary's attendance.

Gary absentmindedly dabbed three full stops on his clipboard. Sadly, for Gary he was cursed or blessed with the annoying habit, depending on which side of the curate's egg you sided with, of always forgetting and remembering in the nick of time an important question. A bit like the great TV Detective Columbo. Except Columbo did forgetting and remembering on purpose and with great dramatic effect, style and panache. Gary was sadly just a tad forgetful or today just a bit hung over! He then spoke… "Well, ladies, you have been most helpful, thanks again. Oh, one final thing. Do any of you happen to know who his doctor was?" Ginger wig who he now knew as Agnes came good.

"Yes love, Gibby's doctor was the same as me! I would see him the odd time over the years in the doctor's waiting room along with all them other 'sickos' and 'hippie anoraks' and them other 'brew' dodgers… It's a Doctor Navid of the Templemore Avenue Clinic… He's a lovely foreign gentleman so he is!"

Things were all going swimmingly for Gary, these ladies were an amazing source of information. "I can't thank you all enough for your time and patience ladies. I have your details if I require anything else from you." This went down well with the ladies who allowed themselves a modest titter followed by another spectacular gummy smile. Gary was always a hit with the elderly women, God had been good to him that way. Green coat, who Gary now knew as Letitia spoke next. She appeared to be the leader of the group probably from her days as a supervisor at the mill. As she spoke, she subtly stalled Gary's approach to the front door of Gibby's house. "Ya know, Canstable, he was in the war, so he was. I hear tell he won a medal for being brave n all. He would never talk about it though. He was a very private person you understand. Some of the men were like that, others would never shut up about it. You would think some of them had won the war all on their own single handed! (Allowing herself a cackle.) He took nathin to do with the Legion or Remembrance Sundays and all that. Oooh, but he was a handsome big critter in his day. He coulda had his pick o the crap!!" Gary bit his lip struggling for composure.

Ginger wigged Agnes jumped in. "He coulda parked his slippers under my bed anytime."

Gary surrendered and laughed with his new besties. A shrill pitched gum infested chortle erupted among the three. Black coat broke in, her name was in fact Mabel, "Gibby never took up with anyone and there was plenty of interest in him. Sure after his parents died, he had til take care of his wee sister. What was her name nae? Mmmm…aye it was Meta. She was in a wheelchair all her days, you would see her sitting out front of their wee home when the weather was good reading her bible n all. She had a beautiful wee face, aww she was awful kind. She was a great wee knitter ya know. She would knit for all them wee orphans and them wee starving children in Africa. I never seen her with a pattern once! And she was devoted to her church. She attended the Iron Hall in Templemore Avenue. Never missed a Sunday service. Aye and she taught in the Sunday School for years, the kids just loved her. Both Sunday morning and evening services with Gibby wheeling her. They were both always well turned out, 'maculate'. You would see them out walking around the area in all weathers. Gibby pushing her in her wheelchair happy as could be, aye, and then when Meta passed (Mabel shaking her head sighed heavily.) Gibby stopped attending, probably too upsetting for him. (Now mournfully gazing upon Gary.). You know how it is, Canstable…"

Gary nodded, exuding a suitably sincere frown. He was trapped with no chance of escape.

Ginger wigged Agnes seized the opening. "He was devoted to her, aww bless she died in the early seventies. Gibby told me just short of her sixtieth birthday. It wrecked him so it did. He told me it nearly done for him." Letitia then regained centre stage.

"Then after a couple of years, he got himself that wee dog. It just turned up at his door one day. A wee white and brown terrier mix. No collar and covered in fleas it was. What did he call it nae? TRUDY, was it?" Ginger wigged Agnes seized the baton.

"NOOO, silly it was wee Rudy, when no owner could be found Gibby took him on. Got him cleaned up and sorted out with the vet n all… God help anyone calling at the door. Rudy would go mental! I'm telling ye, Canstable, that wee dog, given half the chance woulda ate ye alive and no word of a lie, it's God's honest truth. There was no chance of 10 Woodlee Street ever getting burglarised. Gibby just loved that wee dog." (A faraway look fell upon ginger wigged Agnes's countenance. Gary in fact wished she was ALSO now very far away!) "They were inseparable, you would see them all over the place. Well wee Rudy finally got old and sick and had to be put down a couple of months ago. Gibby sorta went downhill from then on so he did. Well, and so it's come down to this now, hasn't it, Canstable?"

Letitia spoke next, quietly, falteringly looking down at the pavement. "Well, Canstable, do ya think he's tattie bread, dead I mean?"

Gary spotted his chance to escape. "Well, that's what I'm here to find out ladies, I don't expect any of you know if Gibby had any next of kin or the whereabouts of a set of spare keys to his place?"

A wee huddle ensued followed by a few. 'Eh he's' a couple of, 'I'm not so sures' finishing with a unanimous 'absolutely'. Green coated Letitia spoke, "Gibby had a second cousin, she's a wee girl called Melissa, mmm, Melissa Saunders. Her mammy was a right old cow, in til' everybody's business so she was. She's married to a lovely wee fella. He's a plumber. Works for Shanklys on the Woodstock Road so he does. I think they live not too far away in Halcombe Street, aye and she has a wee job in Gordon's Chemist in Castlereagh Street. You'll maybe catch her there!"

A final thanks was offered by Gary to the old dears, fonts of all knowledge regarding East Belfast. If the occasion ever arose for them to grace that ever-popular TV Show, Mastermind their specialist subject would surely be... "'The Life and Times of Gibby Jenkins', thank you please Magnus!! Gap fillers extraordinaire!" Ginger wigged Agnes in parting said.

"Yer more than welcome Canstable God bless yez all, the lot of yez. I don't envy yez yer jabzz!" She flashed Gary a winning smile displaying her toothless mouth in its best light. Gary returned the smile. The ladies shuffled on, cackling as they went. Sailing off into the sunset down Woodlee Street and onwards, towards the Beersbridge Road. Their National Park, their Serengeti...

"Salt of the Earth," Gary said to himself. Gary looked into their vehicle to check if our Shelley was still alive. She had assumed the relaxed position. Her eyes were closed and her usually chattering mouth lay open with a spot of drivel making good its escape. *Bless*, he thought, *my wee pard is resting in the coiled spring position*. None shall pass! After an anxious moment's contemplation, Gary knocked gently on Shelley's driver's side window. The savage beast stirred. An eye began to open. Gary quickly mouthed that he was going to try to get into 10 Woodlee Street. He tugged on his ear and pointed to the radio asking her to listen out for him. A thumbs up appeared and quickly disappeared as the eye again closed.

Gary had his portable radio on him, but he didn't want it blaring on and off while he was dealing with all this. On first inspection, 10 Woodlee Street looked in fine fettle. Its front doorstep was polished. Cluttered only by the six milk bottles in various stages of decomposition. The window frames had been recently painted black and the windows were spotless. The view to the inside was obscured by a brilliant white net curtain. No way in the front... Gary then walked around to the back entry carefully watching his every step. The entry was bogging and stank. Gary located the rear entry door for number 10. A turn of the handle and the door opened easily. The rear yard was spotless. Everything in place and a place for everything. He tried the back door handle, his luck was in, it opened easily. He began to get the feeling this all was more by design than luck or good fortune!

Gary gingerly eased himself into the kitchen... He called out, "Hello, POLICE, is anyone here?" He repeated this several times. Nothing, he became aware of classical music, barely audible coming from the area of the living room. He knew he was required to search the property, but he wanted to establish if in fact Gibby's dead body was there! He moved quickly and quietly through the kitchen and downstairs living room. Gary spotted the source of the music, an old radio by the living room door. He moved to switch it off but changed his mind. It was strangely calming and comforting, still no sign of Gibby.

Gibby's place wasn't too smelly. He had been in houses where dead bodies had been found which had smelt gross. Maybe Gibby was away on a break Gary hoped as he made his way up the spotless stairs. The toilet was located at the head of the stairs. Many a seated corpse had been found there thought Gary, thinking of his idol Elvis. The King! Gary swiftly opened the door. EMPTY. A fresh fruits of the forest fragrance filled his nostrils. Very pleasant! A quick look into the separate bathroom also found it to be empty. Gary made his way past the rear bedroom door which was closed. He found the front bedroom door open and empty. In the Covenly Three's own words it was 'Maculate'. It was clearly Gibby's bedroom evidenced by the men's clothing in the drawers and large wardrobe. A large photograph of a young Queen Elizabeth gazed upon the young constable from the back bedroom wall. Beneath it hung a simple wooden plaque with the inscription. 'PER MARE PER TERRAM'.

Latin wasn't Gary's strong point.

Gary made his way back to the last remaining room. The back bedroom! The door bore a beautiful name tile with painted flowers and the name META inscribed. Last chance saloon. He gently turned the door handle and entered...

Gary paused and took a sharp intake of breath… In a whisper, he said, "Hello Gibby."

Gibby had clearly passed. He was sitting on an old cream coloured wicker chair located next to a charming woman's dressing table. A beautiful vanity set consisting of a brush, comb and mirror rested on top. A tub of talc sat next to them. Gary caught a whiff of peach. A large brown envelope with an object inside sat on the table next to Gibby… It was inscribed in black marker 'TO WHOM IT MAY CONCERN'.

"That, Gibby, my friend would be me. Hang fire old chum, I've a call to make."

Gary returned downstairs. It never ceased to amaze him how he always tip-toed around a dead person's house and whispered in communications. It was daft considering he was the only living (barely) person there. Gary spotted the old black Bakelite phone resting on a tiny stool in the hallway. He could have used his radio but never liked the notion of blaring deceased details over the air. He felt it inappropriate and a smidge disrespectful. He checked on Shell again through the front window. His pard was still in coiled spring mode. It would take a brave betting man to punt on who looked the deader of the two! Gary happily whipped off his super cosy turtle shell flak jacket, he would be here for a while. Picking up the phone he dialled 650222. After a short ringz, he got the police operator.

"Extension 26500 please." Another few rings and, "Good morning, Mountroyal RUC, how may I help you?"

Gary recognised the voice on the other end as one of a dynamic duo of Station Duty Officers or Guards as they were commonly known. They were Victor Snape and Harry Sweetlove. They were responsible for the Enquiry Office and all its nuances. They issued radios and weapons to the crews, maintained records in the appropriate registers and took calls from the public attending the station or by phone. They were the chief custodians of the C6 or the 'Occurrence Book'. Affectionately known as 'Waldorf and Statdler' but mainly 'the two Grumpy Old Bastards'.

It was now just short of 11.00am. Gary spoke, "A very good morning 'Vic the'." A shortened version of Vic the prick. A term of endearment only a few of his besties were permitted to use.

Vic was a senior constable in his forties with 25 years done. He had been happily divorced for 12 years. He now had two new loves in his life, a threesome you could say, "Gina and Tonica…" A match made in Cirrhosis Chat Heaven! He had been around a few stations and had been eased into Mountroyal 8 years ago following a gun attack which happened when he was stationed in New Barnsley RUC Station Belfast. Vic had been shot in the back that day and lost two of his colleagues, Sally, a female Sergeant he had been seeing, and a probationer constable, young Neville a week out of the depot. Vic had amazed his surgeons when battling for his life in intensive care, he really hadn't been expected to pull through. Amazingly, five months after the shootings Vic returned to work. Sadly, a large part of who Vic was died the day of the fateful shootings and the murder of his friends. Vic was now permanently on light duties and could no longer go out on the ground. Vic had his demons and he battled them every day!

Vic relaxed and spoke. "Bout ye, Gary, how's it hanging. Well what news…. Is yer suddenly deaf, dead or what?"

Gary updated Vic in a short space of time and requested he contact Doctor Navid at the Templemore Avenue Surgery. Gary needed to know if Gibby had been seen by any doctor within the last 28 days removing the need for a post mortem. He also requested Doctor Navid's attendance at 10 Woodlee Street to formally pronounce Gibby as dead. Gary pushed his luck further and asked Vic if he could get a hold of Melissa Saunders giving the information given him by the 'Covenly Three'. Melissa would be needed to formally identify Gibby to him legally for the benefit of the coroner. Vic as usual was sound as a pound.

"No worries, Gary, I'll get on with all of that, I'll also give Wes a shout at BRC to update his log. I'll get back to you on your landline there!" Gary smiled.

"Cheers, Vic. Oh and by the way, where's Tweety Pie, I don't hear any whistling or shitty classical music?"

Vic chuckled. "Tweety is bouncing in and out of the radio store with sheets of paper. He's been swearing profusely in about 10 different languages, I think he's doing a wee job for the big boss. Top secret and all that. It keeps him honest."

Gary laughed. "Everyone loves a bit of Tweety Pie all right, laters Vic."

Gary hung up and returned to the living room plonking himself down on the worn settee. A moment to himself was required. A catch up, had he missed anything? He carefully gazed around the room, spotless. He raised his eyebrows in amazement, no television set, just the ancient radio for company. The small Alba radio continued with its soothing classical sounds. Numerous religious plaques adorned the walls. An old mantle clock tick tocked against the heavy mood. Gary got himself up. Time to search.

A systematic search began throughout the downstairs. Nothing of any value or of use to the Pathologist was found. He headed out into the hallway intent on searching upstairs. Perfect timing, the phone rang just as he passed, he nearly shit himself! Composure returned Gary lifted the phone, "Hello, Gary Weaver here."

It was Vic. "Hi Gary, a sitrep (situation report) on your last, Gibby hadn't seen any doctor in two years. You've got a post mortem being lined up. I've informed the Coroner's Office. They're getting back with me shortly regarding the where's and when's, though it will probably be tomorrow chum. Doctor Navid's aware and should be out with you within the next 30 minutes, oh and by the way I think the new skipper's calling out with you. He's just left in the supervision vehicle, the red soft skin Escort!"

Gary appreciated the warning.

"Cheers, Vic, catch ya later."

The self-preservation society kicked in. Gary skipped out the front door and to their vehicle in three strides rapping Shell's driver side window. The creature from the black lagoon leapt like a trout, banging her head on the lowered sun visor which had been protecting her cute snow-white face from the glaring sun. A 'busted bake' followed just ahead of the look of death, Shell blurted, "What the fuck, Gary. You trying to kill me!"

Gary laughed. "Listen pumpkin, the new skippers on his way, get those creases ironed out of your face pronto, your eyes are a gooey mess and a bit of lippy wouldn't go amiss."

Shelley frowned. "Fuck me Gary, are you looking into my knickers or what!"

"Camaraderie!" They both laughed.

Gary quickly slipped back into Gibby's place while Shell transformed herself from beastly to beauty just as the red Escort turned into Woodlee Street. There wasn't a sinner about. The red Escort parked immediately in front of theirs. The young Sergeant disembarked lightly.

No flaker, no forage cap and no side arm. Here was A Section's newly promoted Sergeant. The very dashing Tony Speers. It was his second week with his section. Everything was new to him. The proverbial fish out of water. A complete change of scenery, job role and way more responsibility. To say he felt wet behind the ears was an understatement. Like a novice skater on ice, Tony was slowly letting go of the sides. But Tony could bluff for Ireland. He had a master's degree in hanging tough! To Shell, he looked like a Roman god. She gave a low growl and sprung out of her vehicle. Shell let fire with all her assets as she sashayed towards the young and gorgeous Sergeant. She would show no mercy; he wouldn't stand a chance! Eyes flickering, a flashing smile with her recently applied 'Sexy Scarlet' lippy (by Avon). She thrust her chest out for maximum effect as she closed in. What a difference a minute can make...

Tony had been hit right between the eyes. If it had happened in the boxing ring the towel would have been thrown in. He was now liking being a Sergeant very much, these perks and they were perky were never mentioned in the job description! Tony smiled at Shelley, perhaps a couple of degrees warmer than a friendly smile. A man on a galloping horse would never have spotted the difference. But Shelley felt everything getting warmer. Shelley's heart was now thumping like a Lambeg drum on the 12th of July! Their eyes collided like a reckless car crash and quickly disengaged. "Morning, Sergeant Speers, lovely to see you, what brings you all the ways out here?" Shelley fawned, licking her lips! Tony smiled. "Good morning, Shelley, how's it going, and please call me Tony, only Sergeant when members of the public are around. I'm here to check that you pair are OK and have got everything you need."

Shelley was now convinced she wanted to have his babies, "I'll just pop in to see how Gary's getting on. Catch you later Shelley. Oh and keep the good work up." Tony had been brushing up on his likeability phrases for newly promoted Sergeants. Shelley gushed as Tony approached Gibby's front door. He gently knocked it and went in. Gary and Tony met in the downstairs hallway which was bathed in the hushed tones of Beethoven's Moonlight Sonata. Gary updated Tony as to the current state of play and led him upstairs to Meta's room where Gibby was.

"Here's Gibby skipper..." Gary said as they entered the room. Both paused for a moment and respectfully gazed upon Gibby. His eyes were partly open and in a far off gaze. What seemed to be a soft smile quietly set had been one of Gibby's final acts. His short grey hair was combed neat and tidy. His skin tone an alabaster blue. "You're right ladies, he had indeed been a handsome man," Gary whispered softly.

Gibby looked to have been around six feet one. A large frame with no excess baggage.

His hands were like shovels and somewhat callused. A lifetime of wheeling

Meta Gary supposed. Eyeing the folded down wheelchair in the corner. Gibby had taken the time and effort to go out smartly. He was wearing a dark blue shirt and tie, the tie had gold type badges through it. Gibby wore a blue woollen jacket with grey slacks. On his feet, he was wearing immaculately polished or bulled black oxford shoes. Gibby was holding a green beret in his left hand which had a metal badge to the front matching those on his tie. Resting on his lap and lying open was an old and obviously well used bible. Its pages were open at the Book of John, Chapter 10 with verses highlighted in yellow. A faded letter addressed to Gibby was placed between these pages.

Both officers gazed around the room. It was like stepping back in time. Three faded framed photographs hung on the wall. The first of a mother and father and two small children posing outside what was obviously 10 Woodlee Street. One of the children smiling for the camera was in a wheelchair. The children couldn't have been any more than five or six.

The second slightly larger photograph was a full face image of a stunningly beautiful woman, a young Meta. She would have been in her twenties with long straight blonde hair. Her eyes were large and an amazing turquoise blue. Her smile was soft and angelic. She looked so very happy.

Both men stood up close to the image which was further enhanced by a shaft of sunlight elevating it even more. "Wow, stunning," said Gary. Tony nodded in agreement. "That portrait must be over 50 years old." *Meta had been gone over 10 years now,* thought Gary.

The third photograph was slightly smaller. It showed a handsome soldier in full uniform wearing a green beret like the one Gibby was holding now. He was on his hunkers beside a beautiful blonde-haired woman in a wheelchair. It was obviously a young Gibby and his beautiful sister Meta. They were both laughing and looking lovingly at each other. Meta was holding a medal in her hand.

The medal was an ornamental silver cross with straight arms ending with broad finials. It hung from a plain suspension bar. They could see imperial crowns on the front face with what looked to be the 'Royal Cypher' in the centre. They noted the year 1944 showing on its lower limb. Attached to the medal was a ribbon which bore three equal vertical stripes of white purple and white. What looked like a parchment with writing on it rested on her lap?

At the base of the photograph, the following was inscribed …

'PER MARE PER TERRAM, 14th September 1944…'

Tony then spoke, "Ahh, PER MARE PER TERRAM… Latin for BY SEA,

BY LAND. Gibby must have been a Royal Marine Commando during the Second World War. That's their motto."

Gary nodded, now he knew what the wooden plaque in Gibby's bedroom was all about.

The time was now 11.20am.

The front door knocker rapped briskly several times. "Hello hello it's Doctor Navid from the Templemore Avenue Clinic!" Gary had made it to the front door just as the good doctor had finished his sentence. Doctor Navid was a man in his mid-fifties and of Indian descent. He was just under 6' in height and of slender frame. He wore thick rimmed glasses which had the effect of making his eyes look huge. He was stylishly dressed, and every item of his attire was a version of brown right down to his classic brogue shoes. He had lived in Northern Ireland for over 40 years and had got his medical qualifications from the world-renowned Queens University Belfast. Doctor Navid had worked at the Templemore Avenue Clinic for 23 years. He was a kind, patient, caring and a most professional of medical practitioners. He had a disarming sense of humour and when he spoke, he spoke with a rich Indian accent which was occasionally mugged by a Belfast twang. He was adored by his patients.

Gary led him upstairs and introduced him to Tony and to Gibby. Gary showed Doctor Navid the only medication he had found regarding Gibby, a tiny amber plastic box containing white tablets. The box was labelled Amlodipine Tablets. Doctor Navid examined the tablets and slowly shaking his head spoke, "I'm so very sad. I've looked after Gibby and previously his lovely sister Meta right up until she passed 10 years or so ago. They were so very kind to me when I was a young doctor just starting out." He chuckled. "These tablets constables, they were for his ever so slightly high blood pressure. I had to barge him to take them. He would never complain. You see he was a very fit man for his age, we would cross paths over the years, me doing house calls and lost, and Gibby doing his post rounds and pointing me in the right directions many many times, I remember one time especially, it was back in 1969."

"The Troubles here had just started. Everyone was angry and afraid. Both sides really beginning to hate each other. Me, a young Indian doctor unsure of everything trying to do my rounds. Well, this day I was driving up the Lower Newtownards Road, Belfast. It was really kicking off. The area was full of smoke. Cars and lorries were burning in the road. Masked men were on the streets from both sides. Petrol bombs were flying from one side of the peace divide to the other. The woman and the children were screaming and crying. It was terrifying. I was really really scared for my life.

The next thing is my car is stopped by a gang of masked men. They are armed with clubs and hammers and bars. One of the men, he shouts at me to get out of the car. He called me a 'Paki bastard!' He tells me they're going to burn it. I am thinking I am going to die and my beautiful new shiny blue Triumph Herald is going to go up in flames. They then are grabbing me and pulling me out. I'm thinking this is the end and am saying my prayers to Allah when I hear this almighty roar coming from somewhere close. I am hunched and cowering when looking up, I see one of the masked men flying over my bonnet. I hear a smack and another man is knocked the spark out and he is lying fast asleep beside my driver side door.

It was Gibby in his posty uniform with his wee post bag across his shoulders. Well, the masked men were not liking this and ran off. Gibby was shouting at them to lay off me and that I was the young doctor. Praise be to Allah that day for sending Gibby to my rescue. Gibby got the masked man up onto his feet that he had knocked out and gave him such a shouting. He told him to tell all his UDA mates to lay off me or he would sort them out. Gibby kicked him up the backside and sent him on his way. He then turned to me and smiled and asked me if I was OK, he then gave me a quick thumbs up and off he went with his posting of letters. Until my dying day, I will never forget that smile. I tell you it came from heaven. That day Gibby possibly saved my life. We would see each other over the years, both of us doing our rounds out on the streets. We always gave each other a wave, sometimes a quick chat, "The Indian Doctor and the Belfast Postie."

A tear welled from behind Doctor Navid's thick rimmed glasses. He took them off and cleaned them with a crisply ironed beige handkerchief he had on him.

His gentle eyes looked tired and sad from a life of care. He then gently placed two fingers to the side of Gibby's neck feeling for the pulse that he knew had long ceased and then removed his hand. "For me it is a heart-breaking task but also a great honour to be the doctor to formally pronounce Gibby's life extinct, sleep well old friend, may you fly with wings to your God...I pronounce life extinct at 11.30am..."

Gary made a note of the time on his clipboard. Doctor Navid glanced at the wall and spotted the photograph of the young, decorated soldier and then gazed sadly at the serenely still Gibby. "My goodness me, a man of great service, to his country, to his family and to his people. Who would ever have guessed, Gibby was such a very private person?" Doctor Navid was aware that a post mortem for Gibby was going to be held probably the next day. He handed Gary a sealed brown envelope marked for the attention of the pathologist containing an overview of Gibby's previous health. He then left the house quietly, head bowed.

Gary then rang Mountroyal Enquiry Office updating Vic. Vic, following Gary's instructions, rang Wes at BRC to update his log. The coroner's office was then also called and updated.

On receipt of the news on Gibby a post mortem was scheduled for 11.00am the following day. This was to be held at Forster Green Mortuary at Newtownbreda, Belfast. Wes then contacted the staff at Mallon's Funeral Parlour on the Beersbridge Road who worked on behalf of the Coroner and Police. Their role was to collect and convey Gibby's remains to Forster Green Mortuary. Their estimated time of arrival for Gibby's collection would not be for another hour and a half due to other commitments. It was now just short of 12.00pm.

Vic telephoned all this through to Gary who was happy enough. He was on to 7 bells anyway! An hour and a half to wait. Tony on hearing this smiled and said, "Sure Gary, when you're marching you're not fighting." Gary was beginning to really like his new Sergeant.

Tony continued, "Well Chumlee, time for you to open the brown envelope and see what's inside…" Gary lifted the envelope and opened it. He then placed the contents on Meta's dressing room table. There were four items, an Ulster Bank Savings book, a small maroon leather case, a sheet of parchment type paper with writing on it and finally a handwritten letter from Gibby. The first item Gary examined was the Ulster Bank Savings account book showing a credit of £8542.14. Gary then lifted the small maroon leather case and carefully opened it. It was Gibby's medal. It was the Military Cross. The medal that the young Meta was proudly holding in the photograph on the wall.

Gary then lifted the parchment document. It was Gibby's Military Cross Medal Citation. Gibby had taken part in the Normandy landings. Code name Operation Overlord. The date was 8 June 1944. On that day, the allied forces landed in France and the liberation of Europe commenced. Fierce fighting began by land, air and sea. Every inch gained was paid for in blood! This eventually culminating in the axis forces being driven back to Germany. The German war machine was eventually drained of arms supplies and critically men. The eventual death of Adolf Hitler followed and the German surrender. This spelt the end of the Nazi movement and the end of the war in Europe. Many many lives were lost. On that day, Gibby held the rank of Sergeant. He was a member of Number 3 Commando Unit. Number 6 Troop. They were involved in heavy combat in Normandy. France.

Gary then read the Citation aloud to Tony.

"On the morning of 8 June 1944, Sergeant Jenkins and 35 other men were holding a rear-guard position in the village of Radeval, Normandy, France. His Senior Officer had been seriously wounded and Sergeant Jenkins had assumed command. His troop then came under a heavy and sustained attack by a company of German Infantry. Sergeant Jenkins with total disregard to his own safety led a counter assault with a Sten submachine gun and grenades. During this time, he accounted for a number of the enemy. Sergeant Jenkins inspired his men to clear the enemy from their position. 15 of the enemy were killed and 12 were taken prisoner. Owing to Sergeant Jenkins' courage and leadership that day our own losses were three killed and three wounded. Our success and survival that day was largely due to Sergeant Jenkins leadership."

"Wow!" Tony gasped... Looking at Gibby, he said, "What a man, what a life!" Gary nodded in agreement, then spoke. "And now to our final item... Gibby's letter!" Tony sat down on the edge of the bed and listened...Gary cleared his throat and began reading...

"Dear Sir or Madam,

I'm awful sorry you've had to find me like this. I've cleaned the house as good as I could for you. I was born and raised here in a happy and very loving Christian home. Sadly, I'm the last of my family, the last of the Jenkins.

I've not much to leave but all that I do have I leave to my wee second cousin Melissa Saunders. She's looked out for me and had me over to her place many's a time, Christmas's and all that. If you'd give her my medal and Citation, I'd appreciate it, and also my wee bank book. Would you please tell her that I loved her very much and tell her I'm awful sorry how it all ended?

My Solicitor is a Mrs Courtney Davies of Belam & Davies Solicitors on the Ravenhill Road, Belfast. Courtney is a great wee solicitor but mad as a hatter. She has my will and all my policies. Courtney knows my wishes and will attend to the business side to my funeral…

I've also set money aside for a wee do at the Blades Club after my funeral, in case anyone turns up!

Many thanks,
Gibby Jenkins."

Tony shook his head sadly. "Gibby, you were an absolute star!" Gary nodded in agreement.

"And it all started and ended here at 10 Woodlee Street!"

The time was now 12.30pm. Gary and Shelley had another hour to wait before the Mallon funeral crew arrived to take Gibby to the Forster Green Mortuary for the following day's post mortem at 11.00am. Tony arranged for a packed lunch to be brought out to them. As Tony was leaving to return to base he spun around and said to Gary, "Good work today, Gary, Gibby was in very capable hands. When Gibby's collected at 1.30pm don't forget to return to Mountroyal and take a proper break. After all, you pair are on till 7.00pm tonight.

"Regarding tomorrow, I believe you're on a 7.00am–3.00pm, don't come in for 7.00am. Just head straight to the post mortem at 11.00am. I'll put you down for files and enquiries all day tomorrow. I'll see you the day after!" Tony gave Gary a subtle thumbs up and a wink and left waving in at Shelley as he passed. Gary was chuffed… "Best wee sergeant ever!"

Gary remained downstairs and listened to the soothing classical music until the Mallon funeral crew arrived at 1.30pm. The Mallon crew were very professional and respectful.

In all, they took 10 minutes to have Gibby placed into their vehicle and were gone. Gary rang Wes at BRC and gave him a final update for his log. Before leaving Woodlee Street Gary gave the house one final inspection. He closed all the windows and drew the curtains. He locked the yard door and then the back door. He then turned off all the appliances. And when the tiny alba radio ceased playing its soothing classical music, a heavy and very sad silence descended. The silence of ending, the silence of finality. A feeling as though the house itself had passed! Gibby, the last of the Jenkins was gone…

Gary gathered up Doctor Navid's letter for the Pathologist. Also Gibby's medal with his citation, his bankbook, his hand written letter. And finally, his house keys for Melissa. He paused a few seconds waiting for any Columbo moment. None came! Gary quietly locked the front door securely and left.

Gary and Shelley were back at the station for 2.00pm. Shelley rang Control (BRC) and put AM70 on a Code 50/73, their break. While Gary was in the Enquiry Office completing the C.6 Occurrence Book Vic saddled up beside him giving him the latest news on Melissa Saunders.

"Got a hold of Melissa at Gordon's chemists a short while ago. She was awful upset and took the news badly. Had a wee cry! Anyhoo... Regarding the Formal Identification of Gibby, she's meeting you at Forster Greens Mortuary Reception tomorrow at 10.45am. Lucky you, bro, she knows where it is and she has her own transport..." Gary responded, "Happy days, Vic, you're a star."

They could hear Mozart blaring from a radio coming from the firearms/radio room. Tweety was whistling furiously oblivious to the din lost in concentration. He was a man on a secret mission for his uber boss the SDC. His research was proving difficult but becoming interesting.

On hearing the horrendous sounds, Gary looked over to Vic with a what's going on face. Vic laughed and said, "Please don't ask for fuck sake!" with a twinkle in his eyes.

48 Hours Previously

Gibby Jenkins climbed the stairs of his lifelong home one last time. He was clutching a large brown envelope which he had marked... TO WHOM IT MAY CONCERN...in bold writing.

He had spent the last few days scrubbing and polishing his home. He wanted the place spotless for whoever came. Since wee Rudy had died, he had slowly lost interest in things he used to enjoy like the fresh air, a wee sociable pint at the Blades Club with his select few mates and a plate of good ole Norn Iron grub. All these things had now become onerous. Gibby now felt useless and surplus to requirements. He was dog tired. He felt very low. He was very down or maybe just sad. Whatever it was Gibby knew his tank had run empty and this would be his final journey...

Gibby approached Meta's bedroom door and knocked gently and went in. The room was silent and Gibby felt at peace as he wearily sat himself down in the old white wicker chair beside her beautiful dressing table. He placed the brown envelope beside Meta's brush and smiled as he stroked a few strands of her hair that still clung to it. Gibby then opened the bedroom window slightly to let the air in. He smiled as a gentle breeze played with the white net curtains and the dappled summer sun lit up the beautiful photograph of his sister. He felt himself welling up looking at her beautiful image, she was ever beautiful and he was old, alone and done. Gibby sighed heavily and looking at his sister's face spoke, "Well, sister, it's time and I hope it won't be long till I join you, God's given me a good life for which I'm grateful for, but I feel I've let him down. I've achieved absolutely nothing and have left no trace or mark on this world. I never married, oh how I would have loved to have had kids, to raise them, to play with them, to love them and to encourage them, to see them make something of themselves which dear sister I never did. Well, none of those milestones in life ever happened to me, sure I have done my bit in the war, got myself a medal. Big deal. I would rather have my comrades back. What a waste of so many young lives and so very many friends. Me a hero, what rubbish..."

"You see wee sister, you were the real hero, not me. It was you who in spite of all of your physical setbacks served your Lord all your days at church. You influenced so many young children, educating them in word but also by your beautiful example. I know many of them have become doctors, teachers and nurses. You must have knitted hundreds of clothes for those wee children at home, as well as those far away throughout your life. Never seeking any reward or thanks. I never heard you complain once, not even near the end when you were very sick. You stayed strong for me. Oh, how the children in the area loved you."

"I recall coming home from work many a summer night and turning into Woodlee Street to find you sitting outside in your wheelchair reading them all kinds of wondrous stories."

"Transporting them from their hardships and worries to all kinds of magical worlds, their wee eyes bright like saucers and mouths wide open. You held them with grace and love in the palm of your hand freeing them to the oceans of their untapped imaginations... All I did was wheel you around and loved every breath you ever took (now sobbing)."

"Ohh Meta, how I have missed you."

Gibby recognised Meta's well-worn bible sitting on the dressing table. He hadn't touched it since she had passed over 10 years ago. He had found it too upsetting. It had been such a huge part of her life, she had treasured it. Sobbing, he reached over and picked it up for comfort. As he did so a faded envelope escaped from between its well-thumbed and worn pages. Gibby reached down and picked it up. He immediately recognised the faded handwriting as that of his beautiful sister Meta. Tears running down his weary cheeks Gibby once again looked up at her beautiful photograph. The faded envelope was addressed to ….

THE GOOD SHEPHERD… MY BIG BROTHER GIBBY.

Hands now trembling and tears tripping, Gibby gently opened the faded envelope.

With short gasping breaths he began to read Meta's words to him from beyond the grave…

The room appeared to glow as the setting sun cascaded through the brilliant white net curtains.

My darling big brother,

I hope this letter finds you well and I hope you have found it at the time of God's choosing.

I want you to know that I held on for as long as I could but eventually the good Lord called me home.

I have gone to a better place where I no longer need the use of a wheelchair…

When our parents passed, I would have been put into a home had it not been for you.

You took care of me completely and never complained.

But for me you would have fallen in love. Married, had beautiful children.

Your life would have been so very different. You went off to War and came back a decorated hero. The world was your oyster.

You were my big brother and my hero. I was so very proud of you. I Love that photo of us together the day you got your medal. We were so very young then. It's never been off my bedroom wall close to my bed and ever close to my heart.

All of Belfast was proud of you…

Yet you shunned all the fame and all the glory and took care of me and all of your people in our area. You were far more than just a Postman. Tales were always getting back to me from church friends and neighbours about your kindness. Lifting spirits with your craic and going the extra mile for them. And that was from both sides of our political divide.

Both Protestant and Catholic. There was no such thing as a NO GO area for you dear brother. Wee Doctor Navid swore to me that you saved his life which you never once mentioned. Modest Gibby to the very end.

My life, my church life and service. My work with the children both at home and abroad would never have happened had it not been for you wheeling me in all weathers.

My words can never fully express my love for you.

I know that our heavenly father is well pleased with your life's sacrifices and service...

One final request from your wee sister.

Since you have my bible in your lap, please read the following passage which I have marked in yellow highlighter for you... His word can probably express what I have been trying to say so much better than mine. I am tired now and will close off dear brother.

Thank you for my great life with all my love in this world and the next.

Meta xxx"

...My Good Shepherd Brother...

Tears softened and Gibby's breaths calmed as he opened his sisters well-worn bible which had not been opened in many years. He then read the following highlighted passage ......

> *JOHN Chapter 10 verses 11–18.*
> *I am the Good Shepherd. The Good Shepherd lays down his life for his sheep.*
> *I am the Good Shepherd. I know my own and I'm known by my own.*
> *Even as the father knows me, and I know the father.*
> *I lay my life down for the sheep.*
> *The Father loves me because I lay down my life, that I may take it again.*
> *No one takes my life away from me. I lay my life down myself.*
> *I have the power to lay down my life and I have the power to take it back again.*
> *I have received this command from my father.*

Gibby released a huge sigh. He smiled looking up at Meta's beautiful face. She had given him closure and peace from beyond the grave. His eyes remained on hers which had been filled with brilliant sunlight as the light in his own eyes grew softer and slowly dimmed. The World was now a sadder place, because the Good Shepherd was now gone.

GIBBY had passed.

Gary cleared up his paperwork and started his Security Duties at 3.00pm. He was detailed by the Late Section Sergeant as Observer in a land rover AM80. Shelley was detailed driver and Reserve Constable John Alexander or Wee John was an extra in the back. They were parked up in a static position at the bottom of the Castlereagh Street, Woodstock Link Mountpottinger Road junction.

Across the road parked in the Mountpottinger Road was land rover AS82 a crew from Strand RUC Station. Both crews were facing each other from opposite sides of the road! In short, their joint roles were to keep rival factions apart or 'tribal fractions' as Gary would often spoon. Marching season in Northern Ireland was approaching which heightened tensions amongst the political divide. An annual event would slowly evolve whereby children of barely walking age would start throwing stones at each other's side. Winding each other up. Stirring the pot as it were!

Gary's crew were on the Protestant or PROD side of the road; the Strand crew were on the Catholic or Nationalist side. Basically, they were planted there to 'Shoo' the little shites away. Ignored or left unattended things could escalate totally out of control. This ritual had been going on for years and years. It was mind numbingly boring for the police officers involved. Though was great if you wanted to debate world peace, football, sexual positions of the karma sutra, or how to murder your mother-in-law without getting caught. Or alternatively sleep for several hours in a stuffy sweaty metal box wearing a flak jacket. Oh and by the way, it was 'easy money'.

Gary however felt a tad frazzled. 'Suddenly deafs' had that effect on him. Was it all to do with the intrusion, the invasion of privacy when dealing with a complete stranger's death?

Gary didn't possess the intellectual keys to unlock that particular padlock and locked tight it would always remain. Well, Gibby would be properly taken care of tomorrow Gary mused, strangely unaffected by the white noise coming from Shelley.

Reserve Constable John Alexander never uttered a word during these shitty turns. He was like a Shaolin Priest. When the land rover came to a halt at the static point, he would assume the sleep mode. Over the years, Wee John as he was known had earned many many thousands of pounds in this lucrative mode. Occasionally, a stone or brick would strike the stationary land rover. This came with the territory. The little shits did this when they were getting bored and wanted you to chase them. Sometimes out of equal boredom the police actually did give chase.

Many folks have wondered what it would be like to stand on the inside of Big Ben as it chimed away the hours? It turns out that sitting in a police land rover being struck by all manner of foreign objects over many hours replicates that very sensation. Sadly, for the 'Bonnng' addict Big Ben only strikes a maximum of 12 times at the very most in a day.

If you're into your 'Bonnng' highs join the Police for a Bongtastic Career!

Guaranteed also to give you that magical 'Bongraine' from HELL!

6.45pm.

"Ahh, thank fuck!!!" The relief crew had arrived to take over their static point at the Woodstock Link. Night Shift officers in four hours early to take a ride on this mind numbingly boring gravy train. 'Choo Choo'. Gary was leaving the Station! Gary terminated duty at 7.00pm.

It had been one of very many long days in his career.

...Daddy's Home...

When Gary got home that evening, he was cream crackered. It was just short of 8.00 pm. He had been up for fourteen and a half hours. "Daddyyyy..." Wee Maddie leapt into her Daddy's arms... "Coming out to the garden to play daddy. I've made a tent under the tree. We could have a picnic." Gary could see down the hallway and through the kitchen window. A tiny tent fashioned with old blankets and clothes pegs was fluttering gently in the late evening breeze. A child's table and chairs sat out front with little cups and saucers atop, Care Bears, teddy bears and other stuffed creations were scattered over the immaculate lawn.

"Oh to be young and innocent again," Gary whispered!

"I've waited all day for you daddy, are you coming?"

Maddie trailed her knackered daddy out the back. Her tiny frame excited to be showing off her tent to her hero. "Daddy, sit down; I'll make you a cup of tea..." Maddie beamed, smiling up at him. Gary visibly creaked as he sat down on the grass lawn in stages as any octogenarian would! A 12-hour day wearing a heavy-duty flak jacket left anyone stiff and sore. Gary smiled as a tiny plastic cup and saucer was thrust in his hands. "Mmmmm delicious Maddie, that's the nicest cup of tea I've ever had, can I have another one please?"

Maddie and her daddy played happily for a further fifteen minutes. Time together was a precious commodity. From the back door Gary's wife Irene called out, "Maddie, darling, time for bed. Your bath's ready."

Maddie looked up at her daddy with sadness in her eyes, "I'm sorry daddy but I've got to go to bed now. Can we do this again tomorrow?"

Gary heaved himself up, brushing the grass off and said to the apple of his tired eye. "As long as you make me another cup of that lovely tea princess. Do you promise?"

"I promise, Daddy. I can't wait."

Then off she scampered leaving her weary daddy in her wake. Gary ate his tea on his own, it tasted like cardboard! He was so tired; Irene and Maddie had eaten theirs several hours before. A norm in many policemen's homes. Both Gary and Irene were by now well used to this groove. Gary went to work and came home. Irene worried herself to the bone, never letting it show.

Irene and Gary had met while he was on a security duty at the Royal Victoria Hospital Belfast. Gary had been guarding a wounded colleague in plain clothes. The RVH as it was known was located in a very republican area of west Belfast and this was a particularly dangerous turn for a police officer to perform. Some had been murdered performing this role. It was here they met some five years ago. Irene was a Staff Nurse working out of the Critical Injuries Ward which was never short of business, only beds. And the rest you can say is history. A killer combo, the beautiful nurse and the handsome policeman. Irene was a very important cog in the spinning of this family's wheel. She had given up nursing when wee Maddie came along.

A mug of tea and a custard cream together, a quick chat then Gary was off to bed just after 10.00pm. He snatched a quick peek at Maddie who was now fast asleep nestled among her favourite bears!

Gary was asleep before his head hit the pillow. "Cavorting in the land of Zob, dancing with the fling flangs and singing with the jube jubes!"

...Gibby's Post-mortem...

Gary awoke the next morning feeling like a million dollars. He showered and shaved whilst listening to Gibby's classical music channel which he was now a convert to. He popped on a pair of tan chinos, a dark green polo shirt and his favourite brown mole skin shoes. He called them affectionately his, "Brothel Creepers!" Irene detested this title, wee Maddie was still fast asleep.

He had his two Weetabix in warm milk with sugar followed by two rounds of marmalade on burnt buttery toast just how he liked it. All this was washed down with a porcelain mug of hot sweet tea. Irene sat with him on regular cornflakes with cold milk and a mug of instant black coffee. Her face was baldy, her hair a mess but stunningly beautiful as ever! The view out back, pastoral and breathtaking! Life today, at this moment, was good! His new favourite Sergeant had granted him special dispensation, instead of coming in for the gruelling 7.00am start for the Early turn requiring Gary to rise at 5.30am, the wonderful Sergeant Speers had given him permission to take care of Gibby's post mortem with no requirement to show his face at Mountroyal whatsoever that day. And he was on a late shift the following day, which didn't start until 3.00pm.

If all went well with the post mortem, he would be down the road by 12.30pm and home to the beautiful Irene by 1.00pm. What also pleased Gary was that he could make his way to Forster Greens from his home using only the country roads. A very easy on the eye drive of 30 minutes across the stunning south Down countryside. He gave Irene a peck on the cheek and slipped into his grubby silver Ford Escort and was on his way shortly after 9.00am, accompanied by Air Supply's Greatest hits. He had with him the completed forms P1 and Form 19 for the P.M. Also with him was Gibby's envelope containing his letter, bank book and Military Cross medal. He planned to give Melissa these items following her formal identification of Gibby to him. This done, Gary would fulfil Gibby's final wishes.

Gary had attended many a P.M. at Forster Greens and there was a strict pack drill, a way things were done. No P.M. would ever take place without the presence of four sticky buns.

Golden rules had to be obeyed. On route to the P.M. Gary had popped into Whites Bakery on the Gilnahirk Road, Belfast. There he purchased two cream Charlies and two custard tarts. Buyers pick. Sticky Buns mission accomplished. Shortly before 10.00am Gary's escort rattled through the rear entrance of Forster Greens Mortuary. It was a tiny compact structure, built for purpose set in a wonderful woodland setting. To the back was an old overgrown apple orchard. Amazingly when in season it still offered up fragrant blossoms and fruit.

Gary entered through the main front door directly into the general Reception Area. He had remembered all he needed for the P.M. and he had Gibby's brown envelope for Melissa. He was greeted with Abba's Greatest Hits playing over the building's intercom. To the right was the reception counter with a buzzer affixed. A large glass security window spanned the width of the counter where he could see into the main office. The office door to the left of the large window was always securely locked. To his left was another door which led to a viewing room with also a large glass window. Gary always thought that this room was unnaturally dark on the inside. It was from here formal identifications were made by relatives of their loved ones.

The deceased body would be presented to the relative from the mortuary side of the window which was always brilliantly lit and forensically clean. The deceased would be presented to the relative with their face and body covered with a gown. The police officer would instruct the Mortuary Attendant to remove the gown exposing the deceased face. He would then ask the next of kin or relative a simple question. "Can you identify this person to us?"

With the identification made, the next of kin's duty was done and they would be free to leave. The date and time of the formal identification would be recorded. The post mortem to establish the cause of death would begin carried out by a designated State Pathologist.

Gary stood in the Reception Area for a few seconds looking into the main office window. No sign of life (oops!) He hit the buzzer and waited, the door to his left flew open and the dynamic duo appeared very much larger than life. A slender woman in her early fifties and classically attractive for her age paused and smiled, she was the boss of the place, the lovely Sheila Ingram! Her greying hair was swept back in a bun. Her face was beautifully painted, and she wore a very expensive grey woollen suit recently purchased from Nora Bradleys exclusive shop in Belfast, it had cost a small mortgage.

Sheila was married to money and didn't need to work. She however was independent, sharp as a whip and strangely loved her job. "A very good morning, Gary, I hope you bought the buns and not the old Mace crap."

Sheila was in charge of the running of the Mortuary and was very good at what she did. She had been doing the job for over twenty years and there wasn't much in the way of horror and tragedy that she hadn't come across! Sheila was accompanied by Ronnie Adams, a 'Geordie' through and through. Ronnie or Ronaldo as Sheila called him was in his mid-forties. He was short and squat and powerfully built. Ronaldo was single and had previously been in the army. He was a mad keen Newcastle United footie fan, and today he was bursting with excitement. He was blessed or cursed with a wicked sense of humour which he found hard to suppress even at the darkest of times.

Ronnie and Sheila had worked together at Forster Greens for ten years. A perfect blend of Chalk and Cheese! Ronnie was wearing his work clothes, or his scrubs. A pale blue cap and matching over gown and white wellie boots. In his finest Geordie accent, "Morning to you, Gary lad… People have been dying for you to see me." Gary laughed… Sheila rolled her eyes. How many times had Ronaldo rolled that old chestnut out?

"Let's go in and get the kettle on," Sheila said as she turned the key opening the main office door. This wee team had performed this dance a few times before. 'Super Trooper' was now in competition with the kettle as Gary 'chillaxed' on his favourite orthopaedic armchair. "Who's doing the PM then team?"

Gary asked, Ronaldo excitedly jumped in, "Young Saul Petrie, the biker boy. Ooh I can't bloody wait."

Gary glanced up at the security cameras covering both front and rear of the mortuary. Gary's job was now to keep a lazy eye on them. He was the 'flick switch' man! Should Melissa arrive early he would flick the switch next to him and Abba would be replaced by the more solemn tones of Brahms. "Tea's up," Sheila said as four hot cups of tea were presented.

Right on cue, a powerful motorbike eased into view of the rear security camera. A Darth Vader like figure dismounted and made its way around to the front and into full view at reception. Ronaldo couldn't contain himself as the dark figure removed its motorcycle helmet. It was indeed the young Saul Petrie, 33 years old, single and looking for love. State Pathologist extraordinaire based out of the Belfast City Hospital Belfast.

Saul was a master of his craft and had a fast-growing reputation. He had cut his teeth dealing with some of the most horrific cadavers the troubles could produce. Explosions, shootings, torture, punishment beatings, murders and then there was sometimes just the regular unfortunate incident. Saul had been there, seen it and had designed the T Shirt.

He looked older than his 33 years which was mostly to do with his five feet eight-inch scrawny frame allied to a pale complexion and fast receding ginger hair. He had the piercing blue eyes of a hawk and missed nothing. Saul's jacket was already off as Ronaldo grinning like a Cheshire cat let him in. He kicked off his biker boots and was soon standing before them wearing a blue button up shirt minus the tie. Grey Primark slacks which were a size too big and a pair of red and black Denis the Menace striped socks.

Saul, looking around, said, "Morning mother." (He always called Sheila mother, she had looked after him from the start.)

"Hi Gary, how's it hanging?" And looking at Ronaldo, he said, "And you can fuck away off." Ronaldo howled with laughter and delight.

Newcastle United had just signed Tottenham Hotspurs 30 goals a season golden boy for a ridiculous sum. It was all over the papers. Saul was a 'Lilly white' through and through and to him and the Spurs faithful he felt 'The End of the World was Nigh.'

Sheila interjected, "Now, now children, behave yourselves. Gary's bought us buns and here's a mug of tea and here Golden Plumbs, (Handing Saul his work sheet containing two PM's for the day.) is your 'Menu del Dias'."

Gary's one is first on the list at 11.00am, a Mr Gilbert Jenkins. The second one's a wee child, she's down for 2.00pm. It was now just gone at 10.15am, Melissa wasn't due for another 30 minutes or so. Gary handed Saul the official paperwork followed by Doctor Navid's letter. He stole a quick look at Gibby's tablets and nodded. "Anything else Gary, nothing smelly I hope?" Saul said finishing of his cream Charlie. Gary gave a quick retell of Gibby's life and the Military Cross was aired. Ronaldo being ex-army was in awe and garnered special respect for Mr Jenkins.

Sheila spoke… "Mmmm that custard tart was lovely Gary, an inch on the lips, a mile on the hips." She laughed…

Ronaldo looking at Saul said, "Fancy a cancer stick out back before we start sir?"

"Spiffing idea, my good fellow, I'll just get my scrubs on before we puff.

See you out there," replied Saul slipping into the small locker room containing his scrubs.

Sheila shouted after them, "Them fegs il be the death of yez…"

"We'll not have far till go then for our post mortem," came a shout from the locker room!

Gary watched the unlikely pair via the rear security camera having their puff, laughing and joking in their scrubs. He felt honoured to be their colleague and friend. It had just gone 10.40am when Gary spotted what had to be Melissa Saunders' car arriving. Gary flicked the switch and 'Lay all your love on me' instantly became Brahms! Everyone was familiar with the cue. Saul and Ronaldo headed for the main morgue. Sheila popped her shoes back on and Gary, armed with Gibby's envelope, took himself out into the reception area.

Melissa Saunders entered the reception looking anxious as one would expect. She was in her early thirties, slender with dark brown shoulder length hair. Her eyes were a dark brown colour, tiny and pinched. It was obvious by the redness she had been crying. Melissa was wearing a plain green anorak, open and a Gordons Chemist over vest was visible. Gary introduced himself to her and sat her down. Sheila nodded warmly from behind the glass window of the main office.

Aware that Melissa was stressed and her mind was charging like a runaway train Gary calmly went through the previous day's events. He removed the bank book from the envelope and gave it to her. Gary then explained that a Solicitor, Courtney Davies was in the wings waiting to take care of Gibby's estate and funeral. As well as the wee do at the Blades Club. He gave her Courtney's contact number. A wave of relief washed over Melissa's tired face. Next out of the envelope came the Military Cross and the Citation. Melissa read the citation whilst holding the medal in her hand and tears began to quietly flow…

"None of us ever knew, he never told a soul!" she whispered…

Gary gave her a minute to let her settle and compose herself. He then explained the identification procedure to her and led her into the viewing room. Waiting for her on the other side of the glass was a solemn and respectful Mortuary Attendant who when given the nod by Gary gently removed the gown exposing a face. It was now 11.00am.

Gary then whispered to Melissa.

"Can you identify that person to me please, Melissa?"

Melissa replied, "Yes, he's Mr Gilbert Jenkins, my Uncle Gibby from 10

Woodlee Street Belfast." Gary gave Ronaldo the quick thumbs up and led Melissa back out into the reception area. Gary thanked her for her help on behalf of the coroner and offered her a cup of tea. Melissa declined, this had been an ordeal and she wanted away. She thanked Gary for all he had done and left carrying Gibby's envelope and its special contents. As her car drove out from camera view, Sheila flicked the switch.

Braham's made way for 'Money money money'!

Gary, relieved, poked his head into the main mortuary area to thank Ronaldo, but also to ask Saul if he wished him present in the theatre for Gibby's post mortem. The two jokers had morphed and were now in full work mode. A world class Pathologist and his able attendant. Saul in answer to Gary's question said to him, "No Gary, all's good I can take it from here. Call back in a…"

The theatre phone shrilled above the noise. Saul answered and motioned Ronaldo over to the refrigeration bay marked 3. With the phone to his ear Saul motioned Ronaldo to open the bay door and pull the tray out. As he opened the bay door and pulled the tray out, Gary gasped in angst. What looked to him for all the world was a beautiful Angel lying with its eyes closed, not dead, merely sleeping, a child of no more than six years old with blonde hair placed carefully over her tiny shoulders. Her face was the purest white and serene, without a mark or a blemish. Saul could see that Gary was upset, he spoke, "Gary chum, I've seen a lot of gruesome sights but the wee children are the hardest for me. (Looking now at the dead child.) That's wee Sonia, she was going for a message for her Gran yesterday, ran out in front of a car, the driver stood no chance. Her whole life in front of her, how does a family recover from that? Go grab yourself a coffee up in the village at Newtownbreda. Call back at 1.00pm. I'll have Gibby's results waiting for you. Hope not to see you too soon, buddy…"

'Angel Eyes' was belting out as he left his two friends! Saul turned and went back to his work, Ronaldo looked up and nodded as Sonia was eased back into the freeze.

Gary had his coffee at the Golden Crumb in the Village. He tried to read the complimentary rag but his eyes could not get any signals through to his brain. He had attended Forster Greens for Gibby's PM. A man who had lived a full and useful life. But he had been emotionally hijacked at the sight of the dead 6-year-old child whose life had barely begun.

"The Beginning Of An End And The End Of A Beginning!"

Gary was back at Forster Greens shortly after 1.00pm. "Slipping through my fingers," greeted his arrival. He rang the buzzer at reception and Sheila appeared, "Hiya Gary, the boys are away out for a wee dander to get their heads showered before their 2.00pm. You know, wee Sonia, bless her. Saul told me to tell you Gibby was straightforward enough, heart failure or in medical jumbo, myocardial infarction. Here's the paper work. I've already rang the Coroner's Office and they've released the death certificate."

Sheila let Gary into the main office whereupon he rang the Mountroyal Enquiry Office. He got through to Tweety and gave him Gibby's C6 reference number which he located in the Occurrence Book. Details of the PM and the cause of death as prescribed by Dr Saul Caskey, State pathologist, were recorded. The Coroner's Office had also been notified and a death certificate released. Gibby's C6 Occurrence would be written off later that day by Sergeant Tony Speers and countersigned by the duty Inspector. The call was now closed and dealt with. "Cheers Tweety, catch you themara…" Gary said to which Tweety replied, "Enjoy your wee fluffy day Gary, you take them when you can get them. There's enough bad days out there."

Gary then thanked Sheila for her kindness as per usual, and passed on his love to the boys. Home time! As he left the building, ABBA played him out with…

"Hasta Manana!"

Gary was a different person as he made his way home through the beautiful countryside. His eyes were wider as he appreciated the wondrous sights and colours. The job could be a great teacher and the experiences it offered could at times be life changing sometimes for better sometimes for worse. Gary had learnt so much over the past couple of days.

In Gibby, he had appreciated a life well lived. He had learnt of the qualities of sacrifice, devotion and modesty. An uncluttered life, a life of caring, a life seeking no brass band or fanfares.

In Sonia, he had been slapped hard in the heart. Gary had learnt that life was very precious and should never be taken for granted. Life was a gift and could be cut short. Gary burst in through his front door. Irene was on her knees in the kitchen fiddling with their old hoover.

"Where's my wee Maddie, have you made daddy his cup of tea?" he shouted. From the garden, a wee curly blonde head popped out from the makeshift tent, wearing a pink care bears T-shirt and blue denim shorts and barefooted she sprinted up the garden screaming to her father now standing at the back door, "Daddyyyyyyyyy."

Maddie bounced up into her daddy's arms and gave him a big hug not letting go. Gary could feel her wee heart pounding and tears fell down his cheeks also not letting go. Irene looked up from their old clogged hoover and seeing her tearful hubby raised an eyebrow. "You all right, love?"

Gary smiled. "I'll tell you later, pet, we're away out to play."

...Gibby's Send Off...

It had been three days since the death certificate had been released. Melissa had met with Courtney who in typical fashion and efficiency executed Gibby's will and wishes. The funeral service was to be held at The Iron Hall Church, Templemore Avenue, Belfast on Tuesday the 24 May 1983 at 11.30am. The funeral notices were placed in the Belfast Telegraph as well as the Newsletter. A tsunami of notices flooded in, swamping the obituary sections of both newspapers. These notices came in all manner and form, from all sides of the community, from the great and the good, from the rich and the poor.

An outpouring of love and respect for one of their very own. The Covenly Three had played no small part. Their networking skills would have been the envy of the FBI or KGB, everyone that needed to know knew.

On the day of the funeral, police parking cones had been placed to the front of the church. A strong police presence was also noticeable. Outside speakers were erected. The day itself was in Belfast terms soft. The sunshine wrestled playfully with the white puffy clouds and dappled the tree lined avenue with its light and shade. Pastor Ivan Knox who had been retired for some time but had known Gibby and Meta for many years was to officiate at the service. The Templemore Avenue Brass Band of some 40 plus members also attended in full uniform wishing to pay tribute to Gibby's life and service.

By 10.30am, outside the church and lined down Templemore Avenue, several hundred mourners stood quietly. Inside the church was full, barring six reserved seats at the front. These were located beside Melissa and her husband who were staggered by the turn out.

Gibby's coffin was situated at the head of the church.

Resting on its top was his Royal Marine Commando beret.

Beside it, in its open maroon case was his Military Cross.

With minutes to go before the start of the funeral, two armoured vehicles pulled up outside the front of the church. Six figures got out and went into the church hallway. Pastor Knox on seeing the figures nodded to the organist who began playing one of Gibby's favourite hymns. A hymn that had given him comfort many times throughout his war years.

"ABIDE WITH ME…"

As the organ played, the six figures quietly entered. Six Royal Marine Commandos in full military dress with caps to their sides moved to the empty seats to the front. Each man nodded to the coffin as he passed. Pastor Knox led the service with simplicity and compassion giving a very moving and worthy tribute to Gibby.

Following the service, the Commandos, Gibby's brothers took the first lift and bore his coffin out onto Templemore Avenue and positioned themselves behind the hearse.

Melissa and her family were next followed by the brass band.

Following the band were hundreds of mourners…

A drum roll followed next as the hearse began to move off slowly…

As the commandos began to move in slow time carrying Gibby on their shoulders, the brass band began to play.

Its rich deep tones echoing the length and breadth of the Avenue pulling at the hearts of the followers…

'THE LORD IS MY SHEPHERD'

They were following their Shepherd one last time…

...You've Been Played Love! ...

Charlene Uprichard was pissed off. Her useless bastard of a husband hadn't returned home yet. He had been due to finish his shift at Mountroyal at 3.00pm which usually had him back at their plush home in Bangor some time in and around 3.45pm. She swore he did it on purpose. She had been stuck in the house all day and forced to watch all the usual bubble gum for the eyes crap that spewed forth from their television. Fair enough she had the house to herself when the kids were at school. Oh and she had enjoyed her cardio workout at Peak Perfection Gym where she was a platinum member. Her personal trainer Gavin was delighted with her progress. She had put on muscle, lost weight and several inches off her waist. She loved her gym time; there she would network with all the other MM's or the Mummy Mafia as they were known by everyone except themselves. They were indeed a very select group. Membership by the girth of hubby's payroll only.

Her husband Stevie had been a big disappointment to her. He was better than average looking, reasonably intelligent but dull as dishwater. The bottom line was he just couldn't keep her in the manner she wanted to be accustomed to. She had sacrificed everything for him. She had given up her day job as a nail technician at the famous 'Nailed It' Salon in Donaghadee for him. She was a top technician, appointments to see were as rare as hen's teeth. Between them they had two children, Oscar who was 11 and Olivia who was eight. Her children, in Charlene's eyes, were super everything and highly everything else. In reality they were overweight, over indulged and unpopular spoiled brats. Whatever they wanted they got. If they didn't get what they wanted, they gurned and hissy fitted until they did. If their father ever tried to intervene, which was rare, they went squealing to mummy.

Charlene was bored with her life, she wanted more excitement, more thrills. Back at her gym there was a group of women who were all single, separated or divorced. Charlene had observed them over the weeks and months and tut tutted at their hedonistic attitude to life. Wholly inappropriate and unbecoming of lady members at their prestigious Peak Perfection Gym. They would arrive en masse at spin or cardio classes throughout the week ready to put some serious effort in. All faces made up to the nines. Fully loaded in spandex and colour coded gym gear with matching designer trainer's sweatbands and water bottles. They flirted outrageously with the fitness instructors and tossed sexual innuendos about with unfettered abandon. Even more infuriating to the Mummy Mafiosi was at the end of their gym sessions they would meet up at the club bar. There they would gather in loose groups settling in strategic positions, all the while sipping on their gins and slimline tonics and nibbling on healthy green and orange sticks. They were in complete contrast to the MM's by virtue of their attire. They were usually dressed in the most desirable high-end fashion whilst dripping in gold and jewellery. Should a stray attractive male wander into their path they would noticeably still and preen and pose provocatively for him. Each woman straining her every sinew for their unwitting victim's attention. These Sirens were the mortal enemy of the MM's who labelled them as the 'Cougar Crew' or their abbreviated title the CC's.

The Mummy Mafia saw world order from the view that well. "We're the MM's. We have babies like handbags, little human trophy dolls. We are the best at being mummies. Our husbands are very rich and at the very top of their chosen tree. But by the way, so are our families. We went to the finest schools. We were all head girls. Our dress code is frumpy track suit wear with dull expensive trainers. We just don't have the time or even want to give time to being semi-respectably turned out. Our sack of spuds look is our badge of honour. We live in hilarious chaos and insist on shouting aloud our every word. In so doing we command centre stage as our little tearaways run around wild, unkempt and unsupervised. The Mummy Mafia love making as much a fuss leaving places as they humanly can. They bask in their self-inflicted limelight. Laughing and rolling their eyes to anyone caught in the glare of their headlights. Finally finishing outside, they can be seen loading up countless bags into brand new 4x4s before speeding home to their messy mansions. Leaving a trail of blissful peace and quiet where once was chaos.

All mummies of the past have tried but sadly fallen short of this super mummy. The Mummy Mafia's demands are simple…accept their perfection."

The CC's come from a different planet. They are single, never married or recently divorced. All highly successful in their chosen field and have pots of cash. They are 100% image conscious and if it's not designer or top of the range it's not on. The CC is a magnet to the unsuspecting male species. Everything about her draws him in like a moth to a femme fatale flame. Her presentation is always 11 out of 10. She's into every word he says, never shutting him up. She has a higher sex drive than him. She loves sports and detests the soaps. She is horrified at the thought of having babies and she always insists on either paying or at worst going Dutch. She will never send him a mixed message and an offer of coffee at the end of an evening means torrid sex and a lazy breakfast.

It was one of those not so hectic days at the club, Charlene was nibbling on an energy bar and nursing a latte. She was sat centre sofa with a group of fellow MM's. It was her 15-minute shift to glare across the crowded clubroom café at the hated CC's. A stunningly handsome male entered from the gym area. The CC's went into overdrive preening and fawning to no effect. The stud was oblivious. Six foot plus, jet black wavy hair still wet from the shower and a designer stubble. He was wearing a plain black t-shirt and tight-fitting grey jeans. The only thing tiny about this hunk was his waist. His chest was rock hard and as for his arms they were like the guns of Navarone. A scruffy lumpy duffle bag dangled from his huge shoulder. A fellow MM groupie gasped and said, "OMG, DDFG!" the others, drooling, all nodded in agreement. This male was indeed drop dead fucking gorgeous. Charlene was mid fantasy doing bad things with this Adonis when the mum to her left whispered in her ear, "See him, that's Tony Speers your Stevie's new Sergeant." Charlene nodded, never once dropping her gaze from him as he went to the bar and ordered a pint.

Charlene couldn't get him out of her mind and fortune struck a few days later when she bumped intentionally into him in the gym corridor just between the male and female changing rooms. She was just out of the showers; her hair was still damp and brushed back. Her face fully applicated and pristine which was a clear breach of Mummy Mafia regulations. She had also forgotten to put her bra on which in itself was a sackable offence. All in all, she looked seriously hot as Tony meandered down the corridor towards her noticing her for the very first time. Here before him was an attractive thirties milf with a full on camel toe wearing a tight fitting white top and no bra. Her nipples were thrusting out like blind cobbler's thumbs, he thought to himself. As he went to pass her, she smiled fully at him and spoke, "Hi, it's Tony Speers, isn't it? I'm Charlene Uprichard, Stevie's wife. He's told me all about you." If she could have, she would've licked her eyebrows wIth a slurp. Tony was unprepared for any sensible chat. He was still locked in horn-ball mode and couldn't find the 'back' button. Struggling for a cool comeback the best he could come up with was, "Oh Stevie, yes he's a good lad. A real team player, the section would struggle without him." All the while, his treacherous eyes were darting north and south at Charlene's straining form. Charlene then shook her head, her full damp mane swished back and forth like a dominatrix's riding crop. In a lightning burst, she thrust her liberated chest forward finishing inches away from Tony who struggled to breathe. She then deftly placed a hair clip in place. Smiling up at him, she said, "Stevie's got his papers in again for the regulars, I would be very, very grateful for all the help you could give him if you get my drift." Tony got all her drift with bells on but was now in full flight mode, "Absolutely, Charlene, drift taken. Eh I'll tell Stevie I bumpers, I mean I bumped into those I mean you. See you again, I mean cheerio."

Charlene gushed. No one had spotted her sexy performance and she had Tony Speers by his proverbials. She slipped back into the woman's changing rooms to frump up. First task was to pull her tracksuit bottoms down a couple of inches to saggy arse mode. Next her 'passion killer' sports bra was shoved on. Finally, makeup removal reverting to the full MM Groupie look. Five minutes later, she was in the club bar come café 'frumping' it big time with her fellow mafia mums.

Gazing out across the room at the CC's she secretly yearned for the siren life. For Charlene, if the truth be known, sex had nothing to do with it. She hated it. All that thrashing about. Blow jobs only given when a credit card had maxed out, a hand job quickly administered when he wouldn't take no for an answer. The act of sex was purely for babies, not having to work and continuous membership of the PTA Club. No, for Charlene the only thing she loved was the chase. She never felt the desire or the need to sort herself out. She just loved the teasing, the flirting and the power and control it gave her. When she was caught, the game was over. Sex was not on her shopping list.

"Treat them mean, keep them keen," was her mantra.

A million miles away a young woman was taking a shower, hot water and soap was being lathered over her perfect form. 'Tonight, I celebrate my love for you' by Roberta Flack was playing from a record in the living room creating the right mood. A male had just poured Italian Frascati sparkling wine into two frozen glasses. He shouted into the bathroom, "Honey, I'm just making a quick phone call to make sure work doesn't need me for the rest of the day." The female replied, "They better not, you have several jobs to sort out for me big boy."

The sharp shrill of her home phone caused Charlene to jump. She was now in a state of rage. Oscar and Olivia had been home for an hour and were driving her mental with their incessant squealing and shouting. No amount of chocolate would calm them down. "Where was that useless bastard of a husband, he should've been home by now." Charlene badly needed her afternoon nap. All vestiges of female attraction had been removed in anticipation for his imminent arrival. All make-up scrubbed away and gone. She was in full baggy mode with the 'piece de resistance' her 'Santa's helper' woollen bed socks, half on half off proudly dangling from her feet. He would pay for this.

Charlene snatched the phone up her head about to explode. "Yes." She could hear noises, at first a click, then other phones ringing. Muffled conversations in the background and police radios crackling messages. Finally, a male's voice. Stevie spoke, "Hi pet, I tried you earlier, but you didn't answer." Charlene snapped.

"I was at the gym dickhead working on my body so I could look beautiful for you. I'm all dressed up now for a bit of rumpy pumpy." Stevie laughed. "Just my fucking luck. I've been held on until 7.00pm for a security patrol. We need the money honey. I'm really sorry." Charlene growled. "I don't know what you spend the money on, you're always at work for fuck sake. Well, you can forget about the rumpy loser," Stevie laughed amid the background din, "Them's the breaks. Catch you later. Don't worry about tea, I'll get something here." The phone in Bangor went dead. Charlene fumed. "Useless fucking bastard."

A million miles away a female lay naked spread-eagled on top of fresh ivory-coloured silken sheets. She had placed chocolates on each nipple and one on her freshly waxed Brazilian. She shouted into the living room, "Tea's ready, I hope you are hungry big boy."

In the living room, a tape recorder was quietly being replaced in a backpack and placed down the back of a settee. The male appeared back in the bedroom wearing nothing but a grin. His eyes wide in excitement.

"Absolutely starving, darling."

...Assault and Batteries...

Tuesday 24 May. 10.30am

It had rained steadily through the night and continued on into the morning. The crews were out on the ground dealing with humdrum calls. Tony Speers was in his office pushing paperwork around his desk. Stevie Uprichard's 'Constables Application' form was staring him hard in the face. His recommendations and those of Inspector Derek Grant were sought. There were no doubts in Tony's mind that he would be writing favourably on Stevie but he just wasn't feeling particularly wordy enough at that moment, maybe later. His office door knocked and Stevie entered. Tony quickly shoved the application out of the way.

Stevie smiling spoke, "Skipper, do you mind if I nip out to Arthur Greer's Hardware Shop. I need some batteries for my tape recorder. I'll be back in five?"

Tony looked up. "Where's the other two?"

Stevie answered, "Wee Johns on the back gate and Billy Porters in the box."

Tony nodded. "No worries but make it quick." A quick thumbs up and Stevie was gone. He gathered his anorak out from his locker in the Cons changing room and bounded downstairs into the Enquiry Office shattering the glum depressing atmosphere. Tweety was in the adjoining radio room working on his special project for the boss. His radio was on low but the doleful sounds of Mahler – Symphony No. 9 in D did nothing to lift the air of gloom. Vic sighed from behind his rag, he was bored and losing the will to live.

Stevie lifted the Vacant Property file box down from its shelf and fiddled through it for a few moments and then put it back. Vic, seeing Stevie's apparel, spoke, "What are you up to "Mufti' man." (Mufti is a term used for someone in uniform wearing a civilian item of clothing at the same time.) Stevie laughed. "Skippers let me nip out and get some batteries for my tape recorder. Billy is forever running them down instead of plugging the recorder into the mains. It's not fucking rocket science. Do you guys need anything while I'm out?" Tweety appeared from his den grinning broadly.

"Morning Stevie lad are you going a wee message?" Stevie nodded.

"Nipping out to Greer's Hardware for some batteries." Tweety nodded.

"See while you're out, would you get a smiley face for this miserable bastard here. He's been in foul form all morning. Look at the bake on him." Vic's head surfaced from behind the Ards Chronicle. "Do you blame me, Stevie, working with him all day and listening to his crappy music. Fuck sake, buy me a sharp knife I want to slit my wrists. Even the Queen's covering her ears." They all looked up at the portrait of a young Queen Elizabeth hanging from the back wall. She also appeared a tad sad.

Just then, Pinky and Perky buzzed themselves into the reception area from the main building. D/I Archie Brown paused at the window with Detective Sergeant Cliff Boomer towering from behind. Very much 'Little and Large'. "We're nipping out for some supplies, St Bruno tobacco for me and 'Egor' here's going to Whites Bakery for an apple tart and some 'Cream Charlies' for our boss Catherine. Any of you want anything while we're out?" Cliff rolled his eyes heavenward and shook his head.

Vic spoke, "Nope, sir, all good here." Archie nodded and Pinky and Perky headed out into the downpour. Pinky heading right up the Woodstock Road and Perky heading left. Tweety spun around and returned to the radio room. Vic returned to the Ards Chronicle and found himself secretly enjoying Tweety's latest classical offering, 'The Lark Ascending' by Vaughan Williams. He inwardly chided himself. Tweety shouted out from the depths of his cave, "Der Teufel steckt im detail." The Devil is in the detail (German). Vic went, "Eh!" Stevie realising time was not on his side left shouting. "Laters," as he approached the pedestrian gate, it was buzzed open for Inspector Derek Grant who was coming in. Both men running by each other splashing through ever growing puddles.

Derek Grant just made it in before the huge security door closed. Standing in the reception area, he shook the rain off himself. It bounced off his cream trench coat onto the wet floor below. Derek was holding a dark coloured dry-cleaned item by its clothes hanger hook. Vic eased the Chronicle to his desk. Derek spoke "Boy's a dear. That's a wet one, Vic!" Vic nodded. Air on a G String by Bach was edging out of the radio room. Derek shouted in towards Tweety's man cave,

151

"Are we getting anywhere maestro?" Tweety's head popped out smiling.

"*Lente quidem sed*, Inspector. (Latin) slowly but surely."

Vic spoke stating the obvious. "Dry cleaning I see, going somewhere nice?" Derek laughed holding up the mass swathed in polythene protection. "Aye Vic, it's my monkey suit. The boss wants me to accompany him to the Official Unionist Ball at the Park Avenue Hotel this Saturday night. It's a formal affair crammed to the rafters with MP's, people of influence and other rich bastards. I hate the thought of it but it's a slap up feed and free booze. My main goal is to avoid Vivian Chesney who nabbed me last year. She was complaining about something or another but by then I was half cut. I found myself nodding at intervals whilst hopelessly lost in her cascading cleavage courtesy of her low-cut purple ballroom gown. I actually think she enjoyed it. Perks of the job, I guess. Hey Tweety, (shouting in at the man cave) she speaks very highly of you Casanova. Could you be the one to finally capture this fair maiden's heart?" Tweety popped his head out once more and gave one of his most profound responses, "Nope!" Derek laughed and was buzzed through into the main building.

Stevie Uprichard entered Arthur Greer's Hardware Store which was located at the junction of Omeath Street, Woodstock Road. It was no more than five minutes from the station but the heavy rain had done its worst. Stevie was soaked through. Greer's Hardware Store had been there forever. Arthur had long passed and his son Hughie, now 63 was the last man standing and running the place. The hardware store, as with the police station, had been there for many generations. It was the unofficial supplier of all things to Mountroyal Station ranging from key cutting, sundry tools, nuts, bolts and padlocks, fuses, brushes, mops, buckets and all manner of cleaning products for Aggie and Malcolm. Most items were paid for against production of an invoice by the station's petty cash.

A rich industrial smell played with Stevie's nostrils as he gazed around the packed and highly organised shelves. Hughie was stood at the counter smiling. They had known each other professionally for a while. Hughie coughed in, "Morning son, what can I do for you today?" Stevie smiled.

"Morning Hughie, just a quickie. I need a copy key cut and four C-size batteries," Hughie replied, taking the original key from Stevie.

"Two ticks, son."

The pedestrian gate buzzed admitting Pinky, D/I Archie Brown. The walkway to the main entrance was one huge puddle as the rain hammered down.

As Archie entered, two males slipped in behind him. Vic buzzed the huge metal door open admitting Archie and his two followers. Archie was oblivious as he scuffled into the reception area and was buzzed straight through into the main building. He was dying for a draw at Woody his pipe.

Two very sorry looking drowned rats stood at the counter. Vic was taking a call and making notes. One of the males shouted, "Hello, any fuckin chance here!" He was a thirty something skinhead dripping in at six feet plus and powerfully built. Amateurish tattoos adorned his muscular arms. He was wearing a tatty black t-shirt with frayed and holey jeans. Definitely not the designer variety. His ensemble was completed with black DM boots. Vic unperturbed raised his free hand and mouthed 'one-minute mate'.

The second male was similarly dressed only a scale smaller. He had ratty blonde hair and looked a few years older. His stained T-shirt was brown in colour. He was a walking echo. For the inclement weather outside, neither of them had a raincoat. The first male was a man in a hurry, "Yo, ya fuckin black bastard. Any fuckin chance here." He kicked a waste bin, sending it clanging around the reception area. Shorty followed. "Yo, fuck face. Any fucking chance here!" Vic rolled his eyes at the gougers and continued with his call. Tweety disturbed appeared and approached the counter and stood before the pair. "Morning, gents, how may I be of service?" Tweety gazed upon them smiling pleasantly. He gave everyone a chance.

Tweety became aware of a strong stench of cheap booze. Both males were swaying unsteadily, and their broad Belfast accents were plummily slurred. The taller of the pair turned to his mate and burst out laughing. "For fuck sake mate its Cyclops. Didn't know he was working for the Peelers." The second male howled with laughter totally not getting it. Tweety could take stick all day though it bored him. Tweety sighed. "OK, last chance 'Butch and Sundance' one more go then I'm off." The pair saw that he meant it and settled. The taller male spoke. "Sorry officer. We've been told by our brew office (Social Security Office) to report our giro cheques 'stole' so that we can get an emergency hand-out," Tweety feigned shock and horror. "Gentlemen, how terrible for you. Details please. Names, dates of birth and addresses please before we go any further. Take your time. I can see how upset you both are."

The first male spoke, "Jackie Mahood. 6 April 1952. I live at 12 Ohio Street up the Shankill like." The second male flowed in tow, "I'm Eric Magill. 2 September 1948. I live at 3 Malvern Way, same as Jackie, up the Shankill."

Tweety scribbled furiously before looking again at the pair. "And your brew office is?"

They both blurted 'Snugville Street, up the Shankill'.

Tweety held his hand up to his mouth. "How do you pair know your cheques were 'stolen' from different addresses on the same week? How extraordinary?"

Jackie spoke, "Coz we never got them."

Eric, "Aye, we never got them."

Vic had finished with his call and was watching as the scene unfolded. Tweety spoke, "I can see you've taken to the drink in despair. How sad. (Both drowned rats nodded, wallowing in sympathy.) Sadly, you've called at the wrong station. Your reporting area is North Belfast; we are the wise men from the East. Please go to Tennent Street Police Station, 'Up the Shankill' and they'll record a formal statement from you. good luck, gentlemen, if you hurry you'll catch them before they close." Tweety smiled.

The males looked at each other. Storm clouds were gathering. Jackie leant up against the Enquiry office window inches from the smiling Tweety. "See you, ya one eyed ugly black bastard. If you don't record our complaint I'm going to climb in there and rip your other wee mincer out, comprendi."

Tweety whimpered, "Jackie, I thought we were friends. I have feelings you know." The pedestrian buzzer sounded against the gripping tension. Vic looked up at the monitor and could see Perky, big Cliff Boomer enter, stooping against the downpour. He pressed the release button and the main station door eased open. Cliff plodded in unawares. He entered with a grin carrying a small white bakery box secured with fine cord containing the tart and 'cream Charlies'. "Fuck me, it would drown ye out there!" He then realised that there was something afoot. Tweety spoke, "Cliff, this is Jackie and Eric. They're from the Shankill and they're just leaving aren't you fellas?" The three stood in the reception area, the tension ever increasing. It was like a scene out of 'High Noon'. Eric uncharacteristically spoke first, "What the fuck are you looking at granda?" He then kicked the cake box out of Cliff's hand, sending it crashing into Aggie's recently mopped floor. Jackie laughed and jumped on the stricken box which splatted cake and cream all over the reception area, walls included. Tweety and Vic looked at each other and winced. Cliff rolled his eyes and slowly shook his head. There was cream on his trouser legs and all over his shoes. Cliff looked at the pair and said, "Now lads that wasn't very nice. Look at the state of the place. Aggies just cleaned the floor, and her lovely walls, she's going to be awfully upset. As for my wee box of buns, well I'm going to have to head back out into the rain and get some more. Catherine, my boss upstairs has just made the tea and well, she's going to have to make another pot. At least say you're sorry lads like two good Shankill boys." Cliff looked at them with a pleading expression.

Vic and Tweety were on the edge of their emotional seats. The Shankill duo looked at each other and burst out laughing. Jackie snarled at Cliff the smell of dead booze and fags coming from his mouth. He pulled himself to his full height and tensed his muscles looking Cliff square in the eyes. With clenched teeth he snorted, "Granda, do yourself a big favour. Save your life before I knock your bollocks in. You're way too old for this game. Just fuck away off. I want to deal with this one-eyed gimp and his wee fat friend now." Cliff lowered his gaze avoiding any further eye contact.

He whispered softly to Tweety, "Would you page Aggie to the Parade Room please and buzz me out. Thanks."

The buzzer sounded and Cliff ambled out head bowed. Tweety lifted the tannoy microphone and casually announced, "Aggie to the Parade Room please. Thank you."

Alec roared, "Yeow, fuck away off old hand before I put you in the ground." Tweety stood motionless wearing an impassive expression.

"Lads," he said, "you've made a big mistake. I think his feelings have been hurt. He's very sensitive you know. My advice to you both is apologise to him and then clean this place up. If that big man comes in with his jacket and tie off, well, it's your funeral. Don't say you weren't warned."

The two Shankill men were bouncing with rage. Jackie screamed, "You're first Cyclops." Making a dive at the Enquiry Office window. It was at that moment when the partition door opened. Cliff Boomer filled its frame. There was no jacket or tie. He was smiling from ear to ear. Eric turned and laughed. "Hey Granda's back." Cliff walked over to him and in one brutal move lifted him clean off his feet and hurled him into the heavy metal front door. To say he was winded was an understatement. He couldn't find a breath. He ached all over and began blubbering. He was done. Jackie was now scared. Very scared. He was trapped. He launched himself at Cliff, throwing an overhead right. His fist was caught mid-air by Cliff's huge hand and then it began. The squeeze. His balled right fist was getting squeezed with more and more power. Jackie began to dance and jig like a marionette. He became aware of strange screaming and screeching noises before realising it was coming from himself. He also realised he had lost control of his bodily functions and was pissing himself. He heard himself sobbing and crying like a baby begging for the pain to end. All the while, Cliff was smiling and laughing aloud. Like the bully from your worst nightmare. Then it stopped. Cliff was buzzed back out into the main building.

Jackie and Eric were both sobbing on the filthy wet pissy floor glad to be alive. The partition door opened again, and Cliff entered with Aggie. Aggie was carrying a steaming hot metal bucket containing a heavy-duty cleansing product and a mop. Cliff was holding a black bin liner and a wad of paper towels. He spoke in his usual deliberate style. "Aggie, I would like you to meet Jackie and Eric. They've made an awful mess of your reception area. They want to apologise first and then clean it all up. Don't you, boys?" Cliff fired them a look which was enough. Both men jabbered, "Awful sorry Aggie love. We'd love for til clean this up for you." Aggie not used to being centre stage placed the mop and bucket down rubbing her worn hands down the front of her pinafore. She smiled nervously at the pair and said, "Well thank you, fellas, awful kind of ye." and was buzzed back into the main building. Tweety had noted Jackie's embarrassing mishap and had a crew buy a fresh set of skids, tracksuit bottoms and socks from the Dunne's Store on the Ormeau Embankment. It set him back twenty quid which was inconsequential. Tweety's father had taught him something which he never forgot. "If you're big, be merciful." Jackie and Eric strangely set to cleaning their mess up with a sense of pride and when gently probed about their missing stolen 'brew' cheques confessed all. They had cashed their cheques and drank them away. Stevie Uprichard appeared during the mopping up and looked at Tweety with questioning eyes. Tweety mouthed, "later." With a quick thumbs up. Stevie slipped into the Enquiry Office and hastily removed the Vacant Property Register box from its shelf. He quickly opened and then closed it before replacing it to its original location. No one noticed. All eyes were on the clean-up. He was back in the box with Billy Porter a minute later.

Big Cliff returned to Whites Bakery again through the relentless downpour. On his return, he felt guilty at soaking the boy's lovely clean floor. Cliff presented them with a ham and cheese bap and a polystyrene cup of hot veggie soup. Cliff was like that; he never held a grudge. Raymond was sitting in his new gear holding a black bin bag containing his old stinky gear. A strange period of fun and laughter followed amongst all there as the two villains supped at their soup and ate their baps. The phone rang in the Enquiry Office. Vic answered and began nodding, "Yes Catherine, he's here with us, has been for the past ten minutes."

"Eh eh, yes Catherine. I'll let him know right away. Yep, OK. Sorry about that. Bye now Catherine."

Vic looked up at the condemned man. Cliff was holding court and all in the reception area were rolling with laughter. Vic spoke up, "Cliff, its Catherine. She's looking you!" Cliffs jaw dropped open.

Stricken with terror he lifted his box from the bakery and shouted, "Holy fuck. I'm dead. Awful nice meeting you boys. Now buzz me in for fuck sake." Vic buzzed him through and laughed.

Jackie turned to Tweety and said, "Fuck me, I wouldn't like to meet whoever he's afraid of in a dark alley one night!"

They all laughed. Tweety's shoulders rocking with laughter said, "Jackie mate, no truer word was ever spoken."

Tweety had ordered them a cab from Amber Taxis, destination the Shankill Road. When the taxi pulled up outside the station Stevie buzzed through on the intercom. As they were leaving, Tweety approached Jackie and stuffed forty quid in his hand with a wink or was it just a blink. With Tweety you just never could tell. Vic pushed the button which opened the huge front metal door and in the twinkling of an eye they were gone.

The reception area sparkled. Aggie returned for her mop and bucket and gave a critical eye over the clean. Tweety butted in, "Well Aggie, will it do?" Aggie hummed then smiled.

"Aye Tweety. Nat too bad. Sure they weren't bad critters now." Tweety smiling kind of agreed.

Then there were just the two of them. Tweety noted the rain had stopped and a mild warmth pervaded in the air. Vic stretched back in his chair and returned to his Chronicle. He peeked his head up and spoke to Tweety who was standing leaning on his desk with his back to him. Tweety was reflecting. "OK 'Captain Chaos' I have to know. What was with all the kindness to those pair of losers. You bought replacement gear for pissy Jackie and then you stuff forty quid into his swollen palm as he's leaving. Come on out with it?" A few moments passed and Tweety smiled. 'Clair de lune' By Debussy was drifting nonchalantly through the air. Vic and the young Queen Elizabeth were both hanging. Tweety turned to his long standing pard and chum and with his green eye twinkling, he smilingly said, "Vic, it's nice to be nice. It requires no great intellect to be kind but to achieve all of these every day we must first of all be able to love."

Vic went, "Eh!"

Tweety laughed out loud and said, "Sure it killed an hour anyhoo!"

...The Balls Up...
Saturday 28 May...

The armoured Granada cruised cityward down the Bangor carriageway its driver concentrating on the road ahead. Darkness had just fallen and an ice-cold wind was blowing. Another armoured uniformed police vehicle followed discreetly behind; its occupants were all armed to the teeth. The passengers in the Granada were two senior Police Officers. Both high level 'legitimate' targets for the IRA. The senior officer of the two was superintendent George Sewell, Sub Divisional Commander (SDC) of Strand and Mountroyal RUC Stations. The other senior officer was Inspector Derek Grant, A. Section Inspector at Mountroyal. Both were in formal evening dress. Both wore the striking RUC bow tie bearing the forces colours of deep green, black and red stripes. Their destination is the Park Avenue Hotel for the annual Ulster Unionist Gala Ball. There was small talk but mainly silence. The pair had known each other for over thirty years and were good friends. Silence was inconsequential.

The Ball was to start at 8.00pm with drinks and nibbles from 7.00pm. Their Granada eased into Park Avenue, off the Holywood Road, at 7.40pm and approached the rear car park entrance. A uniformed RUC Constable was there, clipboard in hand as an icy breeze clawed at his forage cap. A high level of security was in place. On seeing that it was his boss, their vehicle was waved in with a smile. George and Derek hopped out at the rear entrance and noted a Police Landover in the rear car park. They observed other uniformed officers patrolling the perimeter grounds of the hotel as torch lights darted and ducked here and there searching for anything suspicious. One of the officers had a large Alsatian which was an explosives dog. George and Derek nipped over to the officer holding the clipboard by the rear gate who greeted them both with a 'Sir'. George greeted the uniformed officer, "Evening Bert, fuck me it's Baltic! Are you lot babysitting us two old wankers tonight?" Bert, a senior neighbourhood constable from the strand chuckled. "Yes, sir, that would be our onerous pleasure, all at time and a half! (Overtime.) We've crews out front and back and further crews satelliting the area on QRF. (Quick Reaction Force) As you can see, we have other call signs out on foot patrolling the grounds. I think you're safe enough tonight to enjoy the tea and tiffin." George then had a quiet word with Bert who laughed and nodded in understanding.

"No problem at all, sir, will do."

From the side of the hotel, they heard high pitched shouting and turned to see what all the fuss was. A rakishly thin silhouette in uniform came running towards them puffing and panting, "Constable back to your post. During briefing, I stressed no fraternising with the guests!" George was bewildered, Derek whispered into his ear, "The plank!" George and Derek waited bemused as the plank approached, all six feet of bluster and pipe cleaner. "Back to your post, Constable, I won't tell you again. Gentlemen, I must ask you to return to the Hotel. There is an ongoing security operation going on here and I'm in charge." George and Derek caught each other's eye suppressing a laugh. George spoke, "Very well. Thank you, Constable, will do." George and Derek turned and headed for the rear entrance. They hadn't gone more than a few yards when they heard a familiar shout, "Gentlemen, it's Sergeant Nigel Norwood to you!"

George and Derek stopped in their tracks and turned to face the plank who was marching towards them oozing arrogance. "Now move along, gentlemen, I won't tell you again." George sighed, the plank who was in charge of security hadn't twigged that he was talking with two men wearing RUC bow ties. George, now exasperated, fixed the plank with a glare then spoke, "Sergeant Norwood, since we are into formal introductions let me do you the honour of introducing my friend here. He's Inspector Derek Grant and I'm Superintendent George Sewell your fucking boss!" The plank froze, petrified. His jaw fell open and he began a series of strangled 'umms' and 'aahs'. George raised his eyebrows waiting for a response. Derek looked hard into the ground trying his best not to laugh. The worm had turned. George continued. "Nope, cat got your tongue then Sergeant Norwood. Let me offer this little nugget of information. You may well be in charge of this operation whose objective is primarily my safety and that of Inspector Grant. We're all in agreement that the IRA would love to take us out. But I would presume that an ASU (Active Service Unit) nutting squad would at least know what I looked like, unlike yourself. Bert the constable at the gate knew who I was and was briefing me as to the security because I asked him to.

160

Have I made myself clear, Sergeant Norwood?" The plank nodded, head bowed. George winked at Derek who was shaking his head. He snatched a quick peek at his watch and saw the time was 'Pint O'clock'.

He waved over at the back gate and shouted at Bert, "Thanks again, Bert, see you at the bowling club next week." Bert waved back. Looking at the plank, he couldn't resist it.

"Run along now, run along!" Sergeant Norwood turned and disappeared into the night.

George looked at Derek in despair and said, "What a fucking plank! Right chum, chest out and best foot forward. Remember who you are and what organisation you represent. I'm giving this 100% for two hours then Tweety's picking us up at 9.45pm. Bert's in on this to give us the nod. As far as the plank's concerned, Bert will inform him our sudden departure is a headquarter's matter which will wrap up operations here. We'll be in the Hop House snug for 10.00pm and a deserved nightcap."

Derek swooned. "I love you, George. You think of everything."

George replied, "I certainly do. That's why I brought you. You're my shit deflector tonight. You're here to field any shitty questions that come my way. If Madam Chesney makes a beeline for me, I expect you to throw yourself under her proverbial train!"

Derek sighed. "Now I hate you!" George laughed. "Let's go, there are pints with our names on them." The pair entered and got their hands on a pint and found an innocuous corner to stand in. They were small fry in this gathering.

The night went swimmingly for our pair who remained in the shadows offering small chat through clenched teeth to anyone that passed their way. When the great and the good realised they were only police and of no use they eased away in search of more verdant pastures. An Ulster Tatler journalist was doing the rounds accompanied by a snap happy photographer. George and Derek slippery as eels avoided them like the plague. A very pleasant meal followed, then there were a couple of thank you speeches to party members on their last legs. Finally, the customary charity auction where the 'Big Time Charlies' could show how rich they were by bidding huge sums of cash for tat to the accompanying gasps of the rest of the peasants. George and Derek kept their hands firmly in their pockets. Claptrap and memorabilia fit for the skip was bid for and bought with wanton abandon.

The hour was 9.30pm when it happened. The pair had dropped their guard, taken their eye off the ball. They had after all consumed a few pints followed by a couple of glasses of 'gloopy' red wine with their meal. The simple and undeniable truth was that their eyes were focussed on the winning line and Tweety at 9.45pm.

They heard the unmistakable Chesney shrill. "Oh there you are gents; the night wouldn't be complete without a few snaps with our boys in blue." Chesney approached cutting a swathe through the ballroom floor. Mere mortals parting like flotsam and jetsam in her wake. Unfortunately for the boys, she was stunning in a 'Cruella Deville' kind of way. Her dark hair was flounced up in loose curls held in place with a diamonique tiara and matching earrings. Her face was stunning and had been professionally applicated for the evening, though maybe more of a bordello look than Vogue. Her ballgown of silver and purple sequins left little to the imagination, its plunging front displayed her magnificently appointed breasts and a large split ran from the hemline to just below her underwear. Oh and by the way, she wasn't actually wearing any, her little secret. Her patent black stiletto heels click clacked across the floor, creating the attention she craved. Derek whispered into George's ear, "I most definitely would, yes please, mister."

George replied in the nick of time, "Pull yourself together 'Jell-O Man'."

Cruella or Vivian, had them where she wanted them and motioned Sammy the Tatler photographer in. She spoke to them as if they were a matching pair of bedside table lamps. "Right, you two gents, either side." Which they did meekly and without protest transfixed by her curvaceous form. She thrust her chest into the eye of Sammy's trembling lens and let loose with a dazzling smile. Several flashing light bulb moments later and he was gone leaving the trio alone. Vivian allowed herself a quick sag back to normality and spoke to George for after all he was the big cheese. "I needed that for this week's column in the Tatler. It's to do with the Self Defence Courses for women they're starting up at the Cregagh Technical College. I'm the driving force, what with being a black belt in judo!" George and Derek eyed each other impressed. Vivian continued, "Not that I am exactly, I'm a yellow belt actually or I was when at school a few summers ago." She giggled. "I'm sure I have the police's backing with this one. Call it a joint publicity exercise. You lot are in serious need of a bit of positive publicity. Apparently, some of the women's groups want to see you boiled in oil Commander Sewell. (George wriggled uncomfortably.) Anyhow, it's the best I can do for you until you get this horrible man caught." Derek piped in, "Ah, and that's what the photographs were all about." Vivian smiled, her mission accomplished. She had no further use of the two 'Plods' and had several other fish to tease onto her hook before the night was over. Vivian raised a sarcastic eyebrow and said patronisingly, "Oh Inspector, we'll make a Detective out of you yet." And then she was gone leaving the pair feeling slightly mugged. George was mega pissed at being rolled as well as feeling slightly tarred and feathered. Exasperated, he hissed, "Bitch."

Derek's eyes still locked on her voluptuous ass stammered, "Absolutely, boss."

Bert appeared like a phantom from behind deep blue velvet drapes and gave the pair the thumbs up. Salvation in the form of Tweety Pie had arrived. A minute later the pair were in the back of Tweety's rust bucket, bow ties off and top buttons undone. Mozart was playing softly as George spoke, "The Hop House my good man and don't spare the horses." Tweety smiled. Fifteen minutes later, the trio were in their snug on the first floor of the Hop House. They had the place to themselves. The pair had kicked their shoes off and their dogs were barking. Both were nursing a pint and were knackered. Tweety was on a ginger ale and lime. George moaned, "Infamy, Infamy, those women's groups have got it in for me. I'm doomed, boiled in oil. Oh the thought of it all, I'm ruined." Derek and Tweety chuckled. the boss was getting it in the ear from all directions. George took a long swig from his pint and when he surfaced, he looked pleadingly at Tweety. "Any crumbs of comfort for a grovelling SDC mighty Tweety see-er of all things?" Tweety looked to the ground and sighed heavily. He fidgeted and slithered in his seat which was most un Tweety like. He gazed at the pair, got up and began an anxious lap of honour. Derek howled, "For fuck sake, out with it Tweety. Don't leave us hanging."

Tweety settled and broke the ice, "What I'm going to say makes some sense or no sense based on one thing and one thing only."

George was hanging in there, "Yes maestro, continue."

Tweety carried on. "OK, if our man's a policeman serving at present in our Subdivision then, based on my extensive research he can only come from one Section. If that's the case the field is narrowed down considerably." Derek brow furrowed whispered with dread, "And whose section would that be then Tweety?"

A tense moment lingered then Tweety replied, "A. Section. Your Section and mine, Derek." The three took it all in numb with dread. George spoke almost in a whisper, "What's the no sense bit all about then?

Tweety squirmed again and looked at his mates from a side on view. "Well, all this is useless if he is a policeman from another area altogether. All he would need is to have access to a police radio enabling him to listen in on our net when he's carrying out his dastardly deeds. If that's the case, what's his fascination with our area? Was he raised here and has excellent local knowledge? Maybe he was stationed here in the past. God only knows, I've wrung the knickers clean out of this one."

George heaved a huge sigh searching for any answers hiding at the bottom of his empty pint glass. Looking at Derek he whispered, "Two little un's for the road?" Derek nodded his mind grinding on Tweety's words. George raised a motioning hand to Paddy the faithful barman and mimed his request. Paddy winked in acknowledgement and drew two Bushmills Blackbush whiskeys from an optic. These he bruised with the tiniest drop of ice. The liquid cups of gold were presented to the pair on an old tin tray but looked magnificent. George handed Derek his glass then raised his own to his nose and breathed all the way in. Its rich peaty aroma set of fireworks in his befuddled mind. He then took a reverential sip with his eyes tight closed. "Ahh, there is a God." The deep gold hug slid down his throat and embraced him for a few seconds before releasing him back into the present. Looking at Tweety, George asked the $65,000-dollar question, "What's your best guess maestro?" Tweety looked sadly back at his friend and boss and replied, "Sorry master, me no do guessing." George drained his whiskey and sighed once more, "The good lord giveth and the good lord taketh away. Keep digging, we need a break. Home time gents." The three weary travellers got up and left.

It had just passed midnight as the Value Cab stopped outside 4 Ravenhill Park Gardens. Ms Vivian Chesney struggled like a walrus escaping from a trawler's net as she wriggled herself out of the rear passenger seat. Her tight-fitting gown was made for a more lithesome creature and the catwalk. Definitely not for this less than glamorous taxi ride home. Her driver stole a peek at her cascading boobs and chirped, "Eight-pound ninety, love." Vivian rolled her eyes and handed him a tenner. She leaned forward giving him the best view in the house. "That will be one pound and ten pence change love."

He waited for the usual imbibed response of, "Keep it and thank you." Alas not this time and not with this dame. Up close, she looked to have a sour bake on her, he thought. Her eyes were rolling as the Mexican standoff ended.

Vivian's unwavering palm received her change. The taxi moved off bellowing exhaust fumes into the chill of the night leaving 'Cinders' at the top of her driveway. It was then that the cold air and booze really hit her hard. She abandoned her statuesque strut and 'farmers wifed' it down the drive. Vivian was glad that she had the good sense to leave some of her downstairs lights on. She happily let herself kicking her shoes off in the hallway and tossed her fur coat over the banister. Feeling rather pleased with her evening's work Vivian felt that a nightcap was in order. A brandy and vintage port would do very nicely. Shuffling penguin-like past the front living room door, she headed for the kitchen. Vivian could just make out music playing as well as a steady humming sound. A puzzled look played on her face then was gone with a hiccup and a shrug of her shoulders. She must have left the radio on as well.

From her spotless kitchen, she grabbed a large pint-sized tumbler from the sink and poured herself a strong one. The measures of brandy and port would have felled a rhino but Vivian's greedy gland was in overdrive. Taking a large gulp, she headed for the front living room. Opening its door, she could hear the song *Who's sorry now* by Connie Francis playing and that low annoying humming sound. She moved over to her music system to tweak the volume, setting her tumbler down. Surprised, she realised that it was turned off.

Then an explosion of pain. Punches rained down to her head and body. Her hair was yanked with such force that huge clumps were torn out. The tiara was ripped off shredding more hair and thrown into the corner. Vivian fell to the ground unable to breathe, blood pouring from her nose. Glancing up, she spotted the source of the music. A small tape recorder was sitting on top of the fireplace. Horrified, she found the source of the familiar humming. Her little secret. It was her vibrator. Humming defiantly and mocking her. "Please stop. I have money, jewellery. Have it all," she pleaded. Vivian howled in pain as she was kicked with sickening force to her lower back.

A masked male then eased down beside her breathing heavily. He was all in black and wore woollen gloves. He had her drink in his hand. When he spoke it was with a dark menace? A voice full of hate and loathing, "Well, Lady Muck, to coin one of your phrases, do you know who I am? Well do you, stuck up bitch?"

Vivian sobbed. "Please stop. I won't tell anyone, please just stop. I'll give you anything you want." The male laughed. Her face was now a grotesque mess: a mix of blood, tears and smeared makeup. Mocking, he shouted, "Drink your fill my lady, you're going to need it!" Vivian felt her hair brutally tugged and the tumbler forced to her mouth. She gulped and swallowed, fighting the pain and gasping for breath. When she thought she was finished, he forced more into her. She was completely paralytic. Alcohol and adrenaline soaked with helpless fear was now all that was left of the once proud Lady Vivian. Weak and intoxicated, she slumped to the floor.

Her attacker calmly got up and switched the tape in the recorder. He then pressed the play and record buttons together which meant it was now recording. Standing over her exhausted cowering body, he spoke, "Vivian, I just hate stuck up bitches like you. You don't have to give me anything, because I can just take it. I really don't fancy your chances of telling anyone about all of this because you see, corpses can't talk! Are we singing from the same hymn sheet Lady Muck?" A brutal kick struck her in the chest causing an involuntary screech of pain. The male laughed.

"Do you want to live Vivian? What's it to be?"

She lifted her head slightly and sobbing whispered, "Live, I want to live please." The male laughed.

"You'll have to earn it. From now on, I'm Master to you. Call me Master and obey my commands and you might live. Who am I bitch?" Trembling Vivian looked up at the masked monster.

"You're my master." The male then picked up the vibrator eyeing her all over.

"Right answer, Vivian, now strip for me. Slow and sensual, like a woman that's born to it. Up you get now, show me what you got." Vivian slowly stood up feeling that her humiliation was complete. If only she knew.

The male watched with wide leering eyes as Vivian began to sway back and forth before him slowly undoing the buttons of her gown. He laughed. "Go on girl, let's see a sexy face." Vivian struck a pose as her gown slid to the floor and continued swaying at him seductively.

He laughed out loud, "No fucking knickers on her and boys a dear there's no razors in your house! What a sexy tease you are." She knew better than to stop undoing the clip to her bra, releasing her enormous breasts. Her nipples were hard as his mouth fell open in amazement.

"Don't stop now my lady, turn around. Let's see your wonderful ass." Vivian turned in a slow dancing motion not realising the male was removing his black leather belt. With her back to him, she began to writhe and shake sexily with her hands above her head. The searing pain caused by the belt on her rear was incredible. This was quickly followed by several more lashes to the back. Vivian tried in vain not to scream out as more strikes hit her streaked cheeks. "Do you know who I am Lady Muck?" the male screamed with laughter.

"Turn around, those big hangers are going to get the treatment."

Vivian was going to faint. Her naked body ached and shook like jelly. Her nipples remained hard and much to the males liking. She screamed as the belt struck hard against her soft stomach. She moaned in pain as tears continued to flow but kept going. Many lashes followed. Firstly, on the thighs and then on her breasts. Huge welts began to develop. Her choice was a simple one, satisfy him or die. Suddenly, he growled, "Stop slave that was adequate. We'll finish with a blow job. Make my eyes pop out Lady Vivian. It's your lucky day, because one good turn deserves another; I'm going to give you a haircut while you're performing so no false moves. I would hate to slit your throat so close to the end. Now lick those big scarlet lips and say 'My pleasure, master'.

Vivian sank to her knees before him massaging her aching welted breasts. She was utterly broken, all vestige of pride gone. She would do anything just to live. "My pleasure, master," she stuttered.

Then she began, blow jobs were a thing she excelled at and enjoyed giving, for her it was about the power she felt, but not this time. Closing her eyes, she set to work. Her head was swimming as the alcohol and adrenalin took grip of her body. She was in a dream world, a mixture of terror and the fight for survival drove her on. She could hear scissors clipping and hacking away at her hair as lengths of it fell to the ground around her. Within minutes, she was all but crudely bald. No precision cuts or styling here, more of a brutal sheering. Several minutes passed before Vivian felt him approaching the end but he stalled her one more time. He held her shorn head up and said, "Jesus, woman, you've got my vote at the next elections. Finish the drink off and then you can do the same for me." The glass was placed to her lips and poured. She drank, gulped, coughed and slurped until it was done. She wretched several times trying to hold the vomit down.

A fresh rush of alcohol hit her system. She wanted to pass out, she needed to sleep. Her bald head was then forced back down on him. Everything became a blur as she thrust her head up and down. She jumped as she felt the sporadic searing pain return. More vicious lashes as fresh welts emerged on top of older ones. She was numb to it all now and completely wasted. Then she felt his thighs tighten and stiffen as he arched his body upwards, his buttocks began to clench. "Yes, Lady Vivian, you've got me. I'm coming, I'm coming." He pulled his length out of her mouth and came all over her face and bald head. Vivian waited exhausted. What was coming next? Several moments of silence passed bar the humming of her tireless vibrator. Then the male tidied himself away. He then grabbed one of her freshly exposed ears and dragged her unceremoniously across the floor crawling on all fours to a waiting settee. A cushion was set down and he forced her head onto it. She was on her knees in a kneeling position with her legs spread. Her severely whipped backside was facing the window. "One final touch Lady Vivian. We want you found looking your best, don't we?" Her attacker then knelt down beside her and whispered softly in her ear, "Well Chesney, I know who you are and what you are as will everyone else when they find you like this. Oh the shame of it. What will your God-fearing constituents think? Aww, don't worry I'll get someone out to you. Go to sleep now, you've earned it."

Vivian was done. The adrenaline had gone draining every ounce from her. The drink was still coursing through her and on the rise rendering her a comatose mess. He stroked her crudely shaved head until her eyes dipped and slowly closed. She fell into the arms of a drunken stupor. Vivian began to snore loudly through her bloodied nose making all manner of strange noises. How great the mighty had fallen. The user and abuser herself used and abused. The monster smiled at his work. His final act was to remove one of her earrings and place it in his pocket. This had been the best one yet. Now for another project. Someone closer to home. A sweet innocent perhaps. Someone 'Heavenly'. He turned the tape recorder off thinking of the pleasure it was going to give him and placed it into his green backpack. Moving over to the front window he opened the curtains slightly before leaving. He left the light on for effect. Quietly opening the front door, he checked to see if the coast was clear. All was good. Carefully he placed Vivian's front door key in the outside lock creating the appearance of carelessness. Mission accomplished, he quietly left under the cover of darkness his best friend and ally. The time was just shortly after 1.00am.

Twenty minutes later, Wes Lamont a Police call handler at BRC (Belfast Regional Control.) received a strange anonymous telephone call from a male caller.

"Good evening, this is the Police; how may I help you?"

"Hello, the Police, good. Listen boys, I'm not messing with you. Go urgently to number 4 Ravenhill Park Gardens. Something's happened there. I'm sure you know who lives there. She's never off the fucking television or out of the papers. Make it snappy now."

Wes the call handler continued, "We need some details from you first sir. What's your name, date of birth and address? Also what seems to be the matter at that address?" The caller laughed coldly down the line, then spoke, "Let me give you a clue with this wee song, "How much is that doggy in the window, the one with the waggly tail, how much is that doggy in the window. I do hope that doggie's for sale." That's your lot. Get your asses out there or there will be hell to pay." With that, the caller hung up. Wes put a trace on the call. It came back to a public phone box in Dundonald a 15-minute drive away. The caller on leaving the phone box dropped a key into a drain close by. Wes Lamont checked the electoral register for 4 Ravenhill Park Gardens and his attention was grabbed when he saw that the key holder was none other than Ms Vivian Chesney, Official Unionist MP for East Belfast. Wes, trying not to flap, dispatched the main Mountroyal response crew to attend. He urged the utmost caution and made them aware of the strange clue in the form of the song.

The Mountroyal crew radioed in their arrival at Ravenhill Park Gardens at 1.15am. As a safety precaution, they parked up at the far end of the street. The two men then separated taking to different sides of the pavement. This was a suspicious call and could well be an ambush or as the police of the time called it a 'Come on'. Circumspectly, they made their way towards 4 Ravenhill Park Gardens alert to anything suspicious or untoward. When they met at the top of the driveway, they could see the downstairs front living room light was on and the curtains half drawn. One of the officers remained at the top of the drive while the other officer who was the observer carefully made his way towards the window. It was bitterly cold as a blustering wind threw up twigs and leaves in all directions and buffeting him as he arrived at the window and peered in. What he saw made him shudder. Chesney was motionless in a kneeling position against her settee. She was completely naked. Her back and rear were facing the window. Her shaved head was resting on a cushion. Her naked body was covered in welts and sores. He now got the clue and could see that the scene ha d been carefully staged. "Sweet holy fuck!" was all he could manage before he kicked into action. He burst into the house and checked that Vivian was alive. He heaved a huge sigh of relief when she belched once after he shook her preferring to sleep. He found a duvet in her hot press and covered her modesty. He then radioed a 'sitrep'

169

(situation report) back to Wesley at Belfast Regional Control who updated the log. Wes whispered quietly to himself as he took the details down, "Holy fuck not another one." Wes kicked into action. A Crime Scene was established. An ambulance was called to take care of Vivian. CID and SOCO (Scenes of Crime) were tasked along with a police sniffer dog to have the scene thoroughly examined for evidence and clues. None were found.

As if by magic, the media machine arrived. Cameras appeared and live news reports were delivered. The shit was hitting the proverbial fan and the fan was pointing in one direction only.

Shortly after 2.00am, George Sewell's bedside phone rang causing him to jump. He was momentarily confused and felt slightly groggy. He answered it with a "Eh, what's up?" It was Wes Lamont at BRC. He listened quietly, slowly turning white as Wes gave him the chapter and verse on Vivian. It hit him like a needle full of adrenaline to the heart. He sobered in an instant. His mouth went very dry and his heart started thumping in his chest. "But Wes, I was with her earlier at the Park Avenue Hotel. She was fine th…" George realised that he was jibbering, as did Wes who let it pass. George was briefed as to all the agencies at the scene and was updated as to the media presence. He noticed his hand trembling and caught his reflection of his bedside mirror. A scared old man in striped pyjamas was staring back at him. What felt like a lengthy silence hung on the phone as Wes waited for any instructions. Everything had been taken care of. George found a tone of authority and thanked Wes for his usual professionalism. He finished the call off with the well-worn and hackneyed, 'keep me updated on any new developments'. George hung up and collapsed into his pillow, a cold sweat forming on his brow. He stared at the ceiling for a while then turned his bedside lamp off for there was nothing else he could do. Tomorrow he would have to face the music from many directions. He was after all the Big Cheese, and he knew the buck stopped with him.

He was officially fucked. He forced his eyes shut and whispered to himself, "I'm fuckety fuck fuck fucked!"

Ms Vivian Chesney Official Unionist MP was the latest victim of the sexual predator stalking the streets of her constituency of East Belfast. Just like the other victims, she was both medically treated and forensically examined. When deemed fit she provided a thorough account of her ordeal in written statement form. Her Tatler article regarding her Self Defence Courses for Women ended up in the shredder very much like her political career. She was quietly replaced.

The old Vivian had left the building along with the brash self-serving egotist. What was left or what remained was an insecure wreck of a woman. A woman filled with fear and terror. She would lose all interest in her appearance and life in general becoming a social recluse. Her new diet was a mix of Valium and cheap wine and her once splendid home fell into disrepair outwardly reflecting the total breakdown of Vivian herself. They say when you're down you find out who your friends are, Vivian found out that she sadly had none, reaping what she had so selfishly sown in life.

She held the highest profile of all the females and was the fifth confirmed victim to date. He was reaching the 'Bogey Man' status and women were afraid to go out alone. Vigilantes were out looking for him along with the Loyalist Paramilitaries. In the shadows, he remained protected by the blackness of the night and the filthy bin lined entries.

Unknown, elusive and with every attack more vicious.

Malcolm in the Middle...
Monday 30 May...

A dark cloud hung over Mountroyal RUC Station. Every officer was feeling the heat from the very top all the way down to the very bottom. The rugs had been beaten black and blue and every conceivable avenue exhausted. To date they had been led a merry dance by this monster who attacked the females in their patch with impunity. As yet they had absolutely nothing to show for their efforts. One thing was for sure though the calls for police had lessened considerably especially during the hours of darkness. Folks were staying in, lying low. Especially the women folk, his preferred target. Day time calls were usually a mix of road traffic accidents, minor thefts, sudden deaths and barking dogs.

This particular day was a quiet one. The C6 or Occurrence Book hadn't as yet felt the weight of an A. Section pen. Vic and Tweety were chilling following their brekkie. A tangy lemon marmalade with rind and toast for Vic. Cremated toast skimmed with butter and smothered in marmite for Tweety, washed down with their personal mugs of tea. Tweety had dibs on the radio channel until 9.00am which was always classical stuff. Vic was a radio 2 man. They took turns every two hours. It was 8.15am and the weather outside was as grey and lifeless as the mood inside. Even her Majesty hanging from the Enquiry Office wall looked royally blue. Vic had resigned himself to yesterdays 'News of the World' paper while Tweety fustled about looking for stimulation. The partition door buzzed open and in gilded Woman Constable Stephanie Gates or 'Heavenly' to her mates in the station. Her angelic beauty was beyond compare, she floated in as if on casters. Smiling radiantly, she nodded at the two guards and quietly updated the Accident Register.

Tweety chimed in, "Morning Heavenly, how's it hanging?"

Heavenly looked up and smiled at Tweety, his one green eye twinkling from behind the dark blue lenses of his specs, "Hi Tweety, all's good with me bar a small talk I have to present at the School of Instruction tomorrow before our Late turn starts. The skipper wants me to discuss the subtle differences between 'Behaviour likely to occasion a breach of the peace and good old Disorderly Behaviour'. Oh and lucky me… It's my birthday the following day as well. Just a wee 15-minute talk, nothing too hot and heavy. Any chance of a hand Tweety old pal old chum?"

Tweety's face lit up. Something to do. Smiling broadly, he spouted in his finest Albanian, "*Qiellor, kenaqesia ime absolute.*"

Heavenly laughed aloud. Tweety finished off with, "Heavenly, my absolute pleasure."

Within ten minutes, Tweety had rattled off their legal definitions, their differences, points to prove and relevant stated cases. All this and a closing summary. He was a handy man to know if you had a lesson to prepare for the next day. Such was life for a genius with a photographic memory and several law degrees under his belt. Vic and Heavenly were enjoying a good old chinwag when Tweety quietly handed her a large brown envelope containing her lesson notes for the following day. She smiled broadly at him and mouthed, "Many thanks, chum,." and blew him a kiss. Tweety soared like an eagle for he liked to see this very special girl happy.

The pedestrian gate buzzed open and in shuffled Lionel laughing as usual with his driver for the day Arnie Savage. Both were in stitches. Just catching the gate in time, a third figure nipped in head bowed. Tweety at once recognised Aggies alternate cleaning partner the legendary hellraiser 'NOT', Malcolm Mackie. As much as Aggie was blessed with an abundance of joy and laughter, Malcolm cast a ghostlier figure. Here was a man who was painfully shy, a man who walked the earth in abject terror. Malcolm was somewhere in his early forties. Looking at him, a man on a galloping horse would see a 5' 11" or so male, medium build, slightly swarthy with large doleful brown eyes. He had a full head of lustrous brown hair which was always kept just so. Unless you actually knew him, he wouldn't look out of place in the 'attractive to the female' species box. He was always well turned out with what could be mistakenly construed as a slightly military bearing. Malcolm was an only child and lived with his widowed mother. Sadly, she was in declining health, and he was her full-time carer. They lived in a compact semi five minutes from Mountroyal Station in Roseberry Gardens. He had been job sharing with Aggie for the past five years and his meagre wage was a life saver at home.

Malcolm was as previously stated painfully, painfully shy. He was very popular with the station party but was a gift for a wind up or the odd caustic comment due to his crippling shyness. The women folk in the station protected him from the naughty boys. Catherine Mercer the CID Admin boss kept a very tight rein on the CID gang especially Pinky and Perky who could get carried away with themselves. As far as A. Section was concerned Heavenly and Shelley afforded him the utmost protection. To them Malcolm was fawn-like, a Bambi type figure. They just wanted to mother him and take him home. He was a hard grafter and was a match for Aggie in the cleaning stakes. When he had his immaculate overalls on, he was at it nonstop. His head was always contritely bowed, and his sad brown eyes fixed firmly to the floor. Here was a man in total fear of the merest form of social intercourse. For Malcolm, eye contact was a strict no no. He enjoyed, if enjoyed is the correct expression, a 30-minute break for his lunch which he took in the Rec Room. He would sit in a chair in the corner facing a blank wall afraid of any form of human interaction, his legs jigging up and down with nerves. This was when Malcolm was at his most anxious, for here he was a sitting target. Many tried to befriend him, bring him out of himself with idle small talk and the likes. All topics such as current affairs, television and sport were tried on him but ran helplessly aground. No one could find the key to unlock the splendid isolation Malcolm existed in. He had one small pleasure in his terror ridden life though, he loved his music. Anything melodic or uplifting. His sole companion and best friend in life was his little tape recorder. You would hear his tunes about the building and know that Malcolm was in the vicinity grafting hard ever the unsung hero. Nobody ever heard him hum, sing or whistle and as far as a 'Tra la la' was concerned dream on.

Malcolm did have an enemy in the station. Someone who quietly sabotaged his work every now and then. These happenings only ever occurred when A. Section were on. Occasionally, a room he had just cleaned and left spotless was found with the contents of an ashtray or the like tipped over the floor. This stressed Malcolm out as it reflected on him. He was terrified of losing his job and worse still having to speak to someone about a mess he hadn't tidied. He was therefore in the habit of continuously checking and rechecking rooms he had cleaned. He mentioned these events to Aggie once and she assured him nothing like that had ever happened to her. Malcolm then figured it was personal and that someone had it in for him but didn't have the foggiest as to why. A while back he returned to the male locker room shortly after cleaning it. He met Stevie

Uprichard at the door who was just leaving. Malcolm eyes down let him pass. Stevie grunted, "Shift your ass weirdo, some of us are busy." On entering the locker room, Malcolm found it trashed and reasoned as to who the culprit was. From that moment on Malcolm kept a watchful eye out for Stevie Uprichard and all of his strange comings and goings.

Tweety and Vic also kept a lookout for Malcolm and greeted him warmly that day as he arrived. Malcolm nodded at the pair and stole the swiftest of looks as the faintest glimmer of a smile played on his lips. Vic hit the buzzer freeing the door to the main station. As the door opened, Heavenly cried, "Hold her open there, Malcolm. Let's you and me have a wee cuppa before you start." Heavenly floated out of the Enquiry Office and threw her arm over Malcolm's shoulder disappearing towards the kitchen. Arnie Savage had a pop. "Our Malcolm's a regular babe magnet, wish I knew what aftershave he wears." He had a wee chuckle to himself. Lionel suppressed a laugh, "Aye that's right Arnie, all you need is a splash of Malcolm's après rasage lotion and 30 years' worth of anti-aging cream and you might be in with a chance."

The Enquiry Office erupted just as Sergeant Tony Speers sauntered in from the main building. If his troops were happy, he was happy. Smiling broadly, he said to the gathering, "Too much merriment methinks. Back out on to them mean streets the lot of yez." The partition door buzzed again from behind him. In bounced the lovely Shelley. She had been out on the beat with the Preacher and what a couple they made. The Saint and the Siren. Shelley was less elegant than Heavenly but no less attractive in an alter ego kind of way. Heavenly being the Dom Perignon to Shelley's Bucks Fizz. Shelley lumbered into the centre of the gathered throng looking every inch the beautiful beast of burden. She was wearing her forage cap which was slightly askew adding to her natural allure. A heavy duty flak jacket with metal plates front and back, underneath a dull green dartex raincoat and her green woollen skirt. Clear tights and black polished shoes, no heels, definitely not permitted. She rested her backside on Tweety's desk and whipped off her cap revealing her jet black hair tied back in a bun and her gorgeously animated face. Shelley was never one to beat about the bush and with her fun was to be found a short twinkle of the eye away. She flashed a brilliant smile at Tony and then drawled, "Sergeeeaaanntt."

Tony responded immediately, "Definitely not Shelley, 100% no." Shelley laughed with excitement. "But I haven't even asked you yet. You see, I was just planning a wee birthday surprise for Stephanie tomorrow. Well, tomorrow's not actually her birthday it's the next day but we're on rest days then so tomorrow's the only time we can do it. The gang are all in on it, we just need your permission."

Tony felt slightly uneasy feeling himself slowly being sucked into a vortex. "Go on then." Shelley's eyes widened. "The plan is for when she's doing her wee talk at the school of destruction tomorrow. We'll have a tape recorder hidden away running quietly for her first ten minutes or so, then George Formby's going to blast in off the tape singing Happy Birthday. (Her brilliant blue eyes flared with glee.) Catherine and the CID gang are up for it. They will have the tea and tiffin ready and a candle lit cake. They will bring it all down when they hear the singing. Pretty pretty please, what do you think Sarge? Are you up for it? Come on, she's a wee pet. She'll love it. Say yes…" Tony felt all the gathered eyes on him made worse by the Preacher who buzzed in and eased next to him. Their eyes met, the Preacher smiled his eyes laughing. "She's got you by the short and curlies, boss." Tony blurted out, "George Formby, have we nothing better, and what about the Inspector. Has anybody rolled your cunning plan past him?" Snap went the trap. Shelley's eyes sparkled with 'Gotchaa, Inspector Derek says it's down to you Sarge. What do ya say then?" The earth had stopped spinning awaiting Tony's response with baited breath. His eyes darted around the sea of expectant faces, "All right all right then. Shelley, it's all down to you. My only condition is we're all done and dusted for our Late Section briefing. And that includes all the tidying up."

Shelley leapt from the desk and threw her arms around Tony's ambushed shoulders. She thought about planting a smacker on his lips but decided against it. She was going to quit while she was ahead. Looking up at his terrified face she cried, "Best wee Sergeant ever. Malcolm's on tomorrow and Aggies coming in for the birthday surprise. Between them they've kindly offered to tidy up, so all's goodly good good great. I can't wait to see her wee face." She released Tony from her clutches and spun around winking at her adoring fans. "Come on Preachy Baby, there's crime to be fought out there on them mean streets of darkest East Belfast," Shelley planted her forage cap on at the same jaunty angle as before proving that it was no fluke but a fashion statement. The Preacher smiled, shaking his head, "Lead on girl wonder." The dynamic duo departed through the heavy front door with the Preacher following in tow. As they approached the pedestrian front gate, Shelley turned her head back to him and said perkily, "Preachy, does this skirt make my ass look like the size of an elephants. What do ya think?" His comeback was priceless.

"Not on your Nelly our Shell, not on your Nelly." The Enquiry Room erupted with laughter. The Preacher shot a thumbs up for the benefit of the camera as they disappeared from view headed for them mean streets.

Tweety loved these priceless moments of friendship and fun. It was the glue which forged tight sections who got going when the going got tough. Malcolm smiled from the stairwell he had been polishing with his usual pride. In his own way, he was one of them. For they were all a rag tag band of brothers and sisters during those dark days of terror, conflict, fear and uncertainty. They were all very much in it together. Lionel shaking his head and still laughing spoke to his skipper, "Sarge, that's those bail checks done. They were all in and well behaved. We've stopped a few out there but no one even comes close to fitting the bill of our man."

Arnie chipped in, "Aye skipper, for what it's worth, the punters are giving us mega grief about what we're doing about it all and why haven't we caught the bastard. We've got the C.I.1 forms done on all of our stops."

Tony frowned. "All we can do is try chaps. Keep casting your nets. We might just strike it lucky." Lionel nodded and headed out the heavy front door, Arnie shuffling close behind. "Onwards and upwards, Arnie my son. Onwards and upwards."

And then calm. Tweety twiddled. Vic went back to the News of the World. Tony was scribbling a few lines of his own in the A.6 or Accident Register when Inspector Grant buzzed himself in from the main building. He cautiously stepped into the Enquiry Office giving nods all around. He looked about warily to see if the coast was clear, and once more for good measure before he whispered to all present, "Gents, can you keep a secret?" This was all very strange. Three sets of ears nodded slowly wondering what great secret of the universe was going to be revealed. Derek was like a man on a mission. A supreme mission which was about to end. Checking around one final time, he carefully withdrew a large brown envelope he had secreted inside his tunic. He then tossed it onto Vic's desk and leapt back like a man released from a great burden. Vic looked up at him puzzled, eyes searching for further enlightenment. Tweety was loving the suspense of it all. This was all very un-Derek like. Tweety caught Tony chewing a smile. Derek squeezed a supressed sentence out, "For fuck sake, check the envelope out. Open it up, you great numpty." Vic felt himself tighten and gulped as he flipped the top open. His eyebrows raised as he quietly examined its contents. There were 20 black and white photographic stills of a beautiful young long-haired woman. She was completely naked and in various elegant poses. These images were obviously taken in a professional studio and done in an artistic manner. Nothing smutty here. Vic smiled and handed them to Tweety who nodded in appreciation. He was into classical art and these were very tastefully done. Tweety spoke as he viewed the images before handing them across to Tony. "Very nice work. Nothing crude or lewd, quite spectacular actually. These weren't taken yesterday, Inspector. What's the story?" Derek shrugged. "I dropped a file down the back of my cupboard yesterday and when I pulled the brute back to retrieve it, I came across this little envelope and its delicious contents. It could have been there for years. That's as much as I know."

The partition door buzzed and Heavenly entered, catching the four art critics red faced and red handed. Derek wanted the ground to open up and swallow him whole. Anyone but Heavenly! Tweety's lenses steamed up as he flustered and flapped with the stills he had. She had a file in her hand and walked over to Tony who was holding several of the nude images. Tony hanging tough casually said, "Look what the Inspector found down the back of his cupboard yesterday." He then casually held them out to her. She gave him a puzzled look and took them from him. "Oh my goodness," Derek squirmed.

"Oh my my." Vic and Tweety were melting from embarrassment. Heavenly took Tweety's batch and carefully studied each image. "Well, aren't these just beautiful. Amazing camera work and what a stunningly beautiful model don't you think?" A sweeping wave of relief hit the office as each man fought for air space spewing forth 'Absolutely'. And 'Perfect use of light and shade'. Finishing off with 'True art at its finest'. Derek gathered himself together and said, "I really didn't have the foggiest what to do with them, still don't." Heavenly looked at the four males and smiled. "Well, they're from a different era. Historical nudes and breathtakingly beautiful. Don't you dare throw them away. That would be a sin."

The partition door buzzed again, and Malcolm entered head bowed as usual. This time, the four men and Heavenly panicked. Vic slipped his images under his newspaper, Tony blindly followed suit. Derek stuffed his down his tunic. Tweety delirious sat on the blank brown envelope for no good reason at all. Heavenly could do no better than hiding hers behind her back offering her widest smile. "Morning, Malcolm," they all inharmoniously chimed with cheesy grins usually saved for raiding apple orchards. Malcolm completely unawares was struck with terror. Five people launching themselves at him all at once. Horror of horrors, one of them was the station Inspector. Malcolm trembling whispered to the room, "Morning all." And began to nod his head up and down at breakneck speed. Still looking earthward, he set his tape recorder on the Enquiry Office counter and planted his thumb awkwardly on the play button. For a few seconds, the musical strains of 'Tie a yellow ribbon around the old Oak tree' by Tony Orlando filled the now deafening silence. Then the cassette tape mangled itself on the recorders turning spools screeching and wailing before grinding to a strangled halt. For Malcolm, if there was a hell he was in it. He lifted his head up and glanced at the mangled tape in his precious recorder. Pressing the stop button put an end to the strangulating strains but alas he was too late. Popping the eject button, he discovered that not only was his favourite tape mangled, but it had also snapped. It was during these fleeting moments of despair and disaster, while poor Malcolm's back was turned that the images were all hastily returned to the safety of the large brown envelope. He would be none the wiser. He forlornly turned to the gang shaking his head, his pleading sad eyes looking even sadder. He spoke the following words which for Malcolm were a soliloquy. 'Me tapes fucked'.

Syrupy sweet condolences and support came from all corners of the room. Something was afoot but Malcolm just couldn't figure out what. *They're being too nice, he thought*. Heavenly spirited towards him, "Ohhh poor Malcolm. Your lovely music, how we'll miss it for the rest of the day. Won't we, boys?" The faintest fracture of a glare followed, spurring the boys into spasms of nodding and, "We sure will!" Malcolm crestfallen tidied the Enquiry Office in deathly silence.

There would be no warning of Malcolm's imminent arrival that day. For that was the day Malcolm's music died to quote from another song. Malcolm finally departed leaving the five mulling over the latest turns and twists of events. Out of the blue Vic came in a bit off keel and abstract, "You gotta admit he's a bit weird."

Tweety looked at him with his one good eye, "Who?"

Vic let out a groan, "Malcolm for fuck sake, Malcolm. Who the fuck else is weird around here?"

Tweety, rather wounded replied, "Well, the plank for starters. What about that wee bollocks out in the box, Mr Sweep aka Billy Porter and as for Stevie Upritchard! He creeps me out at times. I always get the feeling he's just half a cog out."

Vic nodded slowly. "Fair point, Tweety. It didn't take a genius to work that one out."

Derek laughed. "No, it didn't but he did!" They all shared a titter. Vic pressed on. "Okay, guys and gal, we've all had a butchers hook at those racy pics. What do you think our Malcolm would do if he had the opportunity for a quick peek?"

Heavenly ever protective of her Malcolm got her oar in first. "I know Malcolm, he would run a mile. He wouldn't be into that sort of thing. No way."

Tony mmmd into the fray. "He's a flesh and blood man. I say he'd sneak a peek given the chance."

Derek nodded. "Agreed."

Heavenly cocked an eyebrow at him to which he responded, "Just saying."

Vic hummed and haa'd. "Na, he's too odd. Besides he'd be too terrified to take a butchers." He then looked across to his faithful pard, 'Tweety?'

Tweety sighed. "There's only one way to find out. Lay a sting for our Malcolm. We can take bets on it. Those who think he would versus those who think he wouldn't. The CID gang would love it; even Catherine I'll wager. Losers buy the winners a drink at our next Eastenders soiree. Oh and by the way, I think he would cop a butchers. Well, what do we all think, are you all on board the Malcolm train with me? I have a cunning plan running around in my head and I just think it might work."

The Enquiry Office was deadly silent for a few seconds, but it felt like ages, then Derek got the ball rolling, "I'm up for it. I've got to know. Would he or wouldn't he?" Heavenly shrugged. "Me too I suppose. Only to prove my point though. For no other sordid reason." She gave Tweety a cheeky wink. Tony jumped in, "Let's do it for scientific research!" They all laughed. Tweety's cunning plan was simple. The sting would happen the next day while the Section were on their Lates. The racy images would be left on top of the Sergeants briefing desk in the Parade Room creating the illusion they'd been accidentally left there. They would be displayed so that only the top half of several of the images would be showing. The beautiful siren would be tantalisingly peeking out, luring and offering more delights from the vaults within the brown envelope.

The Parade Room was directly behind the Enquiry Office and could be observed through a tiny serving hatch located in the radio store to its rear. The hatch was seldom used and was a left over from a bygone age. Its tiny wooden doors were held closed by a simple snib which had several coats of gloss paint slapped over it. Vic's Swiss army knife and a bit of elbow grease soon had everything up and running again. Tweety's cunning plan was to use this hatch as a secret viewing point for the sting. The hatch opened by the smallest margin would give ample sight of Malcolm's actions, good or bad.

Malcolm was a creature of extreme habit. In today's currency, he would comfortably lounge on the autistic spectrum. Back then, ignorance sadly surfed on its own blissful wave and to common folk he was just plain weird. You could however confidently set your clock by him. Malcolm started his cleaning in the Enquiry Office and vigorously worked his way around Mountroyal Station never wavering in his order, approach or routine. He would always finish with the Parade Room. Everyone gradually became aware of his routine and also that the kitchen was the last room he cleaned before arriving there. Therefore, it was a simple matter of placing the stills on the desk just as he was finishing up in the kitchen. Tony and Derek would casually keep an eye on Malcolm's progress the following day. When it came to the kitchen, they would masquerade by way of taking turns making coffee or washing dishes. When the time was right, they would signal for the stills to be displayed. Vic who was in the 'Wouldn't Camp' and Tweety who was in the 'Would Camp' would silently observe the unfolding drama from the darkened radio closet behind the ever so slightly open hatch door.

As the day rolled on, the plan was relayed to the rest of the section members as they came and went. All perused the images giving them a better picture so to speak, while Vic and Tweety canvassed hard for their particular side. By the end of the shift, it was eight votes apiece. Tweety's 8 'Woulds' including himself were, Derek, Tony, Lionel, Stevie Uprichard, Billy Porter and last but not least both Pinky and Perky. Vic's eight of 'Wouldn'ts' consisted of himself, Heavenly, Shelley, Catherine, Aggie, Gary Weaver, Wee John and the Preacher. Malcolm seemed to have cornered the female vote. All would, like the salacious images themselves, be revealed.

While bomb scares, bombs and murders were running riot that particular shift, the security forces men, women and associated civilian staff at Mountroyal were coping magnificently. Whether they were heading to a murder scene, dealing with a bomb call, attending a road traffic accident, standing at a cordon or standing in a Security Box, only one thing was on all of their minds...Malcolm, would he or wouldn't he. Freud and Jung were espoused coupled with dashes of nature versus nurture. The seductive Salome who danced into the pants of King Herod and got poor John the Baptist beheaded found its way into the debate. By the end of the shift, two participants had switched sides. Billy Porter switched to the "'Wouldn't' side. After some serious sweeping, he bought into the argument that Malcolm was a sweet innocent, as pure as the driven snow. Nothing bad or untoward had ever been said about him. Equally, Saint Malcolm had never uttered a bad word against anything or anyone. Shelley was the other turner; she went from the 'Wouldn't' to the 'Woulds'. Her switch was less considered than Billy's. When challenged, she proffered the acronym, "AMAB, and dirty one's at that!" All men are bastards. The Wouldites were a bit hurt at that one but secretly couldn't disagree with the sentiment.

Shelley had organised the loan of Stevie Uprichards tape recorder for the birthday surprise. He was aware that Tweety would need it for the following morning. At 3.30pm, thirty minutes before the end of their shift, he darted into the empty locker room. He quickly fed the numbers into his combination lock and opened his locker door. Looking around, he grabbed his recorder and saw that there was a tape inside. He pressed the play button checking to see which tape it was as well as to gauge the strength of the batteries. His recorder burst into song shattering the silence. Stevie quickly hit the stop button and then eject button whispering to himself, "No no no, silly boy." He lifted the tape out of the recorder and checked there was nothing written on it. Stevie then dropped the tape into a pedal bin at the entrance of the locker room. He quickly placed a brand new C60 tape fresh out of the wrapper into the recorder. All was sorted. He secured his locker again and made to leave with his tape recorder under his arm. On leaving, he collided into Malcolm at the doorway who was making his way in. Malcolm had been doing his customary final checks whilst leaving air fresheners in each cleaned room. Tony was startled. "For fuck sake, Malcolm. You nearly gave me a heart attack. Out of the way, you creep." Malcolm mumbled apologies as Stevie barged past him, nearly knocking him over before disappearing downstairs. Malcolm warily entered the locker room nervously expecting to find some area trashed. He lifted his normally prostrate head and gazed anxiously around.

There were around fifty or so lockers which were set out in aisles. Waste pedal bins were positioned at the end of each aisle. Malcolm walked each aisle expecting to find a mess somewhere. Everything seemed fine. The last possible place for sabotage would be the bins. He had emptied them all and placed fresh bin bags in them not more than ten minutes previously. With every tentative check, his mood brightened. Everything was fine and dandy as he approached the final pedal bin located by the door. Malcolm pressed his foot on the pedal and the lid sprung up. "Empty thank fuck. Uprichard or UBastard hasn't done any trashing today!" Then Malcolm caught sight of the tape cassette nestling at the base of the fresh bin liner. He reached in and gently pulled it out. A C.60 tape. No writing on it. Malcolm was puzzled not for the first time that day. He carefully examined the tape from every angle, even holding it up to the light. It looked fine. He could stick an hour's worth of tunes on it, if it worked. Excited, he dashed down to his tiny storeroom and hurriedly placed the cassette into his recorder and pressed the play button. Malcolm's face lit up like a child on Christmas morning as one of his favourite tunes played. The tape already had tunes on it. Malcolm was delighted. The day for him had been a bit too topsy turvy but it had ended on a good note or notes. Wearily, he got out of his work clothes. Tidied everything away in his locker. Put his overcoat on and left the station and home to mum. Head bowed eyes down.

The following day would be an 183ctionn packed one. The duty sheet had A. Section down for a school of instruction starting at 12.00 midday followed by their Late Shift at 3.00pm and terminating at 11.00pm. But there was way more to it than that. Tweety had to get the George Formby rendition of Happy Birthday recorded at Aggies house before the school of instruction began. Stevie had handed him his tape recorder fully loaded just before close of play the previous day. The batteries had been checked and all was good to go. Tweety had arranged to call with Aggie at 10.30am that morning. He had already run the tape silently for ten minutes leaving it ready for the Happy Birthday recording as planned. All went swimmingly and a dummy run went without a hitch. The tape when played from the beginning was deadly silent for its first ten minutes and then George Formby crashed in, ukulele and all with his cringe worthy rendition of Happy Birthday. Aggie loved it and gradually so too did Tweety, whatever would Mozart have thought!

Heavenly's stomach was doing summersaults. It was the monthly school of instruction at Mountroyal RUC Station and her entire section was present including her new sergeant, Sergeant Tony Speers. Tony was sat in the back row with his feet planted firmly on the floor. His feet were covering the tape recorder which was playing, its tiny spools quietly turning the tape through its first ten minutes of silence. Even looking at him made her nervous or was it excited, she wasn't at all sure. He was looking very serious to her not realising Tony was filled with tension, terrified of giving the game away.

Her task was to deliver a short talk on the difference between a Breach of the Peace and Disorderly Behaviour. Her mouth was dry, and her knees were knocking. She smiled at the sea of faces waiting expectantly. All they could see was a vision of serenity. The old parade room had taken on an entirely new presence. It now felt more like the Royal Albert Hall, and she was the main act. She caught a glimpse of the wonderful Tweety. He gave her a faint nod and a thumbs up. The Preacher was smiling up at her the way he always did, exuding his usual carefree warmth and simplicity. Stephanie always felt safe when he was around. Shelley was tapping at her wristwatch smiling broadly and then mouthing, "Any fucking chance." She giggled, took a deep breath and began. Heavenly to the gathered throng exuded a quiet confident class. A mix of grace and elegance and a subliminally powerful sexual attraction. She worked confidently from Tweety's template firstly giving the legal definitions of each of the offences. Then breaking them down outlining their differences. She was relaxing now and getting into a flow, allowing herself a little light banter during some questions and answers with the gang. Tony sitting at the back began to chill. His job was nearly done as the clock ran quietly down. He unclipped his tie and undid his top button while gazing at Heavenly quietly thinking to himself, "A woman very much to be loved." The Preacher smiling from a different pew looked upon the same beautiful vision. "If only you knew Stephanie." Gary Weaver and Lionel caught each other's glance. Lionel mouthed, "She's pretty good." Gary thumbed up to that. Wee John let it wash over him, he was on twenty quid an hour. Billy Porter bored, fidgeted and scratched at his dense thatch of blonde hair. He hated these classes. They had nothing whatsoever to do with him. He forlornly gazed out of the Parade Room window jealously watching the last of the cherry blossoms and ragged leaves dancing and darting mocking him from outside. Arnie Savage the senior constable in the section knew the offences inside out. He was simply enjoying the view and wishing he was twenty years younger and Heavenly was looking at him while wearing the female equivalent to beer goggles.

Heavenly noted Stevie Uprichard in the front row. He was the only one taking notes and seemed genuinely keen. She smiled at her star pupil now and again, grateful for his interest. Tony too was impressed by Stevie's attitude and made a mental note to finish off his report recommending him for the regulars. He had shown him more than enough.

Stevie Uprichard was on top of the world. He felt as though it was game set and match with regards the regulars. If he played his cards right, he might make the depot before the end of the year and shut the fat bitch up. From behind closed eyes, he sneered at all the ass holes around him. If only they knew. Stevie smiled sweetly at the Heavenly Stephanie. She caught it from the corner of her eye and smiled right back mid-sentence. Stevie's imagination took hold as he eyed her up and down. The things he would do to her given half the chance. Who knows, the way she was eyeing him she might just be up for it? His mood darkened as he watched her beautiful lips moving and how her smile lit up the room. What he imagined that beautiful mouth could do. Stevie mentally hit her mute button and was lost in a dark fantasy watching that sexy mouth and those beautiful lips. He was snapped back into the present by the Parade Room door bursting open. In entered a stern-faced Inspector Grant.

The room fell silent. The colour drained from Heavenly's rosy cheeks as Inspector Grant took a seat at the front of the class. He spoke in a clipped tone. "Pray continue with your lesson Woman Constable Gates. We're all here to learn." Derek was fit to burst; he had got in just in time. Heavenly now felt sick as she cleared her throat and took a breath. Suddenly, the musical strains of George Formby and his plucking ukulele exploded from the tiny recorder. A large cheer followed accompanied by everyone in the room standing and singing 'Happy Birthday' to her. The shock nearly killed her and then the tears came as she realised the whole thing was a set up. Shelley bounced up and gave her a massive hug and shouted, "Gotcha babe!" The pair shared a teary embrace. Seconds later the CID gang arrived with the tea and tiffin. Archie or should we say Pinky was beaming as he carried in a huge candlelit chocolate cake. Its top was adorned with a pair of angel wings crafted from icing. He carefully placed the angelic cake on the sergeant's desk and stepped back motioning for the deed. Heavenly skipped up to her cake and in one huge blow put out the candles to another rousing cheer. She held up her hands and shouted above the din, "Thanks, gang. You're all so kind. What a wonderful surprise."

Catherine then kicked into action. She was masterful in quiet delegation, and everyone had a cuppa and a plate of assorted goodies in a jiffy. Derek and Tony high fived which a teary eyed Heavenly spotted then shouted, "I'm going to kill you pair, just you wait." They laughed, shaking their heads feigning innocence while pointing accusing fingers at Shelley. Aggie who had been hiding in her store room excitedly appeared on hearing the cheering for no station party would be complete without her. Along with Catherine, she was one of the matriarchs of the station and part of its heartbeat. Their value and worth with regards to their kindness and love was priceless. Pinky and Perky plates piled high grabbed a quick hug before disappearing back upstairs but would soon return.

Tony, Shelley, Stevie along with Tweety ended up alongside Heavenly just before the party ended. Tony, draining his tea, smiled at Heavenly and asked, "Well, what's the birthday girl up to tomorrow?" Heavenly smiled. "Oh, same as last year Sarge, same time, same place. Excuse me a second, Aggie wants me." Heavenly drifted over to Aggie who was beginning to clear up. Tony noticed the pair shedding a tear and a hug. Malcolm appeared head down. He was flanked by Pinky and Perky. Big Cliff Boomer chuckled. "He thought he'd get away with it. Come on, Malcolm, you're part of the team." Malcolm was touched and quickly shuffled over to the two women. He wished Heavenly a Happy Birthday before thrusting a bunch of late blooming daffodils at her. Both women cried again and threw their arms around the horrified Malcolm. Big Cliff saved him with a plate of sarnies and a cup of tea. Looking at Shell, Tony said, "OK, what's with all the tears between Aggie and Heavenly. They didn't look like happy tears to me?"

The usually bubbly Shelley sighed, a wave of sadness gently arrived. She gazed up at him, her beautiful blue eyes never looked more serious. "Sarge, they share a unique bond. They've both lost the men they loved too soon. Aggies Alec never returned from the Second World War and well, you know about Ozzie. That's what she meant when she said about tomorrow. Stephanie visits Ozzie's grave on her birthday and has done so since he was killed. She makes a point of being there with him at 2.00pm. That was about the time he was taken, if you know what I mean. It's a lovely wee quiet graveyard just on the outskirts of Comber at the All Saints Church of Ireland Church. It's on a lovely plot down at the back wall with a lovely view of Scrabo Tower and beyond. It's so quiet and peaceful. There's never a sinner about. I expect because it's so old. I've offered to go with her, but she insists on going on her own. Anyhow, we're meeting for dinner at the Clandeboye Lodge tomorrow night. I'll get her laughing, don't you lot worry."

Tony nodded. "You're a good woman, Shelley, and a great wee friend. There's more to you than meets the eye." Shelley laughed. returning to full on Shelley mode. She leaned towards him in a playfully seductive pose. Tony was scared. "And don't you forget it Sarge… Any chance of files tonight?" They all laughed. Malcolm and Aggie began the clear up as the curtain came down on

Heavenly's Birthday surprise.

In the background among the white noise, Stevie Uprichard gathered his trusty recorder from the back of the Parade Room. He slowly made his way upstairs and returned it to his locker. He stood quietly facing the outside window, lost in thought while the cogs in his head turned. An opportunity was presenting itself to him. He was uber confident and felt invincible. He was in possession of all the facts. He had a date, time and a place!

The Late Section briefing was carried out at breakneck speed. Time was of the essence if Operation Malcolm was going to run. Tony sprinted through the notable occurrences in their patch since they were last on. Areas out of bounds and stolen vehicles and or vehicles of interest quickly covered. Break times and most importantly the code for the outcome of Malcolm's actions which would be released over the air one way or the other. The agreed code was simple. If Malcolm behaved and resisted, a message would go out to the AM70 crew from the Enquiry office that a Mrs White would attend the station the following day. If, however, he transgressed the message would be the same except it would be Mrs Black. White for good and Black for bad. The message would be heard by all of the other call signs working on the AM or Mountroyal net. The world record for a section briefing was shattered. The briefing started at the usual time of 2.45pm. By 3.00pm, all of the call signs were out of the station and on the ground.

The excitement was palpable. Every time AM70 were called, everyone's ears pricked. Those left at Mountroyal section wise were Tweety and Vic who were the official observers. Shelley, the spare wheel in case someone attended the Enquiry Office at the critical time. Finally, Derek and Tony who patrolled the station corridors keeping tabs on our Malcolm. Come 4.00pm, Tony bumped into Derek in the downstairs corridor. Malcolm was at his penultimate pit stop in the kitchen. Derek mouthed, "I'm going in to see what's what." A quick thumbs up and he was gone like a deep-sea diver plumbing the depths. Malcolm was vigorously wiping down the surfaces when Inspector Derek Grant entered. Malcolm floundered. He didn't like flying too close to the sun. Inspector Grant offered him a warm smile. "Malcolm, I can't tell you how grateful we were for all your help at Heavenly's surprise today. It was most kind of you." Malcolm didn't know whether to stop with his frenetic wiping or continue with his chores. He chose discretion and continued with his frenzy, head bowed, "No bother Inspector Derek thought he saw the semblance of a slight smile. Derek should have gone into amateur dramatics. "Well, the station's gleaming, I take it this is your last room?" He knew it wasn't. Malcolm growing all the more uncomfortable blurted out, "Na, Parade Room in a minute and that's me all done." He was exhausted with all the effort of talking. That was good enough for Derek. "Good good. Good man yourself. Well nice talking to you. We must do this again sometime. Bye now!" Malcolm looked up. "Bye." Bowing his head again then back into his polishing. Derek darted into the Enquiry Office like an excited school girl. "Everyone to their positions he's about to hit the Parade Room. Vic, where's the fucking stills? STILLS, STILLS, HURRY?"

Vic whipped the envelope out of his drawer and thrust them into Derek's outstretched hands. Not a second was wasted. Derek darted out of the Enquiry Office and into the Parade Room. On arrival at the Sergeant's desk, he calmed himself. He then carefully placed the envelope on the desk and slowly eased several of the images out forming a collage of naked nectar. A beautiful face here, a pair of breasts there and a hint of buttocks all on display. He gazed over at the hatch where Vic and Tweety were secreted and smiling gave the thumbs up. From behind the hatch, he heard the muffled giggles and a 'Perfect'. Derek quickly galloped back to the Enquiry Office and squeezed into the cubby hole with Vic and Tweety. Moments later, Tony and Shelley arrived. Shelley had a light bulb moment and whispered a further cunning plan. They loved it, which had them all in fits of laughter. Normally, two bods were a tight squeeze but five! They were packed in there tighter than a can of sardines. Heads were squeezed above each other like a weird totem pole while their bodies were twisted this way and that. All for a better view. But it was sneaky, exciting and giggly hilarious.

Malcolm was exhausted more emotionally than physically. Too much interaction, must do better at avoiding people he thought. He entered the Parade Room unwittingly like a lamb to the slaughter. His cleaning paraphernalia in tow clanging, his weary head as usual bowed. All eyes were on him from the sweaty cubby hole as he shuffled past the desk and plugged his knackered hoover into the socket. The windy contraption squealed into life like a wailing banshee. Shelley, overcome with excitement began to giggle uncontrollably which set them all off. The cubbyhole was roasting and felt more like a steam room. Beads of sweat appeared on their strained brows made all the worse by their attempts to stop giggling. Fortunately for them, the hoover's screams drowned their repressed laughter. Head bowed and oblivious Malcolm rocked the hoover this way and that slowly edging closer to the table. Tweety whispered encouragement, "Come on, Malcolm, it's now or never me old son."

He could feel Shelley's heart pounding against his rib cage and Tony breathing down the back of his damp neck. Tweety gulped as Malcolm arrived at the table and suddenly stopped. He slowly looked at the envelope and its scattered contents for what seemed like ages, then switched his banshee off. Malcolm had taken the hook. The silence was deafening. If anyone laughed now the game would be up. Cramps were arriving like buses and their hearts were thumping like Lambeg drums. Malcolm slowly lifted the brown envelope. Like a heart surgeon his fingers delicately entered and withdrew several of the images. His mouth dropped open and his eyes doubled in size as he ogled the naked pictures. Derek whispered "BINGO! OK Vic, Shelley, do your stuff." Both crept out of the cubby hole. Vic to the tannoy system and Shelley to the other side of the Parade Room door. Malcolm was now parked on the desk inadvertently sitting on top of the brown envelope. He was like a kid in the eye candy shop. There were stills on the table, a few more resting on his thighs and some in each of his sweaty hands. The three amigos Derek, Tony and Tweety were about to explode, if they caught each other's eye they would burst into laughter. Derek fixed Vic with a thumbs up and a nod.

Vic roared down the tannoy, "Malcolm the cleaner to the Enquiry Office please. Malcolm to the Enquiry Office pleaassee." Malcolm leapt like a trout, his heart exploding sending salacious stills floating off in all directions. On cue, Shelley swung into the Parade Room catching poor Malcolm clawing at the air frantically. She stopped in the centre of the room with her hands on her hips. Her face had formed the 'I'm very disappointed in you Malcolm Expression'. Malcolm had been caught with his hands in the honey jar and he knew it. Of all the people to walk in on him he anguished. "They must have fell of the desk." He frantically flapped, wriggling and squirming. Shelley ascending in her Oscar winning role gazed at the images lying around all four corners of the Parade Room floor. Malcolm was now scurrying around picking them up and shoving them back into the envelope. Shelley tut tutted. "Malcolm, Malcolm. It would take a bomb to have gone off for those pictures to have been scattered to where they ended up. I take it you had a little peak?" The cubby hole three had never so unlaughed as hard in their entire lives. It was exhausting. Malcolm looked up at Shelley's raised eyebrow and confessed.

"Just a wee peak. Please don't tell on me!" Shelley smiled, for she had a heart of corn. Enough was enough. She took the envelope from the shaking Malcolm and pecked him on his pounding forehead, then whispered into his ear, "Our little secret!"

A few moments later, a radio transmission sounded from Mountroyal to the AM70 crew and all the other players involved eagerly listening in.

Alpha Mike70 from Alpha Mike, for your information Mrs Black will attend the station tomorrow.

Smiles and chuckles appeared on the faces of each of the crews. For a brief moment, the darkness and dangers of their shift had lifted. Then with grim determination their focus returned. Answer their calls and stay alive until the end of their shift. Then to get home was every police officer's simple aspiration.

Malcolm was loved no less, perhaps he was loved even more. For as it turned out, he was human after all.

...Cheers Bud...

Debbie Dean entered. "Boss that was Sir Jacks' secretary. Your attendance is requested at Knock Headquarters tonight at 7.00pm. Surprise surprise, he's looking for an update on the attacks. The Official Unionists brought the matter up at Westminster yesterday. The Prime Minister, Margaret Thatcher was present. Not good, not good at all. My God George, what are you going to do?"

(The Chief Constable Sir John Hermon was affectionately known as Sir Jack.)

It was 9.30am in the morning but for Superintendent George Sewell it felt like midnight during a power cut. All the lights were off, and he could see no way out. He was dog tired. His desk was strewn with the daily rags all ripping the shit out of him and his officers. Debbie was worried. These attacks had taken their toll on her normally spritely and upbeat boss. They had aged him. He now looked old and sick with worry. George forced a tired smile.

"Jesus Debz, we have nothing new to offer. I'm for the chop, the high jump, the garbage can, the shredder, take your pick. Thirty plus years on the job and all I'll be remembered for is this cluster fuck."

Debbie wrung her hands with anxiety, "Don't say that, George. Anything from Pinky and Perky?"

George shook his head. "Nada, I'll give them a call before lunch. I might need a few pals at the HOP House tonight, post lobotomy." Debbie smiled at her boss.

"I'll make you a wee cuppa. I've got your favourite tea cakes in." The large wooden door closed behind her leaving George alone with the silence of his inevitability.

It had just gone 11.30am. Bud and Preacher had just returned from a dander around the shoreline. It was a soft spring morning and the dew was comfortably settled on the rough waspish grass. Tiny white and purple blooms had arrived

191

and birdsong was on the up as summer drew near. Between them they had gathered a mass of washed-up kindling from the shore. Bud proudly sauntered just a few paws ahead carrying several branches in his soft receptive mouth. Preacher was lost behind a bundle of weathered branches which he carried with his usual ease around to the back of their home. The wood was then deposited into his shed where he had constructed bays for different sizes and lengths. Bud gently lay his largess at his master's feet and was rewarded with a heavy-duty scratch under his smiling drooling chin. Pete was off on rest days for the next two days and there was nothing he liked more than to spend it around the house. He was unshaven which strangely suited him. It gave him a Grizzly Adams come disciple appearance. This look was accentuated by his mass of curly hair which went crazy the damper the air was. He sported a pair of well-worn denim shorts, a navy t-shirt and a pair of trainers that had seen better days. Wood chopping was next then a quick dip in the Lough with Bud followed by eggs and bacon on the griddle with fresh loaf. What more could a body ask for.

Mountroyal CID Office was not the place to be if you were looking for a laugh. Archie or should I say Pinky had just been off the blower. He felt rotten. The Sub Divisional Commander George Sewell, not only his boss but his good friend had been on. He had asked him for any positive updates regarding the attacks. Usually Archie would have the sun, moon and stars to hand but today all he had were grovelling apologies. Nothing. Nada, rien. He would've felt much happier if the boss had given him a proper bollocking. Beat him up a bit, chewed him out. But George had been gentle with him and thanked him for all his efforts. He had told him he was for Knock Headquarters at 7.00pm that evening. A meeting with Sir Jack. Archie released a heavy sigh. His boss was to be the main course on the menu. For George Sewell, it was to be his High Noon and the gallows. Big Cliff, normally king of the wisecracks, had listened in and was silent. It was a sad day for the boss and the subdivision. Catherine Mercer the CID Office Manager breezed in with a tray full of forms. She was humming a fetching melody under her breath. Looking across at the two dinosaurs, she could see that the form wasn't good. Catherine knew from experience to let sleeping dogs lie. She took to her desk and started into her crime stats softly humming away. Archie reached into his blazer pocket, time for woody his pipe. He loaded it up with his St Bruno tobacco and put a match to it, sucking and puffing vigorously until it took. The aroma and the hit lifted him, giving him fresh resolve. George needed him and he was going to give it all he had with what little time they had left. He gazed at the clock on the wall. It had just gone 12.30pm. He looked across at his big mate who resembled a wet weekend in Bognor Regis.

"Come on, you, let's go through these fucking witness statements one more time. We'll divi them up. Maybe we missed something. George needs us!"

Heavenly left her idyllic home in Groomsport just after 1.00pm. The warm spring air against her cheeks and lemon haze slowly shifting from the quaint harbour went unnoticed. Stephanie's mind was buzzing not hearing the soulful cry of the lonely seagull high above. A quick glance at her watch told her she had plenty of time. She had ordered a bouquet of yellow and white roses from Penny the village florist. They were the colours her and Ozzie would have had at their…well, you know. Her heart was particularly heavy as she had arrived at a major decision in her life. It had been three years since Ozzie's passing and she hadn't moved on. She was feeling more and more like the Charles Dickens character Miss Havisham from the *Great Expectations* novel. A woman cruelly jilted at the altar. Dickens wrote of a woman in terminal sorrow. A woman who wallowed in her personal misery never taking her wedding dress off. A woman for whom time had stopped when she was so cruelly jilted. With Ozzie's death, Stephanie too had been cruelly jilted by a murderous fate. However, things in her life over the recent few months had slowly changed. She couldn't quite put her finger on it, but it had definitely started and had something to do with the arrival of the new Sergeant. There was just something about him. The handsome Tony Speers was not her type at all. No, definitely not. It's just those little things she noticed. Like the most mundane of interaction with him that had her heart inexplicably fluttering. She knew he wasn't trying anything on with her, quite the opposite. He had been funny, supportive and very kind. But! Then there was the Preacher. Pete was also gorgeous but in a different way from Tony. Whenever he was around, she felt wonderfully safe and totally at ease. She didn't want to be anywhere else. They totally got each other. They shared the same interests and a shift with him always passed far too quickly. When the shift ended, she immediately missed him and then the fluttering started when she thought about him.

Looking at Malcolm the other day made her realise that they were no different. Each kept their heads down afraid to look up. Both afraid to face their futures. Stephanie was now seizing the day and looking up. It was now time for her to embrace her past without ever forgetting or regretting it. It was also now time for the angelic Stephanie to move on.

Her home in Groomsport would be put on the market and she would start afresh. She knew if Ozzie was looking down, he would wholeheartedly agree. She was both excited and sad at the same time. She called in with Penny and picked her bouquet up shortly after 1.25pm. It would take her no more than half an hour to drive to All Saints Church of Ireland church just outside Comber and to the grave site of her beloved Ozzie.

Malcolm was hoping for a less stressful day. Well, nothing could have been worse than yesterday. Shelley had caught him on literally, with his trousers down around his ankles gawping with those naked pics. God how he cringed every time he thought about it. Thankfully, 'A' Section were on rest days. 'C' Section were on now and they weren't a bad bunch. So far, they had left him alone and were none the wiser about yesterday. The only worry he had was that horrible Sergeant from Strand RUC Station. He was on an overtime turn and doing the early shift with them. "Head down, Malcolm, head down. Let's get through the day with no hassle."

Malcolm was slightly pissed, the cassette tape he had rescued from the bin in the male locker room yesterday had only two tunes on it. He had assumed wrongly that the tape was fully loaded because when he tried it out on his recorder before quitting yesterday one of his favourite tunes played. "That's where assuming gets ye," he growled.

After some serious thinking, Malcolm came up with a doable solution. He figured that he could play the two tunes in each room he cleaned. He would then rewind the tape afresh before starting into his next room. It wasn't ideal but fortunately they were two crackers. One from yesteryear and the other bang up to date. Importantly for Malcolm, it was company and way better than nothing.

Malcolm got stuck into his work accompanied by his deadly duo of melodies. His faithful listeners or latter-day groupies about Mountroyal had become accustomed to Malcolm's wide and varied playlists. They actually enjoyed his stuff unbeknown to his good self. They cocked ears and raised eyebrows of bewilderment as the same two tunes repeatedly floated through the station heralding his presence along with the clanging chimes of his mop and bucket.

In the Sergeant's Office, Sergeant Norwood was reaching the end of his usually short tether. He had taken up residence at Tony's desk for the day and had been swivelling in Tony's precious chair. Sergeant Norwood or the plank as he was called was making good use of his time. He was feverishly going through Tony's vaunted call up registrar. Angrily, he snapped one of Tony's brand new pencils several times for badness and tossed it in the bin. "Where the fuck is that shit coming from?" His tether furiously went twang when he realised Tony's motley crew were outperforming his in every performance category. Fuming, he sent Tony's 'precious' swivelling chair into the corner as he bounced out of the office. "Mr Music Man is going to get it with both barrels!"

Big Cliff or Perky was eating his lunch at his desk. A round of Mothers Pride plain white bread with ham and mustard sandwiches. They were the size of doorsteps and had been made by his own fair hand that morning. If that wasn't enough, he also had a pastie supper from Eddie Spence's Chippy on the Beersbridge Road. He had tucked a load of chips into his already massive sarnie and polished them off with a deep grizzly sounding, "Mmmmmmmm." Archie sashayed over to his buddy's desk and helped himself to some chips.

"You know, Cliff, you're one greedy fat bastard so you are. You didn't need all them chips. They'll give you a heart attack, mark my words. I'm only trying to help you out by eating these for you. No thanks required."

Cliff rolled his eyes replying, "You're too fucking kind wee man."

Catherine lifted her head from her Woman's Own and giggled at the antics of the pair of old stagers. Then she heard the music coming from down the corridor. It was the same tune as the mornings. She loved that tune, one of Rosemary Clooney's best and began softly humming to herself. Archie by now had fired up Woody and was subconsciously joining in. He was no Nelson Eddy. Soft billows of St Bruno settled in the room and like vinegar affected the flavour of Cliff's chips. He raised his eyebrows and pushed the remainder over to Archie who dived in. Cliff had his Daily Mail crossword spread out on his desk. He only had two more clues left to get before he felt he had truly achieved something for the day. Archie ganneted the chips then disposed of the empty chip paper then jigged his way back to Cliff's desk. Cliff knew what was coming but hung tough. Maybe this time it would be different, he hoped. Archie leaned over his desk unwittingly blowing plumes of smoke in Cliff's stoic face.

Chewing hard on woody, he peered at the puzzle. "Struggling today, are we Einstein?"

Cliff sighed. "Nope today would be no different."

Archie smiling. "Catherine love, he needs a wee pull out, his facilities aren't what they used to be. Come on over and give the old duffer a hand."

Catherine giggled. "Archie, stop picking on that wee fella. Do you need a hand there, Cliff?"

Smiling through clenched teeth and mentally waving the white flag, he replied, "Why not Catherine, the more the merrier." The two clues were intensely studied. The first was three across and had seven letters.

Its clue was, "Manifest, evident. What Cliff had so far was O_ _ I _ S. The second clue was five down. It had eight letters, it's first letter was the second letter of three across. Its clue was, eyes repeating themselves, especially when tired. It looked like this to the three cruciverbalists. _ _ I _ K _ _ G." It was then Cliff realised they were all humming that tune. The same tune whose notes were playing from Malcolm's tiny recorder and drifting in from the corridor.

Malcolm had made his way to the top of the stairs after having filled his metal bucket afresh with scalding hot water. He then carefully added the correct dose of lemon smelling bleachy disinfectant stuff. His recorder had been rewound for the fifth time that day. He pressed the play button and started to rhythmically mop his way towards the CID Office. Connie Francis's velvety voice began to play with Malcolm's heart strings. He was all of a flutter as she serenaded him with those timeless words of 'Who's sorry now, who's sorry now. Whose heart is aching for breaking each vow'. Suddenly from behind, the serenely lost in music Malcolm, came a roar which reverberated throughout the station. Malcolm jumped in the air knocking his bucket for six sending water everywhere. It was official, Malcolm was now a red-hot contender for the British Trout Leaping Squad. This was his second record breaking leap in two days.

He turned to find Sergeant Norwood trembling with rage.

"You there. Little man. Switch that garbage off. Who gave you permission to play it anyway?"

Malcolm's heart had just returned from his mouth as he jabbered, "Awful sorry. I'll switch it off."

The sweet sound stopped just at, "Who's sad and blue, who's crying too." Malcolm was a very big yes on both those counts as well as being very very sorry now!

Big Cliff was now very pissed. Was it too much to ask to have your lunch in peace while doing a wee 'crossi' without being surrounded by Thomas the tank engine, a tit warbler and world war three going on out in the corridor? He rolled his eyes and began to rise from his desk when the pennies began to drop. His eyes focussed on the two testy teasers and then the answers leapt before him in more ways than one.

His lips began to move as the white noise continued from the corridor outside.

"Good Holy Fuck. Wee man, follow me. BLINKING OBVIOUS, it's BLINKING OBVIOUS!"

Catherine frowned, "Now now Cliff, no need to swear like that. It's only a crossword after all."

Cliff laughed. "Three across is OBVIOUS and five down is BLINKING. Ha ha, BLINKING OBVIOUS. Follow me wee man, this could be very important."

Archie bewildered then chuckled. "Ah Big Man, no flies on you well done. I take it all back. Where we going?" Cliff smiled and tapped the end of his nose twice and winked.

"Catherine, stick the kettle on. Tea for three and one for your good self if you fancy a cuppa." Catherine knew better than to ask.

Out in the corridor, Sergeant Norwood was lost in his own frothy raging importance. He was tearing poor petrified Malcolm a new ass.

"Hand me that tape. No more unauthorised music for you. What a ruddy nerve. This is a police station, not a bloody discotheque." A bear of a laugh caught him quite by surprise. He spun around ready to dish out more punishment to whoever the joker was. He gasped when he saw the man mountain of a man standing before him grinning broadly. Cliff smiled down at Malcolm who was holding the cassette tape in his trembling left hand.

"Come with us Malcolm, we need a wee chat. Catherine's got the kettle on." He placed a comforting hand on Malcolm's shoulder and gently took the tape from him. Ignoring Sergeant Norwood completely, he led Malcolm towards the CID Office. Archie was standing motionless at the CID Office doorway puffing hard on woody utterly intrigued.

Sergeant Norwood exploded with rage. "How dare you. I'm not finished with him yet. Give me that cassette tape this instance, you big ape. Do you know who I am?" Archie stopped his puffing and gulped as Cliff like a massive train pulling into a station eased to a stop. It was then Sergeant Norwood noticed a wall of back muscles tense from behind Cliff's cotton shirt. Then the leviathan slowly turned. The smile was gone, replaced with something much darker. Then Cliff growled deep, guttural and foreboding.

"What did you just call me?" Malcolm kept moving, his nerves jangling until he reached the safe waters of Archie's side. Cliff then slowly began to walk towards the arrogant Sergeant with the newly found death wish. He repeated his last which rose from his depths to a roar, "What the fuck did you just call me?" Archie whispered to Malcolm under his pipe.

"Not good. This is going to end in tears for that wee pip squeak."

Catherine who was now standing just inside the CID doorway whispered to Archie, "Do something, Archie. Big Cliff will kill that wee arse hole."

Archie nodded. "Another few seconds, my love. It's been a while since I've seen him lose his rag. He never fails to scare me shitless." Sergeant Norwood had turned white with fear. He opened his mouth, but his tongue was tied and his tiny brain had turned to mush. Then the words tumbled out. "I ca, I called you a big ape. I'm sorry. I'm so very sorry. Please accept my heartfelt apologies." Big Cliff stared down at him with a brutal brooding expression. Sergeant Norwood could hear his heart thumping nine to the dozen, his Adam's apple felt like a cricket ball as he awaited his fate. And then just like that the storm clouds passed, replaced with only the faintest of breezes. Big Cliff let go with a huge roar of laughter and began slapping the hapless sergeant on the back. The plank thought his back was going to break as the pounding continued. Grimacing in pain, he nervously smiled back.

Still laughing and slapping, Cliff shouted, "Apologies accepted. No hard feelings eh. By the way, I believe you're called Sergeant Plank. Put it here partner." Cliff held out his huge right hand and smiled looking into the plank's petrified face. Sergeant Plank's knees were gone as he looked into Cliff's eyes which were now full of dark menace. Reluctantly, he placed his tiny childlike hand into Cliff's catcher's mitt. Within seconds, he felt the squeeze come on. Archie grimaced and whispered over at Catherine, "They've made up. Big Cliffs shaking his hand." Catherine put her dainty hand to her mouth, "Dear Lord, not the handshake. Don't look Malcolm." But Malcolm was in seventh heaven as slowly the pressure of the grip increased. It started with a slight jig as the merry Cliff joined in. "Well, Planky me old chum, I just love listening to Malcolm's music about the place, don't you?" The plank was fighting hard not to scream out and was now limbo-ing up and down this way and that.

"Well, I…" The squeeze increased to agonising proportions as the plank screamed out like a boy soprano. Big Cliff laughed out. "You're hilarious, what did you say there?" The plank was now po-going for all he was worth before finally screaming out, "I love it. Yes indeed I just love listening to your music Malcolm. Hearing it playing around, the station just makes my dayyy! Please let go now, you're breaking my fucking hand. Pleeaasee!" But Cliff didn't stop nor did his grip lessen. This particular bully was getting some long overdue medicine and he was going to remember it for the rest of his service. "Please let go. I'm begging you. I'm in agony."

Cliff released his hand causing him to snap back into the wall. He fell to his hunkers fighting back the tears holding his hand up to his chest. He then shuddered as Cliff lowered his face to his ear and whispered to him, "I've met your type before sonny. Your sort inevitably gets themselves killed but not before getting those around them killed as well. I've heard all about you and your shitty antics from a lot of different sources. A wee word of advice son, wise the fuck up. Now apologise to Malcolm here. If I hear one more tale about you, I'll come and fetch you, and the pain you're feeling now will feel like a hug from your favourite aunty compared to what I'll dish out to you. Do I make myself clear?" Sergeant Norwood, shaking, nodded.

He looked up to Malcolm and whispered, "Sorry Malcolm, it won't ever happen again." Cliff gave him one final snarl before disappearing into the CID Office to join Archie, Malcolm and Catherine. Sergeant Norwood was badly shaken by his near-death experience. He retreated to the Sergeant's Office and there he remained for the rest of the shift.

Inside the office, Malcolm was greeted by Catherine who had always been nice to him. She sat him down in one of the office recliners. It was the first time he had ever been in the office that he hadn't been cleaning around them largely unnoticed. Strangely, it was the first time he took in the perfunctory décor and adornments, the family snaps and the Benidorm pen holders. Human hugs amid their world of death and fear. Before long, he was supping a cup of tea and enjoying a slice of boiled cake along with the gang. Archie lightened the air with a few jokes and bantered away with Cliff for several minutes before Cliff waggled the cassette tape at Malcolm, "OK, Malcolm, what can you tell us about the tape. What's the story morning glory?"

Malcolm panicked in case he had done something wrong and blurted out, "I didn't do nothing wrong. I got it from the men's locker room bin yesterday. Someone had just thrown it away. Me own tape had got mangled yesterday and I couldn't believe my luck when I suddenly found it there. When I tested it, I was glad there was tunes on it, though I didn't know til today that there was only two tunes on it."

Archie came in, "Relax Malcolm, nobodies saying you did anything wrong here. We just want to know as much about the tape as possible. You said there that someone had just thrown it away. How do you know that?" Malcolm looked at the faces intently looking at him and was glad that he had real answers for them. He smiled up at them with a hint of pride. "Cos I'd just emptied them bins and replaced the old bags with some new bags about five minutes previous. I came back to check my work because someone in 'A' Section has been messing my work up of late." Archie and Cliff shared a brief raised eyebrow. Cliff growled, "Not very nice, Malcolm son. Any idea who?"

Malcolm beamed, "Absolutely. It was that bastard Stevie Uprichard. He's been trashing my work of late and he was coming out of the locker room with his tape recorder yesterday as I was going in. They used his recorder in Heavenly's birthday surprise you know. That's when I found the tape in the fresh bin bag. As I said, I only just put the fresh bag on some five minutes previous." Cliff nodded slowly and looked across at Archie who had gathered the strands of the situation. He smiled at Malcolm who was sporting his usual worried demeanour. "Malcolm me old son, we can't thank you enough. We'll need to keep the tape and borrow your recorder for a couple of hours if that's OK. One final favour before we record a witness statement from you. Show us where Stevie Uprichards locker is?" Malcolm's heart soared as he got up from the recliner. He felt ten feet tall.

Smiling at Catherine, he softly said, "Thanks for the brew and cake Catherine. It was lovely so it was." Catherine smiled back with that 'You done good' smile she could give. As the pair were heading for the door, Archie called out, "Hey Malcolm, just in case it's important, what was the second tune?" Malcolm laughed. "Youse old fogies. It's one from Tavares. Great wee disco tune. It's called 'Heaven must be missing an angel'." Pinky and Perky froze. The title wasn't lost on them. Cliff grabbed Malcolm by the arm. "Quick Malcolm, where's his locker?"

Tweety had left his French doors open. A soft breeze played with his net curtains, gently lifting them up then setting them down. Tweety had mowed his lawn that morning and the smell of freshly cut grass was amazing. His assorted scones were just out of his beloved Aga Range cooker. The smell was divine as it canoodled with the rich aroma of his Kenyan coffee beans clacking away in his percolator. All the prep work was done, and his patio table was waiting in its finest dinery for the guests to come. Bach danced with the darting breeze adding to the atmosphere. It was a ritual that had evolved from the time Tweety arrived in the street. Once a month or sometimes whenever the chance presented itself, Tweety and his neighbours would meet up and enjoy each other's company. It was nothing pretentious though his guests had a lot of ammo to be pretentious about. His neighbours were all elderly and had been considered important in their respective fields at one time. They were all 'pretentious-ed' out. Tweety's chums wanted nothing more than to impart their gardening latest and share their latest preserves on his revered scones.

Hilary Grimason was first to arrive ringing the front doorbell as she always did. Outside of the job, she was his best friend. Hilary was a retired Physics Professor and lived two doors down. Although in her seventies, she was young at heart and had all the curiosity of an impish child. Tweety answered the door with a smile and a big hug. Today, he was wearing a dapper green and pink Hawaiian shirt. Scruffy denim shorts and lime green flip flops. Hilary laughed at his sartorial elegance seeing the delight dancing in his brilliant green eye obscured behind his dark lenses. Shaking her head and laughing hard, she gasped, "Dear God Tweety, who puts on you in the morning?" Tweety leading her through to the back chuckled.

"All done in the best possible taste, darling." Just then, his phone rang, shattering the idyll.

The preacher had been chopping hard all morning. His woodshed was full but he had kept going such was his joy. It was such a beautiful day, and he was high on life. Gazing all around him, he appreciated his wonderful home and the beautiful scenery. Probably at that exact moment in his life, he would never be happier, fitter or stronger. Bud felt much the same. He was chewing on his favourite stick with his smiling eyes fixed on his master. That was all he needed.

"Come on Bud fella, time for a swim," Pete whipped off his navy-blue t-shirt and kicked away his knackered trainers. Bud stirred. Pete then made a frantic dash for the old jetty at the front of his home. Bud let out a gruff like bark. Pete made the jetty all singing and dancing with Bud in hot pursuit. Bud caught up with him in no time, barking and bouncing with unbridled joy. A final scream rang out as they both leapt off the jetty crashing into the freezing waters of Strangford Lough.

Stephanie parked her silver fiesta in the tiny gravel car park facing the old church and graveyard. Memories squeezed into every emotional square inch she possessed. Happy memories of her and Ozzie. Love and laughter and dreams of a future together never fulfilled. She could see him in her mind's eye, hear his countrified voice and smile at the sound of his ridiculous infectious laughter. Throwing open the doors of their past, she could almost smell him. Sighing and sitting quietly alone, Stephanie opened her tear saddened eyes to this moment and to her new now. Entry to the graveyard was through an old wrought iron gate, weathered by tears and the ravages of time. It was lying expectantly ajar. Stephanie, numb with sorrow felt as if Ozzie had gently opened it for her, as if he had been patiently waiting for this moment too. It was time, time to set each other free.

Tony rolled over onto his side squinting in the low light trying to catch the time on his 'Tag Heuer' watch. "Jeez, it's after twelve. Holy fook!" his black out blinds had done their job. In normal circumstances, they helped him sleep during the day when he was on his night shifts. He felt really lousy, his mouth was as dry as an Arab's flip flop. His poor head was pounding. It had hurt less when he was clobbered with the pool cue a couple of weeks back. "Saved by the Preacher," he gruffly mumbled as his eyes slowly focussed on a spent bottle of Cava lying on its side on the floor. A further two empty Faustino whites lay close by. All death traps for the comatose waddler, he thought. From the depths of his charcoal grey duvet a beautiful smiling brunette's face surfaced. They must stop meeting this way he thought. It was Doctor Chloe, his nemesis. He was trying really hard to walk a more virtuous path. She had turned up unexpectedly at his front door last night with hardly a stitch on. Shivering, cold and wet from the rain, bearing gifts, she was, a diablo pizza and a carryout of booze. What else was he to do? In a humanitarian leap, Tony graciously let her in. And the rest as they say is history.

"That's it there." Malcolm stood back and pointed out the locker. Big Cliff rolled his eyes and growled. "The one with the fucking combination padlock... JESUS FUCKING CHRIISSTTT! I don't suppose by any chance you happen to know the combin...?"

Malcolm shook his head wearing his best 'are you fucking mad' expression, "How would I know the combination. I hate the fuckin bastard and he hates me.

Anyhow he's always creeping about like a lounge lizard. He keeps his locker secure at all times, others don't bother their arse." Cliff blew a fuse and gave the locker an almighty boot. The ceiling shook. Gathering his composure, he looked at Malcolm smiling, "Sorry bout that. I'm a wee bit tense today. Follow me." They left the locker room and scurried back to the CID Office. As they entered, Cliff barked, "Wee man, get Tweety on the blower we need his brains as a matter of great urgency." Archie didn't hang about. He knew the number off by heart.

Still smiling at Hilary, Tweety picked up the ringing phone. "Sweetlove residence. How may I be of assistance?" Tweety mouthed his apologies to Hilary who happily let the rest of his guests in as they arrived. Tweety repeated the same mouthed apologies to them all urging them to carry on without him. Holding up his hand smiling broadly he indicated five minutes. But this was all a façade. Tweety was in turbo mode as Archie relayed the morning's events. His face was set like stone as he listened intently. He nodded gravely as Archie accounted for Malcolm's fortuitous recovery of the tape. He smiled quietly when Archie explained how the tape could only have been there for a couple of minutes and who was last seen leaving the Locker Room. When the two tunes were mentioned, he gasped and Tweety never gasped.

Cliff leant in over the top of Archie's shoulder and whispered into the mouthpiece, "We need into his locker Tweety and it's a combination bastarding one." Tweety smiled. "It's 1,9,2 and 8. Don't insult me by asking. Check it out, hurry. I hope I'm wrong. Chop chop." Archie and Cliff darted back to the locker. Archie carefully fed the combination into the padlock. "Bingo you big bollix we're in." It contained the usual locker stuff but tucked away at the back of the upper shelf in behind a shoe polishing kit Cliff recovered a men's black toiletry bag.

He pulled back the zip and began to rummage, "Holy fuck, dear good God, aww no, no no!" Archie looked at his big pal's frantic face and cried, "Big man, what is it?" Cliff was rattled. "Get me the list. The stuff the bastard took off the victims. Hurry! Is Tweety still on hold?" Tweety was sat in the hallway with his phone wedged between his ear and his shoulder. Hilary not taking any nos for an answer had brought him out a china cup of earl grey tea. It was accompanied by a cherry scone to die for, smothered in raspberry jam freshly potted by Beryl, one of his guests. He was becoming a master of the mimed conversation as he thumbed up, winked and rubbed his belly in a circular motion while all the while formulating a vital course of action. Malcolm was sitting in the office holding the phone aloft bridging the divide between Pinky and Perky and Tweety Pie. He felt a sense of pride. He would never walk the earth with his head bowed again. Cliff and Archie appeared back in the office with the black toilet bag. Catherine had retrieved the list from the casework and began calling out the items as Cliff matched them off from the bag. Vivian Chesney's earring was there along with poor Dot's 'T' shaped necklace amongst all the other trophies. Big Cliff grabbed the phone from Malcolm. "I take it you heard all that Tweety. It was that bastard Uprichard all along. Right under our fucking noses. What I'd give to punch his fucking lights out!" Tweety nodded. "Yep, I got all that. Well done Malcolm by the way, brilliant job!" Malcolm smiled. Tweety continued.

"Right, before we start patting each other on the backs I have a terrible feeling he might at this very moment be out on a mission. Let me explain. It's to do with the second tune on Malcolm's tape!" Pinky and Perky were all ears.

The telephone rang. Tony, wearing only a smile eased out of bed quietly trying not to disturb the sleeping goddess. He lifted up the receiver. It was Tweety. After a minute of stunned listening with his mouth hanging wide open he replied "Holy fuck, Tweety. Yes, I understand. I'll make the call and get back to you one way or another. Yes, I know where it is. Yes, right away. I'm on it!" Tony made the call as per Tweety's instructions and called him right back. The surge of adrenalin had cleared his head as he sprinted back into his bedroom. He may as well have been banging on a big bass drum with the racket he was making getting dressed. Chloe disturbed sat up from her slumber yawning and rubbing her big brown eyes.

"Where you off to, lover boy? I thought we had a day in the sack planned?" Tony had thrown a t-shirt on with his scruffy tracksuit bottoms and was just squeezing into his Adidas trainers. "Sorry, love. Change of plans. Something big popped up at work. Loads of stuff in the fridge. Help yourself. Call you later. I'll make it up to you. Promise." And with that, he was gone. Chloe let out a huffy sigh. Yawned once more then burrowed back under the warmth of the duvet. She was asleep in seconds.

The telephone rang. Charlene Uprichard had looked better. She was still in her 'jammies' as she struggled like a lump up out of her settee. She caught her image in the hallway mirror, no make-up. Her naturally blotchy face stared back at her.

"Yuck!" she exclaimed as she picked up the phone with a cultured.

"Hello." Charlene hadn't the foggiest idea that Tony was standing in his hallway starkers, OMG it was the gorgeous Sergeant Tony Speers. What was he doing phoning her at home knowing fine well her useless prick of a husband was at work? Very interesting indeed. Oh, he hadn't realised Stevie was at work. A few quick apologies and then he was gone. She hung up and caught her jowly face once more as she passed the mirror again. "Uggh, good job he couldn't see me looking like this."

Tony smiled as he hung up. "Good job she couldn't see me looking like this." He immediately rang Tweety back. Charlene squeezed out a trumpety fart and headed for her chocolate supply in the fridge.

The telephone rang. Bud had just paddled back to shore and was shaking himself dry. His big damp ears pricked on hearing the ringing. Peter was still out there not so much swimming but lolloping about. His eyes were fixed on the drifting clouds on high while the soft breeze pecked at his wet cheeks. Bud began to steadily bark and kept barking until Pete noticed. "Coming fella?" A powerful front crawl had him ashore in no time and within earshot of the ringing phone. Phone calls were few and far between at the Majury mansion. Very few possessed his number. He quickly patted Bud's damp head. "Well done, fella." He then sprinted the twenty yards back to his home bouncing in through the front door before the phone stopped ringing.

"Hello Peter Majury here... Tweety how are you, mate? WHAT! Seriously... I don't believe you. You're joking right? OH NO! Yeah, I know it. I was at the funeral. I'm on my way."

The telephone rang. Debbie Dean answered. "Ah Detective Inspector Brown, how are you? Yes, his lordship is in. I'll put you through. George, it's Archie on the line. I'm putting him through. He sounds excited." The telephone rang, a weary George picked up the receiver, "Archie you wee ballicks. What can I do you for?" George sat in silence as Archie's staccato tipped words slowly lifted the heavy gloop his heart was resting in.

"You have the evidence then? Ah ha, the trophies. Chesney's earrings. Ah ha. Aww wee Malcolm. Brilliant. Big Cliff's taking a statement. Fine and all the trophies have been bagged and labelled? Good. Wee bastard. What I'd like to do with him, that fuckers put me through the mangler. What's that? Oh no… Dear God, is she in any danger? OK, we'll get the local plods there right away. Tell Tweety to prepare a press release for me. The way I'm feeling now, I couldn't sign me own name. Please God it will be a happy one. Well done wee man. Give big Cliff a big kiss from me. See you all at the HOP House tonight at seven bells. I might even put my hand in my pocket!"

George put the receiver down gently and allowed himself a heavy sigh.

Debbie shouted in from her office, "Good news then Mr Grumpy?" George smiled and kicked off his shoes. He wandered over to his drinks cabinet and poured himself a 15-year-old Macallan whisky. He took his first sip and let it sit on his tongue and gums for the full 15 seconds. When he swallowed he closed his eyes as he felt a rush of tears coming. His voice crackled with emotion as he poured a second glass.

"Debbie Dean, get your ass in here. I've poured you a special whisky." Debbie appeared at the office door in refusal mode but when she saw her boss's teary eyes, she got all emotional. She smiled bravely and raised her eyebrows at him while taking the glass.

George smiled whispering softly, "We now know who he is. We have all the evidence. All that's left is we have to catch the bastard. Cross your fingers and toes my lovely." At that, they clinked their glasses, took a sip and shed a little tear.

Stephanie entered the old graveyard by the weathered pedestrian gate. It was stiff through lack of use. Generations lay within. The church congregation now was so small and elderly that a slow quiet passing of a once focal point of a community was taking place unnoticed. Because so few attended church, even fewer were buried there. Stephanie knew she would have this time all to herself as she glided serenely over the overgrown paths to Ozzie's head stone. The graveyard was a picture of natural neglect. She clutched the yellow and white roses in her hand as she felt her chest tighten. She was dreading this moment. Mighty oak trees creaked and groaned sadly as a fresh breeze darted in and around the long departed and abandoned gravestones. Some had fallen over, others had snapped. Names on stone worn beyond reading erased by the elements, the seasons and the passage of time. Somehow, she felt like an intruder as she rounded a corner obstructed by an overgrown holly bush. And there he was or there Ozzie's headstone was. Three years since. Stephanie stood alone with her thoughts. Nothing needed saying. She placed the yellow and white roses against his headstone as a tiny card fluttered gently in the breeze. Its message was simple and had been written by Stephanie earlier that day. "Not in the grave but in my heart always. Love, Stephanie x." Tears were softly falling as she turned away from Ozzie's headstone. Time to move on.

A powerful hand suddenly covered her mouth suppressing her scream. A sickening punch followed to her stomach taking all the wind out of her. She bent over falling to her knees gasping for breath. A series of vicious slaps to the head followed, her attacker calling her bitch with every strike. Blood was coming from her nose and had fallen in splatters staining her clothing. She was dazed and in agony as he spoke, "Right, Miss Heavenly, I have been waiting for this moment for such a long time. Your beautiful self on your knees before me. From this point you will call me master. Do you understand me, bitch?" He grabbed Stephanie by the throat and squeezed. Stephanie looked up at her attacker. He was wearing a balaclava and dressed all in black with black woollen gloves just like the statement she had recorded from Dot. She was now choking and fighting for breath as she caught a glimpse of his green backpack lying on the grass. She then heard the unmistakable sound of a police hand held radio crackle.

Playing for time, she gasped. "How do you know I'm called Heavenly?" This was followed by a punch to her right breast. The pain was excruciating. Stephanie dropped to her knees again.

"Don't fuck with me, blondie. Now you've two choices, LIVE or DIE. If you want to live you've a duty to perform but you must put your heart and soul in it like the rest of the bitches. What's it to be then Miss Heavenly?" Her coat was pulled off brutally followed by a kick in the back. Her hair was then yanked hard pulling her head up to the side of her attacker's face. A large pair of scissors were then placed up to her throat. "Well, LIVE or DIE. What's it to be Miss Heavenly?"

Stephanie felt the scissors slicing through the back of her blouse and felt the twang as her bra snapped. These were then pulled from her leaving her upper half naked. Stephanie caught a glimpse of Ozzie's grave which made her mind up for her. "DIE, I choose to DIE. I won't suck you off. I won't beg and I'll never call you Master. If I'm going to die, at least show me your face, you worthless piece of humanity!" The attacker, enraged, ripped his balaclava off.

Stephanie gasped. "Stevie. But why?" Stevie had crossed many lines on his journey to this place.

"Why? You ask me why, you frigid bitch? I'll tell you why. It's because I can. I'm good at it. They're going to find you dead soon and like the rest of my attacks they'll be no further on. Lost in the dark looking for the bogeyman!" Stevie dragged her to her feet seeing the defiance in her beautiful eyes. She had seen his face. She had to die. He was now holding the scissors like a dagger. She knew it was time and closed her eyes. Her thoughts were of Ozzie. Then a loud gruff bark shattered the air as she was bowled over by a huge physical force. She screamed out and when she opened her eyes, she found the preacher lying on top of her. He had been stabbed in the right shoulder blade with the scissors. The vicious strike had been meant for Stephanie. She could see he was in pain as he gave her a quick wink and spun to his feet.

Bud was in full fury at his master's attacker. He bounced this way and that always placing himself between his master and foe. Barking for all, he was worth barely missing the flailing scissor attacks.

The Preacher called out, "Bud, away boy. Away!" Bud growling backed off. Stevie was in a rage as he edged closer to the Preacher lunging at him with the scissors.

"I'm going to take you pair out, Preacher. Hurry up now, the big man above's expecting you. They'll find you pair dead beside each other and I'll be the sorriest guy in the section. What a laugh." Preacher had lost a lot of blood and was getting exhausted. He barely missed the last lunge. The next lunge nicked him on his cheek. He fell back and stumbled on a loose rock which dropped him onto his left knee. Stephanie screamed as Stevie raised the scissors for the fatal strike. "THWACK!" was the sound Tony's baton made as it crashed into the back of Stevie's head. He fell to the ground like a sack of coal. Spark out. Stephanie cried out, "Tony, thank God you got here just in the nick of time." Tony picked up her coat and threw it at her before leaping over to Pete who was now lying on his back exhausted. He looked into the Preacher's eyes, "You OK buddy. Help's on its way." The Preacher was weak and fading, "Thanks for saving us, Tony. We were getting her tight." Tony smiled. "Rest up, Preachy, sure I owed you one from the Cosy Bar incident."
Pete looked Tony square in the eye and gripped his right arm, "Take care of Bud for me please." Tony smiled.

"My pleasure, Pete..." Stephanie used her torn blouse to stem the flow of blood from Pete's back urging him to stay awake.

Pete became delirious thinking he was standing before an angel. "Hallelujah," he shouted, then passed out. Tony lifted the green backpack and emptied its contents. Out fell Stevie's tape recorder running on record mode and a handheld police radio set on the Comber channel. He immediately went on air and requested two ambulances urgently. The next 15 minutes went by in a blur as police backup arrived shortly followed by the ambulances. Stevie, who was still out, was taken away in one and the Preacher and Heavenly in the other.

Tony felt weird standing in his scruffs trying to organise a major crime scene while taking care of an anxious dog. A short time later, Pinky and Perky arrived and applied the finishing touches to the crime scene. Scenes of Crime and Photography appeared leaving Tony and Bud to look on. Big Cliff with Archie in tow dandered over to Tony. "Well done, you pair." Looking at both Tony and Bud. "That was a close call. Five minutes later, Jeez!" Cliff rolled his big eyes. Archie chipped in, "Aye it was all hands to the deck this morning. Everyone played their part from the station cleaner up. Hoist with his own petard he was. Two lousy tunes on a cassette tape done it for him."

Tony shook his head. "Fuck me, lads, the bastard was in my section, and I didn't smell a thing." Big Cliff laughed. "Tony, son, hindsight is a wonderful thing. You saved two lives today and make it three if you count Geordie Sewell. He was to be in front of Sir Jack tonight for a roasting. Thanks to you, that's been cancelled. He sends his warmest thanks and appreciation for your efforts and invites you to the HOP House for a celebratory one at 7.00pm. It will just be me and him, Tweety and the boss."

Tony nodded. "Sounds good. Just a quickie mind. I had to cancel a doctor's appointment today if you know what I means!" Cliff roared. It was like looking at a younger version of himself in the mirror. The three burst out laughing. Tony called at the Ulster Hospital on his way home. He had quickly left Bud off at his mums. Doctor Chloe had been contacted by Tweety somehow. Don't ask! She was waiting for him at the reception with all the information he would need. Stevie Uprichard had regained consciousness but would remain for tests for a further 48 hours. He was under 24-hour police guard. Preacher had lost a lot of blood, but he had been patched up and was stable. He was sitting up and conscious. The nurses and female doctors were falling over themselves for him. He was sooo hot and nice. Stephanie had a couple of cracked ribs and some mild Concussion. She was being kept overnight.

After much pleading, Tony was allowed in to see his two chums. He called with Stephanie first and gasped when he saw how battered and swollen her delicate features were. He gently hugged her and got her a wheelchair whispering soft assurances in her ear. Dr Chloe was slightly miffed. Here was a side of him she had never seen before. They made their way around to the Preacher's ward. When they entered, the look between Stephanie and Pete was one of utter relief. Both had been so very close to death. Now seeing each other somewhat battered and bruised they were just grateful to be alive. They shared a silent hug with tears catching on each other's cheeks. Smiling, Heavenly looked at her two saviours. "Thank you both. How can I ever repay you? You both saved my life…" Tony smiled, fighting back the tears.

"A pint would be nice." Preacher chuckled.

"An orange cordial for me then. On the rocks!" They all laughed.

Their snug on the first floor of the HOP House was a very happy place to be. George was back to his waspish best, dishing the banter out and howling with laughter when he took some well-deserved flack back from Derek Grant. At the start of the day, he would never have guessed it would have ended this way. Sir Jack had even sent a message of congratulations to him and his colleagues which he duly forwarded on to all his loyal foot soldiers. Pinky and Perky were bristling. They had kidnapped the once poor Malcolm who after a few pints was transformed into the driest wit around. Archie nearly had a heart attack when Malcolm appeared with two dessert spoons and gave a hilarious rendition of rawhide. His spoonery had to be seen to be believed. Big Cliff plonked himself down beside Tweety who was enjoying a vintage port. "Well done today, Tweety. You played a blinder."

Tweety took a sip and smiling said, "Aye big man but those injury time winners are hard on the nerves."

Just then Tony and Doctor Chloe appeared. Time stopped as everyone took the gorgeous pair in. They looked like a movie star couple. He was in a tailor made charcoal grey three-piece suit, white shirt and red silk tie. She was in a stunning black Dior dress with an eye drawing split to the side. Black stockings and black stilettos did the rest. Her face looked amazing surrounded by her tumbling brunette shoulder length curls. I think the legal definition is 'Drop Dead Gorgeous'. Big Cliff, the gentleman stood up and did the introductions and got a fresh round of drinks ordered. When he got a chance on the blind side, he mouthed to Tony, "WOW!"

Tony smiled back in agreement mouthing, "Double WOW!" The two chums shared a giggle.

Doctor Chloe plonked herself between Tweety and Archie, she provocatively nibbled on a Cava. Tweety nudged her with his shoulder, "Thanks for everything today, Chloe, you saved us all a heap of worry. Our sections not the prettiest but we're the best and we take care of one and other." Chloe looked at Tweety and felt his aura. Here was a man completely in tune with life. A man on the right page in a universe full of chaos and destruction. It was a weird sensation like sitting having a drink with God and Santa all rolled into one. She nodded. "Yeah, Tony never shuts up about you all. He calls you lot his wee family."

Tweety laughed. "It sure feels like that."

Archie slightly merry elbowed his way into their cosy wee chat. "Hey Tweety, just while we're all here. However, in all this world, did you know that bastard's padlock combination? I gots to know?" The group hushed as Tweety's countenance changed. His slowly blinking green eye gazed around at all their expectant faces. Then looking at Archie whose eyes were wide with excited anticipation he spoke. "Ohhh Archie, I have amazing God like powers not given to mere mortals like yourself. I have an all seeing, all knowing eye capable of looking into the vast unknown expanses of the Universe. It can reach far back in time and then propel millennia into the future. Bow down before me mere mortals." Archie gulped in awe. Big Cliff rolled his eyes and for the millionth time shook his head smiling.

"Any chance of the truth Oh Mighty Bull Shitter?"

Tweety roared, "Ya broke me, Cliff. Simple really. The bastard must have bought the padlock about a year ago. He had the number written on the top of his left hand for about a week as a wee reminder. Uprichard was right handed. It all made sense really." Archie laughed. "And you put all that together in a flash when we needed it, outstanding." Tweety chuckled. "It hardly took a genius!" Everyone laughed. Chloe fixed Tweety in his one good eye. "Tell me this mister. How did you track me down yesterday?"

Tweety laughed again. "As they say in the job. If I tell you, I'll have to kill you!" Archie roared with laughter. "Chloe, love, never a truer word." Everyone burst into convulsions. A grinning Tony interjected, "That's us, folks. We're heading up to the Drumkeen House Hotel for some fine dining. I'm keeping a promise I made to the good doctor here. Hey and thanks again, Tweety for everything. I would've been lost without you these past few weeks."

George Sewell hollered in, "Not correct, Tony. He's been taking care of the lot of us for way longer than that. Here's to you Mr Harold Sweetlove, our very own Tweety Pie." A cheer rang out from a sea of merry faces. Chloe gasped when God or was it Santa replied, "Fuck away of nae."

Stevie Uprichard faced charges of attempted murder and multiple charges of serious sexual assaults. He pled guilty to all those charges at the earliest convenience. A contested public trial would have served no purpose for his future sentence or physical well-being. He was sentenced to 20 years' imprisonment without parole. His wife left him and took up with a prison officer.

Heavenly and the Preacher would make full recoveries and in the fullness of time returned to their work. Bud was glad to have his master back.

Life would go on at Mountroyal for Tony and the gang. They pitched up to perform their earlies, lates and nights in all seasons and all weathers. Each call was responded to with the highest degree of professionalism as well as circumspect caution. Death was always waiting quietly in the wings. Their aim was simple, it was to make it to the end of each shift in one piece and together.

Tweety like the wise old owl would continue to sit and smile.

The End… Or Until the Next Shift Starts!!!
Care to tag along Pard?